WHITE POPPIES

WHITE POPPIES

and other stories by Zhang Kangkang

TRANSLATED BY

KAREN GERNANT AND CHEN ZEPING

East Asia Program
Cornell University
Ithaca, New York 14853

The Cornell East Asia Series is published by the Cornell University East Asia Program (distinct from Cornell University Press). We publish books on a variety of scholarly topics relating to East Asia as a service to the academic community and the general public. Standing Orders, which provide for automatic notification and invoicing of each title in the series upon publication are accepted.

If after review by internal and external readers a manuscript is accepted for publication, it is published on the basis of camera-ready copy provided by the author who is responsible for any copyediting and manuscript formatting. Alternative arrangements should be made with approval of the Series. Address submission inquiries to CEAS Editorial Board, East Asia Program, Cornell University, 140 Uris Hall, Ithaca, New York 14853-7601.

●

Number 153 in the Cornell East Asia Series
Consulting Editor: Doug Merwin
Copyright ©2011 by Karen Gernant and Chen Zeping. All rights reserved.
ISSN: 1050-2955
ISBN: 978-1-933947-23-5 hardcover
ISBN: 978-1-933947-53-2 paperback
Library of Congress Control Number: 2010931924

25 24 23 22 21 20 19 18 17 16 15 14 13 12 11   9 8 7 6 5 4 3 2 1

Contents

∼

Translators' Acknowledgments

We are grateful to Jin Jianfan, of the Chinese Writers' Association, for assisting us in contacting Zhang Kangkang. To editor Frank Stewart, we extend thanks for including "Yanni's Secret" and "Zhima" in *Manoa* 17:1 (summer 2005). To editors William Ryan and Jack Heflin, our thanks for selecting "Are Birds Better at Walking or Flying?" for *turnrow* 4:1 (winter 2005). It is also one of fifteen stories in our anthology *Eleven Contemporary Chinese Writers* (Turnrow Books, 2010).

We thank Mai Shaikhanuar-Cota, editor, Cornell East Asia Series, for guiding the manuscript through the review process.

We are especially grateful to Professors Mary Erbaugh and Mary-Lou Hinman, as well as anonymous reviewers for the Cornell East Asia Series, for their role in this book's path to publication and for the helpful suggestions they offered.

Doug Merwin is a superb editor, exceedingly astute, sensitive, and careful in making revisions. We are very appreciative of his work on this manuscript.

We express our gratitude to Zhang Kangkang for entrusting us with her work and for her gracious and generous hospitality on several occasions in Beijing and Fuzhou.

Finally, the unflagging encouragement extended by those closest to us continues to facilitate our work on translation projects. For this and so much more, Chen Zeping thanks his wife Weng Zhongyu and his daughter Chen Xiaoping, and Karen Gernant thanks Louis Roemer.

∾

Introduction

Karen Gernant

The stories collected here illumine two recent phenomena in China, one of which—the "up to the mountains, down to the villages" movement of the late 1960s to 1970s—author Zhang Kangkang experienced directly. The other—the large migration of tens of millions of peasants into the cities—she observes in microcosm in the person of her housekeeper.

In the "up to the mountains, down to the villages" movement, approximately twelve to fourteen million educated urban youth (*zhiqing*) left the cities to work on farms.[1] It is sometimes difficult for us to visualize such immense numbers. If we imagine all of New York City, all of Chicago, and all of Houston being emptied out, perhaps we can more easily absorb the magnitude of the numbers.

Zhang Kangkang, born in 1950 in Hangzhou, was among these millions. As of December 1974, she was one of the 490,000 young people in northeastern Heilongjiang from other provinces.[2] In much of China, the sent-down youth remained in their home provinces; Hangzhou was one of eight cities that typically sent young people to other provinces.[3] By December 1975, 120,000 educated youth from Hangzhou had been sent down to the countryside; this figure constituted about 13.3 percent of Hangzhou's population.[4]

Over the radio on the night of December 23, 1968, people all over China had heard Mao Zedong summon the educated youth to go down to the countryside.

---

1. Thomas P. Bernstein, *Up to the Mountains and Down to the Villages* (New Haven: Yale University Press, 1977), 24, writes that approximately 12 million young people were sent to villages from 1968 to late 1975. Zhang Kangkang says that 14 million educated youth were sent down. *Dahuang binghe* [The great wilderness glacier] (Changchun: Jilin People's Publishing Company, 1998), revised and published as *Shei gan wenwen ziji* [Who dares question himself?] (Changchun: Literature and Art Publishing House, 2007), 5. Cited hereafter as *Shei gan.*
2. The figures are from Bernstein, 26.
3. Bernstein, 29.
4. Bernstein, 30.

> It is very necessary for educated young people to go to the countryside to be reeducated by the poor and lower-middle peasants. Cadres and other city people should be persuaded to send their sons and daughters who have finished junior or senior middle school, college, or university to the countryside.
> Let's mobilize!
> Comrades throughout the countryside should welcome them.[5]

Among those listening to this broadcast were Zhang Kangkang and her father. As Ms. Zhang recalls, neither of them spoke. Early the next morning, the young Ms. Zhang went to her school and found everything already in a hubbub. "That evening, after dinner, I hemmed and hawed, and then said to Father, 'Anyway, everyone has to go. It would be better to go sooner rather than later, wouldn't it?' Father nodded his head, and I said, 'I want to go to the Great Northern Wilderness [in Heilongjiang]. I would receive wages . . .'" Zhang's father admonished her, reminding her that her mother, then in detention, needed all of the family's support.

Zhang argued, but in the end, this time the decision wasn't hers to make. "My great ambition of going to the Great Northern Wilderness was quickly dashed away like a soap bubble. [This area] was the front line of anti-revisionism, and it was on the Sino-Soviet border . . . No one with a bad background could be in the first group to go there. Those with bad backgrounds were certainly not qualified to defend the great northern gate of the motherland.

"In the schoolyard, I gazed from a distance at the place where people were signing up to go to the Great Northern Wilderness. I felt great despair."

Abandoning her dreams of the north for the time being, she went to a village near her maternal grandmother and uncle's home. A prosperous area, it also had the advantage of being close to Hangzhou. She farmed on a commune there for the period just after Spring Festival 1969 until May of that year.

By that May, "political conditions had relaxed. If you signed up, you would be accepted . . . I walked about six miles alone at night to the county seat, and the next morning boarded the first bus to Hangzhou." There, defying her father, she signed up to go to Heilongjiang. Nearly thirty years later, she characterized the Great Northern Wilderness as "desolate and cold." Yet, she saw it as the only way "to break away from the oppression I felt. It was hope

---

5. Bernstein, 57, quoting from Radio Peking, 12/23/68, *Foreign Broadcast Information Service* no. 30, 12/24/68.

and desire. It was the icy snow and tractors of the wilds and the forests, it was the grass-green military uniforms and puttees. It was a temptation that I had no way to refuse . . .

"... I turned a deaf ear to all the admonitions of my family ... I was crazy about the Great Northern Wilderness, and ice-cold toward my family. I thought that revolutionaries had to be as hard as steel in this test. My decision couldn't be changed." Unable to change her mind, her father refused to give her money for the things she needed, so she asked to borrow sixty *yuan* from her mother's work unit. "When educated youth went down to the countryside, work units didn't dare refuse to lend money." She used the money for "bedding, soap, toothpaste, and other articles for daily use." To repay the loan, her mother's wages were docked five *yuan* a month for a year.

When Zhang Kangkang boarded the train in Hangzhou, she was in high spirits. Throngs of people crowded the train station to see the young people off; those who were departing and those who were bidding them farewell were weeping. But, writes Zhang, "No one saw me off. In order to go to the Great Northern Wilderness, I had had a falling-out with almost everyone." She shed no tears.

In general, the educated youth were organized to go to their assignments with others from their own school. Again, Zhang Kangkang was an exception. She didn't want to be with her former classmates, perhaps because she'd been "badgered" and "discriminated against."[6] She went to the Great Northern Wilderness with a young man she knew from another school. They married on the farm. After a year or two of marriage and the birth of a son, the couple divorced.[7]

Zhang stresses, "I went to the Great Northern Wilderness completely voluntarily. I could have continued working on the commune in my home area ... I could have had a quiet, peaceful life . . .

"But I was restless: the outside world, the distant north country were constantly tugging at me. Perhaps for literature, perhaps for 'revolution,' perhaps for love. Even I don't know why. Anyhow, I had to go far away and carve out my future."[8]

Today, she speculates that she may have chosen to go to so distant a place because of reading a lot of Soviet literature when she was young. If one wanted to go far away, it was the Great Northern Wilderness that was the principal option for the urban youth of Hangzhou. There were also small quotas for

6. Zhang, *Shei gan*, 33, 35, 36.
7. Zhang, *Shei gan*, 281–82.
8. Zhang, *Shei gan*, 35.

youth to go to Ningxia and Inner Mongolia. "I wasn't interested in those places. The Great Northern Wilderness was a much better match for the dreams I had from reading Soviet literature—romance, distance, the collective, and the vast expanse of the land."[9]

Once at the farm, which previously had been a labor reform farm, she worked at a series of jobs. At first, she grew vegetables. Later on, she worked as a mail carrier, dried tiles in a tile factory, and worked in an agricultural technology group. She served as a writer for the drama troupe and for the propaganda office. She liked least the jobs that involved simple and repetitive labor. "I liked work that was a little more interesting, but I never had a job that I liked really well." She wanted very much to be a teacher, but didn't have that opportunity.[10]

In her spare time on the farm, Zhang read. During the first year, "the books I had taken with me became worn from repeated reading. And there were many other good books and 'banned books' that couldn't be taken to the farm." On the farm, reading was limited primarily to the works of Marx, Lenin, and Lu Xun. She lamented to her companions, "There aren't any books here that I want to read. And the books that *are* here, it's a waste of time to read." She mused aloud that she would like to read "all of the world's great literature." Her friends told her that her dream was "unrealistic."

Zhang comments that "it was hard to get good books to read in the Great Northern Wilderness. If someone managed to get hold of a translation of a foreign book, this was precious. Everyone would line up and take turns reading it . . . When I heard that a neighboring company had a copy of [Raffaello Giovagnoli's] *Spartacus*, I walked more than three miles to borrow it."[11]

She went home for the first time in 1971, and stayed about two months. It was the first time the educated youth were given paid vacations to visit their families.[12] At home, too, she spent much of her time reading. Now, for her, Soviet and Russian literature was overshadowed by English and French literature. She read Balzac, Dickens, Merimee, and Hugo. Her mother, who had just been released from confinement, was working in a library, and thus it was easier than it might have been otherwise for Zhang to obtain reading material. She read books by Zola, Hardy, and Mark Twain.[13] The time she spent at home was a "time to refresh my spirit."[14]

---

9. E-mail correspondence, September 2007.
10. E-mail correspondence, September 2007.
11. Zhang, *Shei gan*, 173, 174.
12. E-mail correspondence, September 2007.
13. Zhang, *Shei gan*, 175.
14. Zhang, *Shei gan*, 173.

"Every time I immersed myself in reading, it was as though I had disso-ciated myself from the revolution. The classical European literature seemed to come from a different planet from the propaganda that assailed us all the time ... There was no link between them. Of course, I liked the cultural heritage represented by these 'feudal, capitalist, revisionist' works, but I also couldn't turn away from the magnet of 'revolutionary realism.' ...

"What kind of literature was the best? Why was the literature that was recognized by the current society so at odds with what I loved?"[15]

Subsequent visits home generally lasted about a month. "The educated youth couldn't stay with their families too long, because we didn't have ration cards." That meant that the family had to share a fixed quantity of food with one extra person. For many families, this represented a real hardship.[16]

Zhang went home again in 1975 for surgery; this period of leave was extended to almost two years, during which she wrote and revised her first novel. In 1976, she returned to the Great Northern Wilderness, and during 1976–77, worked in the farm administration office. When I asked whether, from the outset, she had anticipated being in the countryside for the rest of her life, she responded, "At the time, no one could predict his or her future. It seems to me I hadn't really decided to stay there my whole life. But I didn't know, either, what the future would be like. I was too young—nineteen—back then, and couldn't think about so many things of the future."

She stayed as long as she did on the farm, because there wasn't a particu-larly good opportunity, or particularly suitable work, that would induce her to leave. "I was also waiting to go to school. My greatest dream was to go to college. So I couldn't accept just any job in the city in order to return to Hangzhou."

How did it happen that she was transferred to the Heilongjiang Writers' Association? "After my novel was published, the Heilongjiang Culture Bureau was impressed. For an educated youth to publish a novel then was like win-ning a lottery. During the Cultural Revolution, a lot of the old writers had been attacked. In 1978, when all of the provinces' Art Associations and Writers' Associations resumed work, they very much needed 'new blood'—young people. Since I had already published a novel, they felt that I was quali-fied and that I had literary talent, so they sent me to the Heilongjiang Arts Academy. After I graduated two years later, they formally transferred me to be a 'professional writer.'"[17]

---

15. Zhang, *Shei gan*, 175, 176.
16. E-mail correspondence, September 2007.
17. E-mail correspondence, September 2007.

In 1983, after eleven years of being single, she married her present husband, a university professor in Beijing. At that time, she began living in Beijing. She remains formally attached to the Heilongjiang Writers' Association and still draws her salary from it. "I simply transferred my permanent residence to Beijing."[18]

If the young Zhang Kangkang embraced the ideals of the revolution and responded to Mao's summons to city youth to go to the countryside, as did so many millions of young people, the mature Zhang Kangkang looks back on those times with mixed emotions. On the one hand, she is angry, outraged, and penitent. On the other hand, she seems to believe that the legacy of the educated youth in the countryside contains at least a little that is worthwhile.

In the preface to her *Shei gan wenwen ziji*, Zhang writes that it is "agonizing" for her to look back at the past. What occurred in those years "seemed right [at the time] but it was wrong." "Shrapnel was left in my body and spirit. My flesh and blood were ripped apart." At the time, she says, "it seemed to be I, but it wasn't . . . It couldn't have been the real me." Zhang rails, "A person and a generation's youth, time, and lives were sacrificed and wasted."

The educated youth, she writes, "lost the chance to continue our education, and went to work in places strange to us." They brought education to the poor and lower-middle peasants, and treated them when they were sick. They used scientific methods in farming the land. The hard work took its toll on the health of many of the educated youth, causing long-term damage. Some young people even lost their lives. The educated youth sacrificed a great deal, and yet when they went back to the cities, what awaited them was "no education, no skills, no housing, and no money."[19]

An official in the Great Northern Wilderness later told Zhang, "If all the educated youth had taken a holiday for the whole year, we would have sustained fewer losses than with them working here." Zhang adds, "For years, we opened up the wasteland and tilled the land, but we didn't obtain the results we should have on this fertile land. What, in fact, did we contribute?"

Zhang found the time in the Great Northern Wilderness "lonely and desolate." Her support came from her parents, family members, and friends. She gained strength, as well, from reading.

Some people argue that, at least, the sent-down youth movement spawned a generation of writers who had been among these educated youth. Zhang challenges this: "Is there any way of knowing how many talented edu-

---

18. E-mail correspondence, September 2007.
19. Zhang, *Shei gan*, 1, 3.

cated youth were destroyed by the movement? Or how many ordinary people were marred by it? Even though each educated youth gained different things from the long, difficult farm life, there's no way this advantage can offset the entirety of the corrosive experience. There is no way that I—because I've now become a 'writer'—can be grateful to the Cultural Revolution and the up to the mountains and down to the countryside movement."[20]

Still, she finds one redemptive feature to the movement. In the 1990s, when she visited the Great Northern Wilderness, she asked various officials to appraise the movement. On one point, their views coincided: the educated youth had brought culture and education to the Great Northern Wilderness. Zhang notes, "The educated youth had intended to remold themselves, and had gone far away to this frigid wasteland to do that. They didn't consciously become tools for spreading city values."[21] And yet, one assumes, they did so by example—to the point that at least one person told Zhang that he "always looked forward to, and waited for, the educated youth teachers to come back to the farm to visit someday. But they didn't. I was very moved by this, and said you could look for them if you have the chance. He said he had gone to look one time, but the teacher hadn't recognized him."[22]

Though her views of the movement in looking back at it leave little doubt that Zhang Kangkang sees little in it worthy of praise, still, at the time she was there, she now says candidly, "In fact, I wanted to stay there. I wanted to experience more of the life in the Great Northern Wilderness."[23]

The up to the mountains, down to the countryside movement was one major upheaval in modern China, one instance of millions of people being transferred from their home areas—some to nearby places, others—like Zhang—to regions far from anything familiar to them. The furor at the time would have allowed few to opt out. Most of the young people probably went because they could not imagine what they would do otherwise. As Zhang wrote, "If I didn't go down to the countryside, where would I go?"[24]

Another major upheaval in modern China is the recent—and continuing—migration from the countryside to the cities. Twenty years ago, this would have been impossible to envision. Unlike the educated youth move-

---

20. Zhang, *Shei gan*, 6, 284.
21. Zhang, *Shei gan*.
22. Zhang, *Shei gan*.
23. E-mail correspondence, September 2007.
24. Zhang, *Shei gan*, 32.

ment, this one is not official. No fanfare accompanies it. No one urges the villagers to go to the cities in search of jobs. But *circumstances* do, and in this respect, some similarity with the earlier movement exists. In the late 1960s through much of the 1970s, not enough jobs were available in the cities to absorb the youth who were coming of age. Now, unemployment or underemployment remains a problem.[25] And yet the plight of the people in many parts of the countryside is worse. Officials acknowledge that poverty still besets at least ten percent of China's people. Poverty-stricken regions are typically in the interior and in the remote countryside.

Estimates of the number of migrants vary from 120 million to 200 million, out of a total rural population of about 900 million.[26] Close to twelve percent of China's population are migrant workers.[27] If we consider percentages, it's as if thirty-six million Americans uprooted themselves to work in distant places. If we look instead at the raw numbers, it's as if nearly half of all Americans were living and working great distances from their actual residences.

It was in the 1990s that the phenomenon began.[28] During that decade, startling economic development occurred in China, particularly in cities along the coast. Construction projects dominated cityscapes. Wide thoroughfares replaced narrow streets. More bridges were built. New airports were added. Also constructed were new public office buildings, bank buildings, and gas stations. Other construction projects included houses and vast high-rise apartment complexes. Hotels and restaurants, coffee and tea shops increased greatly in numbers. New department stores were built, as were countless boutiques. Supermarkets were established, in some cases replacing the traditional neighborhood markets. Some private individuals now had the means to buy automobiles, and many more taxis were in evidence, as well. The face of coastal

---

25. College graduates have difficulty finding jobs for which their education has prepared them.

26. "No place to call home," *The Economist* (27 June 2007), reprinted online—http://www.economist.com/world/asia/displaystory—gives a figure of 120 million. Citing the State Population and Planning Commission, "China sees soaring migrant population," *China Economic Net* (http://en.ce.cn/National/Rural/20061029) reports a figure of 150 million. (http://en.ce.cn/National/Rural/20061029). And, citing Strategic Forecasting, Inc., IntelliBriefs.blogspot.com/2007/04 reported on 27 April 2007 in an article titled "China: Keeping Track of the Migrant Floaters," that out of 900 million rural residents, some 150 to 200 million of them are "floating migrant workers."

27. Ibid.

28. "Sichuan Tops Chinese Provinces as Largest Source of Migrant Population" (Xinhua News Agency, 6 October 2006, http://www.china.org.cn/english/MATE-RIAL/182986.htm).

urban China was being transformed, and cities along the coast pulsed with a brisk and surging confidence. For the first time in post-1949 China, numerous city dwellers were comfortably well off. Some were affluent.

Migrants from the countryside began to stream into these cities, and others such as Beijing, in search of work. From 1996 to 2006, the numbers of migrants increased twofold.[29] Typically, they find employment doing heavy labor, such as construction, or working in service jobs. Others sell vegetables.[30] As in other countries, they take the jobs that urban residents do not want. Nowadays, "officials have started to realize that migrants are an indispensable part of the city."[31] Liu Jinguo, vice-minister of Public Security, characterizes migrant workers as "an irreplaceable force in China's modernization drive . . ."[32]

Of those migrant workers, approximately 3.57 million are in Beijing, representing about nineteen percent of Beijing's population.[33]

One of these migrant workers is young Guo, who is the prototype for the title character Zhima in Zhang Kangkang's story. She is from a village in Zhumadian in poverty-stricken southern Henan; it is southern Henan that is that province's prime exporter of labor. As of 2004, thirteen million people had left Henan to work elsewhere, and of that number, one-third were from the southern part of the province. And of those, 1.4 million were from Zhumadian. Workers from Henan are in the forefront of the migrant movement. Most work in construction, while others find factory jobs. Housekeeping, such as young Guo does for Zhang Kangkang and her husband, is another major choice.[34]

A visitor to Zhang's home in 2001 notes that young Guo was making *jiaozi* (dumplings), and that she joined the other three for the meal. Over dinner, young Guo told them how she had coped with the one-child policy and had given birth to a second child (a girl). The visitor also noticed that, as in Zhang's story, Zhang and her husband treated young Guo as another member of the family, and interacted with her as if she were.[35] I observed this, as well, when I visited Zhang's home in the spring of 2006.

---

29. "China sees soaring migrant population."

30. "Sichuan Tops."

31. Ibid.

32. "China will improve supervision, assistance for migrant population: police," *People's Daily Online* (16 January 2007), http://english.people'sdaily.com.cn/20070116/eng.20070116_341767.html

33. "China: Keeping Track."

34. Wang Guangze, 18 February 2004, http://www.clibrary.com

35. Yu Xue, 28 November 2001, posted on the Internet.

When I met Zhang Kangkang in the fall of 2003, she told me that she had begun listening carefully to the tales young Guo relates of life in her home village and utilizing at least some of them in her stories. Zhang believes that women who work in the cities are a significant bridge between city and countryside, for when they go back to their villages either to visit or to stay, they take with them some of the urban values and practices. Zhang thinks that over time, this will raise the level of rural culture, which she sees as rather backward, old-fashioned, superstitious, and selfish (in that villagers generally want and often manage to have more than two children).

This insight is compelling, not only for its relevance to today's China, but also in that it resonates with the positive part of the heritage that the educated youth appear to have left behind in the villages. In that sense, it also links Zhang Kangkang's past with her present.

I invite you to turn now to the stories—the first four dealing with the educated youth movement, the last two dealing with rural migrants in Beijing.

∽

WHITE POPPIES
and other stories

WHITE POPPIES

Poppies are usually red or purple. Do you know there are also white poppies?

-1-

One winter ten years ago, when it was almost time for the Spring Festival, a heavy snowfall left the military farm with impassable roads. When I went past a depression in the snow, the shrieking, howling north wind chilled my bones. Falling and stumbling, I climbed the high snow-covered slope. If I hadn't seen the dry sorghum stalks poking out through the vents, I couldn't have found the damn root cellar.

"Lion Head!" I shouted as I climbed down the creaky wooden stairs into the dark cellar. Because of the sunlight reflecting on the snow, I couldn't see anything for a moment.

"Lion Head!" I shouted again at the top of my lungs.

No one answered. There wasn't a sound in the root cellar. The wind howled in the fields overhead, but here it was as still as a graveyard. After I stood in the dark for a while, I gradually made out the long, narrow floor, heaped up with cabbage in one neat row after another. The cabbage was pale green, and gave off a slightly moldy smell. In the darkness, faint rays of light from the few kerosene lamps cast shadows from the wooden pillars. An eerie feeling ran down my spine.

"Lion Head!" I remembered the telegram in my pocket.

A rustling sound of something stirring came from the corridor, and a shadow moved slowly toward me. My hair stood on end: if it weren't for his shuffling feet, I'd really have thought I'd met up with a corpse. He stopped at a pillar not far from me: he was wearing a pointed sheepskin cap, a pair of huge padded shoes and leggings, greasy baggy cotton trousers, and—on his bent back—a tight old padded jacket. All of this made him a very strange figure indeed: his sallow, skinny face, withered skin, sunken mouth, frozen chin, and eyes I couldn't see because he was looking down at the floor of the root cellar.

3

My scalp tingled, and I cursed to myself: "*Erlaogai*—that semi-felon!"

"Buy some vegetables? They're all top-grade," he stammered, still not raising his head.

I could tell from his accent that he was from the south.

"What are you talking about? I'm looking for Lion Head!" I shouted.

He raised his head a bit and glanced at me in bewilderment. Then he turned around silently and headed for the corridor. To tell the truth, it took courage to be underground alone with this thing that was somewhere between human and ghost. In its former incarnation, this place was a labor reform farm. During the Cultural Revolution, when people were released from such farms, some of them didn't want to go back to the cities and be struggled against, so they'd stayed on. On the farm, they did the hardest, most tiring work or the skilled work. We called them "*Erlaogai*"—semi-felons.

Carrying a lamp, the old man walked ahead, a swaying shadow. Had there ever been a soul in this shadow? I thought, *Even if there had been, it has probably long since died . . .*

He stopped at the end of the root cellar, nervously lifting the lamp a little higher, as if afraid that the faint light would illuminate his ugliness.

I heard a sound like a pig snoring. In this root cellar, separated from the world, loud snoring wouldn't disturb anybody. In the corner where the snoring was coming from, a meaty face wrapped in a sheepskin jacket appeared.

I kicked him. This "Lion Head" had done everything he could to get this job of taking charge of the root cellar. Now I understood why. It was such a cushy job that he could sleep soundly while on duty as somebody else did the work for him. Hunh! Had he learned how to hire people? But if you hired people, you had to pay them!

He sat up reluctantly, rubbing his red eyes. He'd been playing poker the night before.

"What's up? You're disturbing my sleep!"

I took a telegram and a crumpled letter out of my pocket and handed them to him. To tell the truth, if I'd had any other options, there was no way I'd have looked for "Lion Head." He was a classmate of mine from the first year of middle school; then he'd had to repeat the grade twice. When I was about to graduate, he finally passed seventh grade. But during the Cultural Revolution he began overnight to cut quite a figure, wearing a watch and riding a "Flying Pigeon" bicycle. Once, he even bragged to me that during one political movement he had personally killed a landlord's wife. Last fall, I'd been sent to this farm in the countryside; I was unfamiliar with the place and the people. I don't know where he came from, but anyhow at least he was someone I knew. Although he wasn't a good worker—he was lazy and greedy—all in all, he was better than the slick guys who reported on everyone.

I sat down on the dirty sheepskin jacket he was lying on. Just as I was about to open my mouth, I heard a thin sound coming from someplace nearby. It seemed to be the old man tidying the stacks of vegetables.

A little uneasy, I pursed my lips and said, "Him?. . ."

"Don't worry. What can he do!" "Lion Head" yawned and shook his head of disheveled hair.

Burning with impatience, I told him I'd received a letter from my cousin in Huachuan, saying that her father in Harbin was seriously ill and had been taken to the hospital. There wasn't anyone to stay with him. Her mother was undergoing political re-education and couldn't go home. My cousin had thought of asking for leave to go back, but she didn't have a penny. She was new in the countryside, and had earned only three *yuan* in six months. It was only because she had no way out that she was making this request of me—her older male cousin—because I earned regular wages. But I was poor: of the thirty-two *yuan* I'd earned this month, ten had gone toward an overcoat, and I'd also bought a hat to get through the winter. It was debatable whether I had enough left to keep me in food until the next payday.

Lion Head said, "Her father's sick. Why doesn't she borrow money from the village office?"

"Her father used to be a police chief. Now he's in big trouble—he's become a 'class enemy.'"

Then he asked, "Why doesn't she borrow from her peers?"

"Who would dare lend her money when they know what her father is now? I'm sweating now because I'm telling you the truth. Hey, Buddy, you aren't going to report me, are you?"

Lion Head stuffed a cabbage leaf into his mouth and chomped on it. He answered lazily, "Of course not. I don't have any interest in getting ahead. Why would I tell on you? Still, it isn't going to be easy to get this money. How much do you think she needs?"

"At least twenty *yuan*."

He jumped up and spat on the sand-covered floor, and said, "Shit! Do you take me for a banker? The little I saved turned into wine poured into the commander's stomach a long time ago . . ."

"Lion Head," I asked pitifully in a hoarse voice, "could you please buy my radio? Even though I assembled it myself, it plays . . ."

The bell for knocking off for the day sounded in the distance. Lion Head's ears were sharper than a hunting dog's. At once, he put on his new but dirty cotton cap and his yellow overcoat. Dragging me along, he ran for the cellar's entrance.

"It's dumplings tonight at the mess hall. Hurry up!" He took the stairs two or three steps at a time.

"Whatever you do, you have to think of a way to help . . ." I was following close behind him. All of a sudden, sand kicked up into my eyes by his shoe blurred my vision and hurt so much that tears gushed out. I had to stop.

Just then, someone tapped me lightly on the shoulder. Then a pair of ice-cold hands touched my face, and held my eyelids open. There was a fresh cabbage smell on those hands, as if soft cabbage leaves had been used for handkerchiefs. They wiped the sand away, and my eyes stopped hurting.

I opened my eyes, and through my tears, I saw him standing in front of me—that old man. He was still bent over, still staring at the floor. It was as though he had never stood straight up. I went up the stairs without saying thanks.

"Ooh . . . ooh . . ." He made a strange sound, as if he were holding in some anxiety and didn't dare talk about it out loud.

I turned around and looked at him. He was squinting at me.

God. What kind of eyes were those? They were like deep dried-up wells sunken in the middle of the desert—turbid, acerbic, desolate, like a pool of ashes in a dried-up well, flashing strangely with goodness, warmth, and light.

I was surprised. Why was he looking at me like this?

He drew something out of the front of his greasy shirt, and stammered, "Don't sell it. Don't sell your radio. Keep it so you can listen to music. It's a good diversion . . . If you need money, I—I'll lend you some . . ."

I was dumbfounded. I couldn't believe my ears.

With his chicken-foot-like hand he nervously took out some money—a thick wad of one-*yuan* notes, old and dirty.

I was secretly overjoyed at this good luck that had descended on me. I'd be able to help my cousin! I was just about to put out a hand to take the money when all of a sudden I came to my senses.

"What are you up to?" I shouted. Even I felt that the sternness in my voice was quite terrifying. "Who wants your filthy money? In your dreams, you rascal! Get lost!"

Huffing and puffing, I climbed out of the root cellar. I was in such a state that I was trembling. Lion Head, kept waiting so long, was impatient.

"What's going on between you and the old guy?"

"Nothing..."

"I heard you." He sneered.

I didn't say anything. Where had my sudden anger come from just now? I was mystified.

"You're a fool!" Lion Head said as he turned around and blew his whistle.

"No. About this, I have at least a few smarts. That old man is an 'erlaogai.' If I borrow his money, and he makes use of me to do something wrong, then what? In any case he's a class enemy..."

Suddenly, Lion Head began laughing weirdly. "No wonder you got so many straight A's in school back then. Class enemy? Ha! Do you really believe each one of them is evil and always trying to overturn the society, the way the books say? How come I haven't seen one? Why would he bother to involve you in wrongdoing? What could he expect to gain from that?"

"Their class is evil by nature..."

"Evil by nature? What does that mean? Let's just talk of this one old man. He's the most obedient person I've ever met. If I told him to drink my piss, he wouldn't dare say no!"

I felt a little sick to my stomach.

"Even he often says that he's been reformed during these years—changed from a monster into a human being. If his wife hadn't divorced him long ago, if his son hadn't been sent down to the countryside, if there were still someone to go home to, he would have gone back to Guangdong a long time ago. If you refuse his loan, you're refusing it for nothing, you dummy!"

He was looking very experienced.

"I won't tell anyone. No one else will know. You'd better understand: he's the only one you can get a loan from..."

When we parted, the stars came out and the snowy ground was sparkling with a cold blue light. Heaven and earth were both ice-cold.

-2-

I had a dream that night. I dreamed that my uncle had died, and that my cousin was weeping as she knelt before him...

I was sweating profusely and my heart was beating fast. I woke up and couldn't get back to sleep again. When it was barely light, I got up and stole out of the dorm, afraid and trembling.

I waited for him on the path to the root cellar. Lion Head had said that Old Si started work two hours before he did every day, and knocked off in the evening an hour and a half later. I knew I could intercept him at this spot at this time.

The northwest wind was blowing so hard that my face stung; frost hung from the brim of my cap. For the first time, I decided to take Lion Head's advice.

Old Si finally showed up, carrying his lunch box, bent over as always.

All of a sudden, I wanted to flee. I wanted to be far away from there. I loathed him, and yet I was going to make use of this loathing to get a favor from him. What kind of person had I turned into?!

When he brushed past me, his eyes were unswerving. He meant to walk right past. I suddenly realized that if I let this opportunity slip, I wouldn't have another chance. I shouted, "Stop!"

He stopped mechanically. When he raised his head slowly and glanced at me, he seemed taken aback.

"Yesterday . . . the thing . . . ," I was incoherent and nervous, "can you . . . still give . . ."

He understood: he nodded his head slowly, his face absolutely expressionless. Was he still upset by the way I'd behaved yesterday? No. Though his eyes looked lifeless, they were kindly.

"I . . ." Terrified and unsettled, he was looking in all directions. I knew that he was either wavering or afraid. Nevertheless, he finally felt around in the front of his garment for a long time and then drew out a small paper packet. He tore the paper open carefully and stuffed a wad of banknotes into my hand. He said, "I was going to send this to my son. It can wait . . ."

Holding the money, my hand shook: did he have a son? He sighed and silently walked away, in the end not saying a word about when I should return the money to him.

I didn't see him again for several months. When he went to work, we were still in bed; when he got off work, we were already in bed. After the snow melted, the root cellar baked in the sunshine. There were just a few stalks of skull-like grain left. I didn't know where he was working now. I didn't receive many letters from my cousin. I heard that my uncle was getting a little better and that my aunt had returned to the city from the re-education camp. As for that twenty *yuan*, aside from my cousin saying she'd "received" it, from then on it was as if she'd forgotten all about it. Naturally, I couldn't bring it up again, either. But month after month went by, and I wasn't able to pay the old man back. My wages were thirty-two *yuan* a month: besides food and cigarettes (I took up smoking after going down to the countryside), I also drank a little to get through the boring hours after work.

Just about every month, I thought about repaying the money, but every month I ended up with nothing left over. When I walked on the path, I was particularly afraid of running into Old Si. I asked Lion Head where he was. Lion Head said, "The new work site was short a cook, so they transferred him there to take the job. But it's almost time for the busy season in the melon fields here. He'll come back soon. This old guy can do almost any kind of work. Back in the old days, he would have been every landlord's ideal laborer."

Lion Head was more stylish now: his wool trousers were trim, his fashionable shoes shiny. I didn't know where he'd gotten them and I didn't dare ask.

It was a rainy day. We didn't go out to work but stayed in the dorm for political study. I was sitting on the windowsill, absentmindedly listening to newspapers being read aloud.

All of a sudden, I noticed a shadow not far ahead. I turned ice-cold and numb all over, as if it were the end of the world. I was right. It was him—Old Si, his face withered and yellow, his form bony. Wrapped in a piece of white plastic cloth, he was like an apparition walking toward our dorm. Why was he coming? He must be looking for me to ask for his money. Had he run out of patience? Oh, God, there was no way I could let the company leaders know about this—at the very least, there would be a struggle meeting against me. No way! I had to play hard ball with him.

I quickly jumped down from the windowsill, thinking I'd stop him outside the door and give him a dressing down. But when I was about to go out the door, I peeped out the window. I was dumbfounded: he was digging out the gutter in front of the dorm. After a while, he finished, and the muddy stopped-up water began trickling east through the gutter. The melon field was on the west side. He stood in the rain without making a sound. When he saw that the water was flowing about the way it should, he turned and left. He didn't even raise his eyes toward the men's dorm.

I breathed a long sigh of relief.

But none of this escaped Lion Head's notice. After lunch, he climbed up on my bed and tossed me a cigarette. Narrowing his eyes, he said, "Hunh, you still don't get it, do you?"

I didn't know what he meant—"get" what?

"Are you still thinking about the twenty *yuan* he lent you? You dummy. Let me tell you, after all is said and done, he's a semi-felon. You took his money. You didn't pay it back. So what? There's no evidence. Who can prove that he lent you twenty *yuan*?! If he reports you, who will believe him? Can't you fight back by charging him with vilifying you?"

I felt suffocated at hearing this. Maybe I wasn't a good person, but I'd never dared to think so shamelessly. How could it be okay to borrow money and not return it? Wouldn't that make me even worse than a thief? How could I be so evil?

Lion Head rapped me on the head. "How come you still don't get it? They and we don't come from the same litter of lambs. We're revolutionary youth; they're sinful criminals! People aren't equal in this world. Hey, look at the company commander, for example: he's forever watching us as if we were thieves. In his eyes, we're hardly human beings. Just like those reform prisoners . . ."

The fields outside our window were dark. It was still raining. I was cold—cold to the marrow of my bones, cold to the bottom of my heart . . .

Not long afterward, in a new wave of the class struggle, a mass meeting was held in the company. Old Si was escorted to the front and stood there. His posture drew guffaws from everyone in the company. They said he was the perfect image of the villain depicted in movies. A child went up and pushed him violently and beat him. The accusation that had given rise to the fight was that a child had been found rolling on the ground because of a terrible stomachache. No one could find the doctor, so the old guy had given the child's mother several wild poppies and told her to steep them and give the brew to the child. Sure enough, the child recovered immediately. But when a crowd of people discovered this, they immediately accused the old guy of plotting to poison the revolutionary people, and this proved that he'd tried in vain to restore the old regime. They wanted the company commander to be more vigilant with him, and make him clean the latrines beginning the next day. The child's mother kept weeping and wailing, saying that from now on she was resolved that it would be better for her child to die of the pain from diarrhea than be tricked again by class enemies.

I sat in a corner, shivering all over, although I wasn't cold. From far away, Lion Head made a face at me, and I understood what he meant. I blew smoke toward the ceiling, and the crowds of people all around blurred in the smoke. Let Old Si go to hell! Since he can never wipe out the debt he owes the people from the first half of his life, so what if I took his twenty *yuan*?

-3-

Beginning last week, I'd become free as a bird: because of a chance opportunity, I was now the company's mail carrier. Every day, I rode a bike to the post office, two or three miles away, mailed everyone's letters, and brought back newspapers, letters, and remittances, and delivered them. Being the mail carrier was a lot of work, but I had no supervisors: I was totally on my own.

One afternoon, as I came back from delivering the mail, I jumped off my bike and was about to go inside when I noticed someone standing in front of the door. He was dressed all in black, his back toward me.

He turned around slowly, lowered his head and looked at the ground, and mumbled something.

Good lord! It was him—Old Si.

He was even more emaciated than the first time I'd seen him, and he was panting a little. One hand was pressed against his chest as though he were being suffocated by a dead weight. He looked at the green mailbag I was carrying, and fumbled for something inside the front of his garment.

My scalp was all pins and needles. I blanched and asked sharply, "What are you doing?"

He shivered briefly, looked up, and then recognized me. He stood there in amazement. A thread of joyful light flashed across his gloomy eyes.

"It's been so long, so long since I've seen you . . ." he stammered. "I've come to send . . . to send a little money to my son." He took out a small, tightly wrapped paper packet.

All of a sudden, I remembered that it seemed he'd mentioned having a son. I asked curiously, "Your son? What does he do?"

"He's like you. He's an educated youth. He's in the countryside in Guangdong . . . It's a poor village. He can't support himself there, he depends on me to send—"

"And what about his mother? How come she doesn't take care of him?"

He lowered his head again. It drooped straight down in front of him.

"After I got into trouble, she left. It's been so many years, I don't even know where she is now . . ."

After handing me the envelope, he turned around and silently walked away.

Something pricked me, I don't know what: I started feeling uncomfortable. I opened the envelope and saw twenty *yuan* and two *jiao*, along with his son's Guangdong address. Below it, he had signed his name: Si Tujing. It was the first time I'd known his full name.

I intended to mail this money the next day.

But lots of things in this world are unpredictable. My cousin—that pretty, pretentious little princess—had arrived on the twilight bus that very day. Her father, who had been in trouble and then rehabilitated, had gone back to his job as a police chief, and so she was going to be transferred to the city soon. She was coming to say good-bye to me. I didn't know why she was still thinking about me—was it because of the twenty *yuan*? She stayed one night in the women's dorm. The next morning, she suggested that I go with her to Jiamusi. I asked for the day off, and happily took the train to Jiamusi. We saw a movie, wandered through shops, went to a restaurant, and had ice cream. Although we had a really good time, a drum kept beating in my heart: when I was ready to get married, I'd better not look for someone like my cousin—in twenty-four hours, she could spend your whole year's wages. As we were about to board the train, she noticed canned anchovies at the station's food stand. Practically jumping out of her skin, she shouted, "Oh, look! This is my dad's favorite food. I have to take some back for him!"

I fumbled in my bag, but couldn't find any money. I searched again: ah, I felt something—a stiff envelope. I remembered that this money was Old Si's remittance.

"Buy ten of them! Ten!"

I was hesitating: I knew in my heart that I couldn't use this money, but just then, my cousin threw me an enchanting glance. I opened the envelope and gave her the money.

On the way back, I made up my mind that next month when Old Si came to send more money, I would send this "embezzled" twenty *yuan* along with it.

But where would I get twenty *yuan*? I was ridden with anxiety.

Lion Head was living extravagantly: he generally came sneaking back to the dorm only late at night. Sometimes he was drunk as a skunk. How did he get so much money? One night, when dice rolled out of his pants pocket, I at last stumbled on to what he was up to.

Lion Head gave a few hollow laughs and whispered, "How about it? Want to give it a try? You can win a lot of money and pay back your old debt!"

I shoved him away, but my heart was beating fast. It was all clear as day: this was the only way to get some extra money! But I knew getting mixed up with Lion Head would lead to no good. I'd heard that he frequently stole from the semi-felons, and then sold the stolen things to buy alcohol. Besides, how could I get involved in something like gambling?

Payday came, but Old Si didn't show up to send money. One day, when I ran into him on the path, I asked why he hadn't sent his son any money this month. He said he sent money every other month. I didn't dare look him in the eye: I was afraid he'd want a receipt for his previous month's remittance. I found an excuse to hurry off. He followed me a little way and asked if I had any mail for him. He said that every time his son received the money, he sent a letter . . .

My heart thumped: I hadn't sent the money. How could he receive a letter back . . . ?

I headed back to the dorm with a long face. Near the truck station, I ran into Lion Head. He must have had a few drinks somewhere, because his eyes were red. When he saw me, he hurried over, grinning broadly, to greet me. Without listening to any protests from me, he dragged me off. I wanted to break away, but he wouldn't let me. Staggering, he pushed me into a small room with a foul smoky atmosphere. It was filled with people.

I was desperate: I'd try it once! I just had to get forty *yuan*, and I could pay my debt and be home free. Forty—that's all I needed.

But Lady Luck didn't smile on me. In the first round, I lost sixty. Could these dice be on to me?

My hands and feet were ice-cold. I was numb all over as I walked out. I really felt like crying.

It was payday again. Quite a lot of people came to me to send remittances. So did Old Si. When he handed me a packet of twenty *yuan*, he dillydallied a while in the corner, and then asked softly, "Isn't there a letter for me?"

I didn't have the heart to look at him. There wasn't any life in his eyes. It was as if he'd emerged from a tomb.

"What's the good of asking? If I had a letter for you, I'd give it to you!" I exploded for no reason.

In order to reimburse Lion Head for my gambling debt of sixty *yuan*, I made so bold as to hold the remittances from four of the semi-felons, including Old Si. This month, not only was I unable to repay the twenty *yuan* I owed Old Si from last time, but I embezzled another twenty *yuan* of his money. How did I dare go on embezzling his money? Probably because he was the only one who never asked me for a receipt . . .

The last goose had flown away, and there was nothing left to look at in the sky. The open fields were mantled with a thin layer of snow. The cold north wind was blowing the fine snowflakes up into the air again, blowing people's moods to hell and gone.

Late that afternoon, I'd carried a large bundle of *Red Flag* magazines back from the branch post office. It was almost dark. I was nervous. On the curving road, I almost bumped into a withered tree at the roadside. All of a sudden, the "tree" was alive; it started speaking in a dreary tone. A little frightened, I jumped down from my bike and focused on the scene: it was Old Si. He was standing motionless in the cold wind. It looked as though he'd been waiting for me for a long time.

"My son—isn't there a letter from him?"

His tone was miserable and sad, like a wounded wolf moaning. He hadn't asked "Is there a letter?" but "Isn't there a letter?" Probably he hoped to trade the worst scenario for an unexpected pleasant surprise.

"No, there isn't. There isn't . . ."

"There should be a letter . . . Nothing could have happened to him, could it?"

He was walking behind me, talking softly to himself. It was as if his body would snap like a withered tree the first time there was a gust of wind. I hurriedly got on my bike and dodged into the darkness.

-4-

The Spring Festival would soon be here. I started getting my things ready to go home and see my family.

Without feeling at all guilty, I made use of Old Si's remittance for a fourth time to balance my income and expenses.

Lion Head was also getting ready to go home. Recently, it seemed he'd run out of luck. I heard he'd lost 100 *yuan*. He'd even sold his bedding and was now sleeping on the bare *kang*. He asked me for money, but where would I get money to lend him? He groaned, and patting my shoulder, said, "Do you take me for an idiot? All the semi-felons' money is in your hands. You ungrateful . . ."

"Bullshit!" I roared.

I hated Lion Head. I also hated my cousin. Most of all, I hated myself.

That day, I went to the post office very early to pick up the mail. I sorted it next to the heater there, as I always did. Suddenly, I came upon a crumpled envelope. A few characters flashed before my eyes: "For Si Tujing."

There was a hole in the envelope; you could see the flimsy stationery inside.

I don't know what provoked me, what made me so uncomfortable. I stole a look in all directions: no one was watching me, so I extended a finger and, with the dexterity honed with slingshots in my childhood, flipped the envelope open.

This is what the letter said:

Papa: I haven't had a letter from you for more than six months, nor have I received any money from you. I've checked at the Kuishan post office, and they said nothing has come. I'm worried. Are you sick? If something were to happen to you, I'd be all alone in the world . . .

Our crew is still doing very heavy labor. In the fall, there was a plague of insects, so the grain was all lost. Now all we have to eat are sweet potatoes and pumpkins. I have a boil on my leg, but no money for medicine. I don't have any money for oil, either; the wok is all rusted . . .

Papa: you have to work hard at reforming yourself—atone for your guilt by doing good deeds. When will you be able to come back and see me? I've already forgotten what you look like . . .

The writing became fainter; I couldn't make it out. What was wrong with me? Tears stung my eyes. I was also a little dizzy. I quietly picked up the heavy mailbag and slipped out of the room.

Above the field, the air was pure, fresh, and clean: the immense, boundless field of snow was like a large white cloth covering all the squalor and ugliness. Who could say for sure what is right and what is wrong in this world? The magpies were calling cheerily, beckoning people to be happy. But the black crows were loathsome, even though in fact they weren't doing anything wrong. No matter what crime Old Si had committed in the past, he had gone through reform for years and technically he had finished his service and been released a long time ago. After all, he was a person, too, a father of a son. Even if he didn't deserve the happiness of a father being with his son, wasn't his son entitled to enjoy a father's warmth?

And I? What had I done to him? How could I have turned into such a callous, ruthless person? His son was an educated youth just like me. Was it perhaps only because he missed his own son that he sympathized with me? I recalled that before I was sent down to the countryside, I read a book that mentioned "humanitarianism." Weren't Old Si and his son people just like me? By comparison, since I'd done those things, how could I still be considered a human? . . .

I rode the three miles back to my company as if I were a wandering, drifting ghost. After flinging down the mailbag, I hopped on my bike again, and fighting a head wind, rode the six miles into town. I rushed straight to the only marketplace there. It was dark before I got back to the dorm. My clothes were soaked, and I no longer had a watch on my wrist. I had sold it for ninety *yuan.*

The next day, I sent a remittance for eighty *yuan* to the Guangdong countryside. I had never felt so lighthearted.

After supper, I took ten *yuan* out from under the mattress—this was my cigarette and alcohol money from my monthly wages—and added another ten *yuan* I had from selling my watch. Altogether twenty *yuan*. I held it in my palm, and then called Lion Head to come out of the dorm.

"Let's go for a walk."

"Where?" He was in high spirits over this mysterious activity.

"The root cellar!"

This year, the company had built a new, warm cellar out of tiles. Old Si was assigned there to keep the stove burning. Of course, I had a reason for bringing Lion Head along: I wanted him to see me return the twenty *yuan* to Old Si.

The moon came out: the snowy field was deathly pale. It was as if the wind had destroyed everything, even the remaining warmth in people's hearts.

The deep snow almost blocked the little wooden door to the root cellar. I knocked for a long time before Old Si opened the door. When he saw the two of us, he seemed quite frightened, as if we'd come to ask for our money back. He set down the willow basket that he'd just plaited, and from a corner pulled out a few potatoes that he wanted to roast for us. Lion Head grabbed a carrot and started chewing it. He was a little impatient.

The damp smell of cabbage was coming from the warm root cellar. In the north in the winter, this was the only place you could still see much green color. Those green leaves, containing moist vitality, were kept by a wizened old man approaching death.

Old Si sat on a block of wood across from me: it was the first time he'd dared face me. He was looking at me with such absorption that I began to feel uncomfortable.

"My son—he must be about your age . . . When he talks, he likes sucking in his breath, just as you do . . ." As he mumbled indistinctly to himself, bright, crystal teardrops welled up at the corners of his turbid eyes.

Inwardly, I trembled a little. Was it possible that it was just for this reason that he'd been willing to lend me money? It had been almost a year, and he hadn't asked me to do anything—not even a little thing—for him in return. Was it possible that this was merely because he felt sorry for a youth who, like his son, was living alone in the outside world?

"Don't I have any mail yet?" He sighed deeply.

"On the way, the letter, on the way . . . ," I said, then choked up.

"Are you saying the letter's on the way?" He repeated this and it seemed he believed it. He didn't want to ask again, fearful of smashing this wisp of boundless hope. The wrinkles smoothed out on his thin withered face, and his dry sunken lips opened a little. His incisors were missing. It was the first time I'd seen him smile a little—if this could be called a smile.

I stood up. My face was burning. Without saying anything, I gently placed the twenty *yuan* in Old Si's palm.

He twitched for a moment and his head drooped. He was holding the money tightly as he stood up, staggering, and walked to the end of the *kang*. He took a tin box out from the base of the wall, and carefully put the money inside.

"With this and what I've saved, I have roughly enough money for my trip. I'm planning to go back to Guangdong and see my son . . . The only way I can feel reassured about him is to go back and see him . . . Ah, I made mistakes when I was young, and I've regretted them for a lifetime . . ." It seemed he was talking to himself.

I happened to look back, and was shocked by what I saw: Lion Head was staring desperately, mouth agape, at the tin box in Old Si's hands. Greed and a savage cruelty were radiating from his eyes. A chill ran down my spine.

The root cellar's door shut behind me. I could hear Old Si coughing. With the moonlight shining on this snow-mantled plateau, it looked exactly like a huge graveyard. But Old Si would walk out of here and go to his faraway native place to be reunited with his son. There wouldn't be ice and snow—or the hardships he faced here.

Suddenly, Lion Head said, "What were you thinking of—returning the money to him? How stupid can you be? Hey, what do you say, if someone like Old Si dies, isn't it about the same as a dog dying?"

I wasn't in the mood to answer.

The next noon, when I went to the mess hall for lunch, I saw nothing on the menu—just plain soy sauce soup for everybody. I heard people talking, saying that someone had died in the root cellar and that no one from the kitchen dared go there to get cabbage and beancurd. My heart thumped and I was weak in the legs. I asked right away who had died, even though I'd already guessed who it was.

"Who else? Old Si. He already had one foot in the grave, and yet he'd been saving money. What for? See, he got robbed. He must have been killed when he wouldn't let go of the money . . ."

All of them were talking about it. In talking and laughing as if this were nothing, they were expressing their own indignation about this semi-felon.

No one sympathized with him: no one dared, no one wanted to, no one could sympathize with a semi-felon.

I was the only one who knew that because I'd returned that small sum of money, he had paid the price of his life: I had taken the murderer with me. But who could I tell all this to? Could I prove my innocence?

I went home for the Spring Festival and stayed six months. The next summer, I returned to the military farm to go through the procedure that would allow me to move back to the city. I happened upon the execution cart parading the robber and murderer Lion Head through the streets of the small town. Lion Head wasn't any thinner than before. His eyes inadvertently met mine, and then he slowly turned his head away. But his expression was still carefree. His indifferent, yet aggrieved, expression seemed to be asking: "Does it count as a crime if you kill a semi-felon?"

The day before I finished the procedure for leaving, I went quietly to the pine forest. I knew that Old Si had been buried there.

He would never be able to go home. In the end, I had to visit his grave: this would be my farewell. But I couldn't find it. I saw only a few mounds with grass growing on them. There wasn't even a wooden tablet to mark his grave. A few crows were circling over the pine forest, cawing sadly, as though singing a dirge for the dead man. Wild poppies were blossoming like snow all over the slope: there was a profusion of pure white petals as soft as water, waving silently in the wilds.

Since childhood, I'd heard that poppies were a drug. People didn't know that if used sparingly, they could act as a healing medicine. This was the first time I'd seen pure white wild poppies, heartbreakingly white. I looked at them in silence for a long time. In my heart, a little something seemed to gradually be coming back to life.

Yanni's Secret

I didn't tell anyone about my idea. For about two weeks, afraid of complications, I did my utmost to keep it to myself. The situation had been vexing from the beginning. People here thought I was like all the other nostalgic types: taking advantage of business travel in order to go back to visit the farms where we had worked when we were young, reliving the splendors of our youth. Every year, the residents of the Great Northern Wilderness would generously welcome these nostalgic visitors returning from afar. Hosts and guests would lean over well-stocked bars together and drink themselves into oblivion. Maybe my plan made me an exception, a wild goose flying north in autumn, though I was aware of the possibility of freezing to death in the snow. It was like clawing under the frost with frozen fingers in hopes of finding a scrap of remembrance. Year by year, events of my time with Yanni were gradually fading, one by one. If by chance I could restore even a scrap, it would resound in my heart like thunder. This was the secret—Yanni's and mine—that we've kept for more than thirty years. But even in old age, even at the moment of death, secrets never lose their hold on you.

Yanni was the only student from Hangzhou who had been left behind on Dayangshu Farm. Of course, I could have asked anyone where she lived. But if I asked, I'd be giving away our secret. And I'd also be violating the tacit agreement between us that I'd kept these many years. No, by quietly returning to the farm in the fall I hoped to keep a little space for my private feelings.

Actually, in these last few decades I'd known all along where she lived—in a place far from the main highway and near the fork of a tributary of the Songhua River. The place was called Keep Watch Village. When you crossed a low, gentle hill, you could see in the distance a luxuriant grove of crab apple trees. In springtime, the blossoming crab apple flowers were like bits of pink cloud falling from heaven. Since locating her so-called father, Yanni had not left this place of livestock and a few thatched huts. At the end of the sixties, Dayangshu had been converted from a prison farm to a rural destination where city students could come to work. A stall had been set aside for treating sick and weak horses, and a few ex-prison inmates who were old or chronically ill worked there. The city students working there dubbed it "the sick ward."

It was in this remote, worthless "sick ward" that Yanni miraculously came across Old Yang, a former prisoner who claimed he was her real father. She believed him with all her heart and eagerly announced this news to me that very evening. In that instant, it was as if a hydrogen bomb had been launched from Russian territory across the river and suddenly exploded, vaporizing me in the blink of an eye. But in the midst of the dark-gray smoke and atomic fog filling the sky, Yanni—with her delicate eyes and eyebrows, her slender waist and thin braids—was shedding tears of joy. She'd suddenly been transformed into a little daughter, as precious as Thumbelina, as charming and gentle as a sprite. I ached from the shock.

I angrily burst out, "That's impossible! He isn't your father! He's a ninety-nine percent con artist!"

She clenched her fists so forcefully that her fingertips turned deep violet. Lowering her head, she retorted, "No. You don't know. There are lots of things you don't know. Old Man Yang really is my father. His last name is Yang, and so is mine. My residence card identifies Xiaoshan as my ancestral home. You've heard his accent; it's a strong Xiaoshan accent. I was born in 1951. He ran into trouble in 1952—not long after I was born."

I broke in. "Lots of old men are named Yang. But you—Yang Hongying—can have only one father."

"I have proof. Really. If you don't believe me, I'll show it to you sometime." Although her voice had softened, her tone was that of someone who would not be swayed, even unto death.

I said coldly, "You'd better ask your ma to visit from Hangzhou. If she recognizes this father, then it can't be a mistake."

At the mention of her mother, Yanni—Yang Hongying—listlessly turned her back to me.

I always felt that Yang Hongying's decision to go to the Great Northern Wilderness in search of her father was so much hopeless nonsense. You could have only one biological father. If he was lost in this vast country of hundreds of millions of people, would it be so easy to find him? It wasn't as if Yang Hongying's father were a splendid river, much less a majestic mountain. He was simply a speck of dust chased away by a broom.

As the swift train carrying us city youth to the countryside left ancient Hangzhou in 1969 she was clutching that immense secret to her heart. She bumped back and forth in the aisle, her gaze catching my swinging pigtails. Finally, breathing heavily in the hazy twilight, she drew me to the platform between the cars. I felt that I was looking at a balloon that was about to burst. This is how she began: "Hey, let me tell you something. No way could you ever guess. I signed up to go down to the countryside for different reasons from the rest of you. I'm going to the Great Northern Wilderness to look for my papa."

Surprised, I asked, "So was your father transferred from military service in 1958? Was he a commander?"

"Uh . . . no."

"Even if he was a colonel, that's still impressive enough!"

"Not . . . that, either."

"Then . . . was he a captain? He couldn't have been just a sergeant."

Shrinking into the folds of the curtain on the platform between the cars, she suddenly began crying on my shoulder.

From her confused narrative and the sound of her weeping, I began to understand. Her father hadn't even been a sergeant but was instead a criminal. When the Communists came to power, he'd been a senior accountant. In the political movements of the early fifties, he was smoked out for embezzling public funds. After his arrest in 1952, he was convicted, and in 1955 he was sent to the Xingkai prison farm in the northeast. Even though he had embezzled public funds for the express purpose of buying a costly down coat for his wife, Hongying's mother lost no time in divorcing him. After his release in 1965, no one in Hangzhou would take him in, nor did he have any close relatives in his ancestral home of Xiaoshan. He had no choice but to move to Dayangshu Farm and work there. Someone carried this news to Yanni's mother, who in turn said to Yanni, "You want to go down to the countryside, don't you? This is perfect. Go to the Great Northern Wilderness and live with him."

Day and night the train swayed toward the northeastern plains. Interrupted by the clamor of crowds shouting slogans to us in the cities we passed through, Hongying told me the story of her life. She said that in her memories there was not the least impression of her father. Her father was like odorless air: you knew it was there, but it was just out of reach. She thought of her father as a shadow in the moonlight: as soon as dark clouds emerged, it quickly disappeared. If she didn't hurry and look for her father now, she probably would never find him. She couldn't bear to imagine herself a father-less girl. Even if she found only his grave, she wouldn't have gone to the Great Northern Wilderness for nothing . . .

Her forthrightness bothered me a little. Perhaps no one had ever warned her that she shouldn't tell a stranger all of this upon first meeting. Her story was interrupted countless times when the train halted for unknown reasons. But I was hopelessly moved by the inexplicable trust she had placed in me. Just think: in the surging flood of thousands and thousands of students heading north to reinforce the Sino-Soviet border, one person named Yang Hongying was different from all the others. Her mission differed from ours. She was going to the Great Northern Wilderness to be reunited with her father. What an extraordinary secret! In its presence, how could I not seal my mouth like a tightly corked bottle? She merely wanted a father, even if he was lacking in status like this one. Everyone had a father, and she wanted to be like all the others—just as, like the other youth, she'd received a padded coat, hat, and boots before boarding the northbound train. I couldn't see anything wrong with her desire. But she might turn out to be very mistaken. It was this possibility that made her secret burn in me. Though I found myself disagreeing with her disordered, absurd logic, I had to scrupulously withhold my deepest doubts.

As the train had been about to pull out of the station of ancient Hangzhou—amid wailing and weeping from the crowd on the platform below—she and I had exchanged glances. At almost the same instant, each of us noticed that the other wasn't shedding tears, unlike the crying students on all sides of us. My nineteen-year-old emotions surged as I thought of the literary education awaiting me. And the seventeen-year-old Yang Hongying, with eyes lit up with joy, looked past the trials of the journey to the hopes of finding her father, who in her dreams had come back thousands of times to kiss her and hold her happily in the golden wheat fields.

Both of us had reasons to be happy, and happiness is destined to lead to friendship. From then on, Hongying and I kept no secrets from each other.

It was much later that I realized that the years are like that terribly dilapidated train pulled by a steam locomotive: traveling along fixed tracks, it has no way to reverse direction.

Now it was August and the hills stretched to the horizon, saturated with the green of soybean fields. I knew for sure that Yanni resided in the village known as Keep Watch. For more than twenty years she'd lived there with the man who supposedly was her father. No one could convince her to abandon that man, and yet no one could prove that Old Man Yang wasn't her father. In the seventies, no one knew you could go to the hospital for a paternity test. In those days, I couldn't do anything; the more I argued with her, the more impassioned she grew. And when I went along with her, I became less and less able to extricate myself from the trap I'd fallen into. With my shallow, self-righteous, youthful intellect, persuading Yang Hongying was terribly difficult. Every time I went to the stable to look for her, all I could do was pathetically hold up a rusty little round mirror. She would turn her back to me as I would say over and over, "Look in the mirror, look in the mirror! Look at Old Man Yang's appearance. What do you look like? Are your eyes smeared with dog shit? Everything about you is delicate: your eyebrows, teeth, and eyelids are like willow leaves. Take another look at Old Man Yang. Everything about him—shoulders, forehead, nose—is square. How can a chunky-looking person have a slim, fair daughter? Have you ever seen a cat give birth to a snake? Or a hair-tail fish spawn a hedgehog? I hereby swear to the great Chairman Mao that Old Man Yang is not your father! This is a con game."

Yanni would grab the mirror and tell me off in her northeastern accent.

It was only after Yang Hongying arrived at Dayangshu Farm that people started calling her Yanni. She seemed to take an instinctive fancy to this nickname. But as I saw it, when others began calling her Yanni, she changed into another girl—a girl of the northeast. And as a northeasterner, Yanni was a little unreal to me. In Hangzhou, when we had boarded the special train for educated youth, people seeing her off had shouted: "Aying, Aying—Little Flower, Little Flower!"

As the train started moving, someone held up to the window the page of a notebook: "To a revolutionary comrade-in-arms, Yang Hongying—Red Cherry." Inwardly, I hoped that was her name. I fancied it would have been best for this slight girl across from me to have been born in early spring when the cherry blossoms were in full bloom, or perhaps in early autumn when the red cherries ripened. But my gaze fell on the card swinging on her flat chest; printed on this ID card were the words YANG HONGYING—Red Eagle Yang.

I asked her, "What in the world is your name? Which *ying* does it refer to? Flower, cherry, or eagle?" She smiled shyly at me, tilted her identity card for me to look at, and said, "From now on, as soon as the train starts, I'm Red Eagle Yang! I am flying to the sky!" Red Cherry's charming petals and fragrance were crushed under the speeding wheels of the train. One by one, they were blown away by the wind.

Choked by the sooty smoke of the locomotive, I indignantly voiced my opinion. I felt that one shouldn't change one's name too often—it was confusing. And red eagle? A big, red bird? The image was scary.

"Listen to me," I said. "That guy over there changed his name to 'Antirevisionism.' The girl over by the window changed her name to 'Resolve.' Others call themselves 'Revolution' or 'Struggle.' None of them has a surname. Lots of Red Guards have gotten rid of their last names—and only without surnames are they completely changed. Why on earth are you still called Red Eagle Yang? It's a really ugly name."

Red Eagle's face suddenly turned pallid—like a young eagle shot from the sky and drained of blood. But despite my words, during that night of endless sounds of train wheels, we snuggled close and hugged each other as we whispered of personal matters. Red Eagle's twitters and moans rushed out with her warm breath, each fluttering breeze hovering over me, besieging me.

When it was nearly daylight, I awakened to see the solemn plains of the desolate landscape north of the Yangzi. I remembered clearly the last words Yanni had uttered during the night. She had said she absolutely couldn't get rid of her surname, "Yang," for it was the only link between her and her father. If she changed her surname, from then on she would be fatherless, and doomed never to find him.

If I could have foreseen the end, perhaps I could have prevented its essential absurdity. If I could have steered her away from her search, she wouldn't still be in the Great Northern Wilderness. She wouldn't have become a slovenly farm wife burdened with a family far from urban civilization.

If, from that day in June 1969 when we arrived at Dayangshu Farm, I could have seen how deeply embedded was this unwavering desire to find her father, then I wouldn't be here, thirty years later, struggling with all the strength of my body and spirit to find Yanni. I might have merely been too young and foolish. All I did back then was repeat the same ineffectual arguments: Old Man Yang was too decrepit and stupid, vulgar and ugly to be her real father. I visualized for her a different father who, even if he were trapped in a disgusting environment, would be gentle and cultivated, elegant and neatly dressed. Then I went back to denigrating this Old Man Yang, who lacked all of these traits. But in the end, I could only say he wasn't her father; I couldn't prove he wasn't.

In the dark coach when she first disclosed her plan to look for her father in the Great Northern Wilderness, I thought of it as a high-minded pact, an ironclad alliance that sealed our friendship from outsiders. Just nineteen years old, I saw looking for a long-lost father as a sweet adventure, washed in the sentimental aura of tears and nostalgia. I willingly accepted that only after hardships and melancholy would the satisfaction and sweetness be attained—

especially because we were looking for an "exile" rather than the kind of lost hero found in movies such as *Children of Courage*. Our quest held a sense of the forbidden that we had to keep to ourselves. We burned with excitement.

In the first days of our secret search, I adopted the "process of elimination": I started by identifying every man between forty and sixty years old whom I could find; and of those, every man with a thick or even a slight Xiaoshan accent who had been kept on to work at the farm after being released. I weeded all the others out. By eliminating each possibility, we made continuous progress in our search. This adventure would end only with a positive identification. But in my innermost being, I dreaded the possibility that the search would end too easily.

In fact, as educated youth sent down to work on the farm, we didn't encounter many ex-prisoners. At the beginning, Red Eagle Yang and I were assigned to the gardening unit, where only a few former prisoners were working. We eliminated them quickly.

Then I requested a transfer to the tile factory because most of the technicians manning the kilns were ex-convicts. Once, Red Eagle Yang was chosen to be a tractor driver—a great job on the farm. But she declined because—as she put it—there wasn't one ex-prisoner in the whole mechanized plowing unit. She wouldn't even consider a job in a place where all the workers were youth like us. Every few days, she would mysteriously appear in the vegetable cellar, the storehouse, and the threshing ground. She was like a mouse furtively chatting with the former convicts. To avoid suspicion, she inquired about their astrological signs and their hometowns—that sort of thing. Her stealthy eyes would take in every gesture as her eager mind absorbed every word murmured by these filthy old guys who had come from all parts of the country. Time after time, she listened to these words and sifted through them.

But it became apparent that our aimless casting about was like looking for a needle in a haystack. It was utterly ineffective, and I was soon fed up.

I shouted despondently at Red Eagle Yang, telling her that there was no bigger place under the sun than the Great Northern Wilderness and this was merely one Dayangshu Farm.

One Dayangshu has to be enough, she consoled me. "Even if it's as big as heaven and earth, it still isn't as big as my eyes."

If I'd been more observant, I would have seen that the evidence had been clear for a long time. Red Eagle Yang's fixation had gone too far and nearly become an obsession. If I had seen this, would I still have helped her carry out her tragic mission?

When winter came, I was sent to reinforce the water-conservancy unit out in the countryside. The unit was a mixed group of students from the northeast and Zhejiang Province. Our job of digging the frozen earth by hand was utterly exhausting. Consequently, my plan to help Yanni look for her father had to be put aside for the time being. But news of Yanni came continuously to the tent in the wintry countryside. Everything I heard gave me the willies.

Someone said that she was acting abnormally. She kept slipping over to the basement where the ex-prisoners lived. She would knit sweaters for them and even drink with them. Someone suspected that she was carrying on an illicit affair with a certain ex-con. Someone else suspected that she was being used and perhaps abused by the bad guys. Another person challenged her political standpoint. Someone even suggested that she might be a Soviet spy. Otherwise, this person reasoned, why was it that every lunar New Year all the other students were anxious to go home and see their families, yet she passed up all those chances and never went back? The stories grew more and more bizarre. The more charitable people said that she'd contracted a weird illness: whenever she heard anyone say "Papa," she burst into tears.

And there were other strange stories about her. A girl from Ningbo wrote to her parents every day, and every day she received a letter in return. It was said that Red Eagle secretly stole the letters sent from the girl's parents, read them, and then silently tore them up. On another occasion, a male student bought a bottle of aged white "Great Northern Wilderness" wine. With money he'd saved, he also bought a piece of red ginseng. After steeping it in the wine, he mentioned to someone, "My father suffers from rheumatism. He told me to soak ginseng in wine and bring it home to build up his strength." Upon hearing this, Red Eagle fainted and fell to the ground. It was said that after she came to she asked people around her what would be the easiest way to commit suicide.

In the tent where I lived, the people who didn't know Yanni talked about her behind her back, and the rumors gradually became venomous. One person said she wanted a man rather than a father. After all, how could someone so desperately want a father? For a revolutionary youth to turn into a sex maniac was disgraceful. This idle gossip ripped away Red Eagle's feathers, one by one, exposing a battered chest that was all skin and bones. My heart ached for her, but I couldn't save her. I'd done my best to guard her secret, but she herself had revealed it to everyone. No one knew where on earth to help her look for the father who was in her heart. I began to wonder even more whether the person she searched for so desperately—the father she claimed was an accountant and an ex-prisoner—was real or fake.

In those days, the water-conservancy unit kept working fast and furiously, allowing me no time off. I entrusted someone with a note to Yanni. I wrote, "The easiest way to commit suicide is to hang oneself from a crab apple tree. But if you do that, you'll never see your father."

I knew that sooner or later I'd see Yanni again. Even after thirty years I knew where to find her. At the end of the slushy paths in the birch grove, in the depths of the fields where the colors changed every season—bright greens, inky greens, golden yellows, then snow whites—was a place where I could visualize her just by closing my eyes. I could still smell the intoxicating sweetness of the blossoming crab apple trees. I knew I could still find her in the village known as Keep Watch. Just three thatched huts, two haystacks, and one well, it held the whole of Yanni's happiness.

In a howling storm in that long-ago spring when I went back to my original unit, people told me that Yanni had moved to the stable. It seemed nobody could do anything with this person who threatened suicide at every turn, yet her madness and perversity had finally aroused compassion in the supervisor. He had approved her application to work in the "sick ward." A shiver ran down my back—not a good omen. Most of the prisoners in the ward—gimpy, humpbacked men, some with eyes blurry with glaucoma—were ugly and disgusting. In the days when we'd gone through the ward on our way to work, Yanni and I hadn't dared even to breathe the air. Was she used to it now?

That damned water-conservancy unit. By keeping me away from Yanni for months, it had played havoc with our plans. But I couldn't give up on her.

Near dusk on the day our unit returned, clouds as fiery as the Red Sea spread across the western sky. Under the setting sun, the tufts of grass that had just greened again on the ridges between the fields were luring me on like a trail of fresh roses. From a long way off, I saw the white fog drifting in the valley, curling upward near the eaves of the huts and rising to the treetops. Then I saw the brick hearth in the yard outside the horse stable. A big pot bubbled with steam, and a burnt smell floated my way. Squatting in front of the oven was an old man holding a poker and raking something out from the hearth.

I couldn't see him well, but I remember that his incisors were long and visible outside his lips, like a grandmother wolf's. His poker speared something round, and he stood up excitedly, calling loudly, "Red Eagle, Red Eagle!"

I saw Yanni come flying out of the stable to hold the potato in both hands. Jumping up and down, she said, "It smells so good—so delicious." She also grumbled, "It's burning hot." Gazing at her with a smile, the old man said, "Hold on. I'll peel it for you. Ah, here's the table salt I ground. If you eat potatoes without dipping them in salt, you'll get heartburn."

Thus, by the time I saw Yanni again, the damage was already done. Father and daughter were the very picture of sweet, warm-hearted harmony. No matter how bitterly I hated the situation, I knew I couldn't change it.

I can still remember Yanni's rapture as she offered me the peeled, roasted potato. She tugged at the old man's cap and said, "Look. Now do you believe in miracles? It's the absolute truth: this is the father I wanted to find!"

The sky abruptly darkened. A half-moon rose from the other side of the heavenly vault. A hint of blue tinted the air—clear, light, crisp. The smell of warm horse dung and hay was flowing over everything. Speechless, I could only lean against the wooden wall of the horse shed. In the palm of my hand, the hot potato gradually cooled, finally becoming as cold as a rock. Then all at once, I screamed. Something soft and wet was licking my neck. Startled, I jumped to one side, then quickly turned around. In the soft yet bleak moonlight, a black silhouette slowly shifted.

A colt about three feet tall was rubbing back and forth against the gate of the stable. Hesitantly, it drew close to the mother horse, pawing lightly at the earth, its long, slender legs trembling. After a while, the mother horse gently whisked her long tail over the little colt's gleaming back. The colt's happy snort echoed in the small shed: *Mama!*

In that instant, waves of tears spilled down my face. I hugged Yanni tight and wept aloud with her. I had lost the power to reason. As long as Yanni could have a father, I thought, who cares who it is!

Like a flash of lightning, Yanni's alleged father had walked into our lives. That night, she and I slept in the same quilted sleeping bag, and she recounted for me the process she had used in identifying her father. It had actually been extraordinarily swift, like checking the seat number on a movie ticket and sitting down—that's all.

She said that last winter, the urban students had been harvesting beans in the snow-covered field. One day, Old Man Yang came looking for a horse he'd lost. From a distance, he shouted at the students. Teeth bared, he looked fierce, as though he thought someone had stolen his horse. Yanni was the only one who could understand him. In his unsophisticated Xiaoshan accent, he was merely warning the young people, *No matter how thirsty you are from your hard work, don't even think about eating the snow! On the soybean plants are black mites—parasites of rats—that drop into the snow. Anyone who eats the snow starts hemorrhaging, develops a high fever, and begins vomiting. The person hemorrhages from spots under his armpits right up until he kicks the bucket.* His warning scared the kids so much that they squatted on the ground and retched.

Stunned, Yanni had been looking blankly at the old man's back: around his neck was the corner of a checked scarf of indeterminate color. And in that moment, a wave of memories overwhelmed her. She told me she suddenly smelled a familiar scent. She remembered that long ago her father had been wearing just this kind of scarf, and after kissing her on the cheek, he had left forever.

Her story burst from her, almost in a single reckless breath. How could she possibly remember things that happened when she was only a year old, I started to ask. But without waiting for my questions and doubts to spoil her happiness, she drifted off to dreamland.

Early the next morning when I awakened in the stable, I had a powerful intuition that this long-toothed Old Man Yang, with his thick Xiaoshan accent, was a fake. He wasn't Yanni's papa—absolutely not! If he truly was, he would truly love her. And if he truly loved her, he would consider her welfare. That is, with his unsavory background, he would not have dared to acknowledge her and thereby jeopardize her politically! If he loved her, he couldn't possibly do that.

I began scheming about ways to trip him up. I knew about genetic traits: that by examining stature, weight, complexion, hair quality, facial features, and bearing, one could find the similarities in any father-daughter pair.

I was persistent in enumerating and exaggerating every fault—for example, his ugliness, his lack of refinement, his fake hospitality. Now and then, offended by my hostility toward him, Yanni grew annoyed. What diabolical skills had Old Man Yang employed to make her so sincerely convinced and so obsessed? Yanni seemed to be completely under his control. Deaf and blind to all the facts I ticked off, she didn't argue with me but instead responded by fawning over Old Man Yang even more. Affectionately calling him "Pa," she did everything for him—washed and mended his clothes and cooked and served him his food. She not only tidied up after filthy Old Man Yang, but also polished his hurricane lamp until it gleamed. Laughing and joking, the two of them played poker in the lamplight, their laughter disappearing high and clear into the night.

Since coming to the farm, Yanni had never been so happy. I had had a hunch, however, that the day she found her father would be the day our friendship ended. For this reason alone, I was suspicious and didn't want to give in so easily. Someone like me, who'd enjoyed a father's love ever since childhood, simply couldn't understand how a father whose authenticity was so difficult to verify could make Yanni betray me and the oath we'd sworn in the dark train car.

I was exasperated and jealous watching Old Man Yang quickly take on a father's authority and use his tricks to charm the gullible Yanni. "Just look at you!" he'd say. "You're made from exactly the same mold as your ma!"

He also used gifts and favors to win us over. For example, he would cut willow branches and plait fish-drying mats. Then he would trust to luck as he went fishing at the bend of the small river. Every day, he caught a few anchovies, catfish, or whatever, kindled a fire with bean straw, and roasted them for us to eat.

He found some discarded electrical wire and bent it into the shape of curlers, which we would put on our bangs before we went to bed. The next morning, when we loosened the wire coils and combed our hair, it looked as though our bangs had actually been permed.

He would cadge black beans and corn from the choice feed provided to the stable by his superiors. He would choose each piece carefully, one by one, and mix them with rice to cook a fragrant holiday porridge for us.

He crumbled and thoroughly soaked the soybean dross meant for the horses. Stir-frying it with vegetable oil and hot peppers, he turned it into a delicious dish. He also collected wild duck eggs from beside the pond and soaked them in brine to make delicious salty eggs for us to eat with our rice gruel. At such times, Yanni would wave her chopsticks at me, despite our conflict over her father, and with her mouth full, she would mumble, "Hey, just look. Isn't it wonderful to have a father?"

On occasions like that, I would promptly forfeit my opinion and fall in with her. The steam from the hot porridge reddened our hungry faces. All of my misgivings and guardedness about Old Man Yang would gradually dissolve in the tasty glutinous fish soup. At last, after I'd accepted countless bribes of food, my tender childish brain turned into a pot of paste, unable to tell right from wrong. Furthermore, I lacked the power to withstand or reject such a warm family feeling. There really is wisdom in the saying that food is contentment. That whole year, from spring until winter, I would slip over to the stable to visit Yanni and—at the same time—to share in her father's love.

Years later, when I recalled those days, I was filled with shame. I knew that in my heart I had never regarded Old Man Yang as Yanni's father. I just let the impression go uncorrected and took advantage of the situation. In the name of a father's love, I mooched food and drink. Not only was I using Old Man Yang, but I was also taking advantage of Yanni.

Once in a while, in a clear-headed moment, I would turn hostile and refuse to recognize him. I'd even hurt Yanni with my sarcasm. I'd say, "Old Man Yang isn't your father! You just want to have a father! If you accept this father, what will you do later on? Can you take him home with you to Hangzhou?"

Biting her lip, Yanni wouldn't utter a word. This irritated me even more, and my words became more venomous. "At the very beginning on the train, you told me you were coming to the Great Northern Wilderness to look for your father. I assumed you were telling just me. Now, though, you've made such a commotion that everyone on the whole farm knows. Everyone knows everything that's going on in your home. How are you going to resolve things? Old Man Yang has led a student astray. If this isn't handled right, he could be convicted again."

Yanni's face turned deathly pale. Then she stood up, and—like a woman martyr going to the execution ground in a movie—she swept back her hair, and as if looking death calmly in the face, she answered, "That's right. It was just to look for my father that I came to the Great Northern Wilderness. So, if I hadn't found my father, wouldn't that mean I came here for nothing? And furthermore, why can't he really be my father? I . . . I have proof."

How could anyone get to the bottom of such talk? The fishy thing was that she never produced the so-called proof. Right up until I left Dayangshu Farm, I never saw anything that could prove a father-daughter relationship between Old Man Yang and her. One day, the authorities sent down a a mysterious workgroup that stayed a few days. I didn't know what they were secretly investigating.

After the workgroup withdrew, a small medical unit was sent down to give the female city youth routine physicals. None of us could stand going through such thorough physical exams. Only afterward, when we talked about it cautiously in private, did we realize that everyone had been dragged through it just to find out if any female students in this wasteland had lost their virginity.

Naturally, Yanni had topped the list of suspects that the workgroup had been sent to investigate. Not long afterward, a girl lashed out at her and her damned father. Behind Yanni's back, she said that Yanni had obsessively accepted a political enemy as her father. Not until Yanni heard this with her own ears did she finally realize how serious the accusation was. Old Man Yang had come within an inch of being charged with seducing a student. Luckily, Yanni's virginity was intact. And so Old Man Yang hung on to his life.

That night, after Yanni realized how close she had come to losing him, she raced back to the stable and sobbed into Old Man Yang's chest. Her sharp, aggrieved crying was like the sound of a *yataghan* piercing the cold fog in the fields. Or like an injured female wolf howling ceaselessly under the moon. I heard her ragged wailing. Every sound seemed to have only two syllables: "Pa-pa." During that black night that gleamed like lacquer, the quivering tip of every blade of grass in the wilderness was shivering and repeating those two syllables: *"Pa-pa."*

From then on, I no longer dared to question or disbelieve: no doubt, this Old Man Yang really was Yanni's father.

Not long after the medical unit left, I was transferred to the farm headquarters' propaganda unit and then temporarily transferred to a substation. A year later, I took some time off to go back to the farm to have a look around. After traveling for miles, I reached my former unit and heard that Yanni had married.

The man was the son of a worker on the farm, a bricklayer. Contrary to usual practice, the bridegroom had moved in with his wife's family. His new home was at the stable. Including Old Man Yang, it was a family of three.

I was speechless.

I arrived on an early autumn morning. Not having slept the night before, I was like a phantom skimming over the fields in foggy confusion. I saw a newly planted crab apple grove on the hillside where the stable was. Taller than a person, the seedlings were sturdy, and hanging on each little tree was ping-pong ball size fruit. The reds and greens were gorgeous.

An old man dressed in black and wearing puttees was walking back and forth in the furrows of the orchard. His blue-veined hands were behind his back, his chest thrust out, his face lifted. Extending his hand, he pulled at a limb, carefully plucked a crab apple, and bit into it. It was so sour he made a face and spat it out. He picked a crab apple from another tree and spat that one out, too.

Just then, he looked up and saw me. Facing me indifferently, he said, "You've come back? Yanni isn't up yet. Don't call her, let her sleep a little longer."

In a bad mood, I answered, "I'll wait."

"Come, help me taste this fruit." Old Man Yang handed me a crab apple. "It shouldn't be crisp or sour. Choose a good tree with fruit that's sweet and soft. I'll find one for Yanni. When she's old and toothless, she can eat the fruit from it."

All at once, my eyes stung.

"It isn't necessary to have a lot of trees with good fruit. One will be enough for her . . . "

Many, many years have passed, and still that hoarse voice hovers in the swaying reeds and on the tips of the grasses in the marsh. It's like the first greening of the crab apples in early autumn. Maybe it's because of Old Man Yang's words that I had to come back and look for Yanni. Old Man Yang had so painstakingly selected the soft-fruit tree for Yanni: did this mean that I should put aside my contemptuous feelings for him?

These past few decades have been vexingly long. But to describe them takes just a few sentences. Not long after Yanni married, I was recruited by a factory and left the farm. Later, I went to college. I don't know why, but not one letter passed between Yanni and me.

One after another of the educated city youth returning to Hangzhou told me about Yanni. After she got married, she gave birth to two sons. Later on, her husband went to work in a coal mine. A few years ago, the mine caved in, and he was crushed to death and his body was never found. Yanni went on living with that "Pa" of hers, who was now seventy or eighty years old and in poor health.

In the eighties, a policy was implemented permitting ex-prisoners to return home, but with no relatives or house left in his hometown to return to, Old Man Yang couldn't go back. In the end, it was Yanni who kept him company and waited on him hand and foot—this must have been due to the karma he cultivated in a previous life.

But it was also Yanni's predestined misfortune. In accepting this father, she put down roots in the Great Northern Wilderness.

Because I insisted on going out by myself without a guide, by the time I found the village known as Keep Watch it was already noon. I was a little hungry. Taking a desolate path through a clump of luxuriant bushes, I looked up and saw a sturdy crab apple tree—one full of red fruit.

Beside a thicket not far from the fruit tree, something like ash was drifting on the breeze. The ground was sprinkled with funeral money. In the clearing in the grove stood a simple, new grave. Some offerings of fruit and snacks were arranged in front of it. The exquisitely carved tombstone didn't seem in keeping with the earthen grave. On it was inscribed *The Grave of My Deceased Father Yang Siyang.*

A woman and two young men knelt in front of the grave for a long time. I stood quietly behind them. When they finally stood up, I called out softly, "Yanni."

She had changed beyond recognition: a wrinkled face, coarse hands, swollen eyelids, dark skin, graying hair. If she'd been walking in the farmers' market, I'd have taken her for a farm wife selling vegetables. In her eyes—once comely and charming—you could no longer see a hint of the Hangzhou student who had come here so long ago.

Her distracted, blunt gaze swept quickly over my face. She stopped in her tracks and glanced at me again. She looked away, then turned sideways and said, "Ah, you're here. I knew that sooner or later you'd come and see me."

Flustered, I stammered, "Yes, I've come a little late. You know, I've been very busy all these years . . . And besides, I wasn't sure exactly where you were living. I never thought that just as I caught up with Old Man Yang—uh, no, your father—he would have died. I came to see . . . " As I was speaking, I walked over to the grave. I felt obliged to kneel and kowtow to Old Man Yang.

Yanni pulled at me fiercely, her hand so strong that she nearly made me fall.

"Leave it at that," she said rudely. "I can tell you now. I deceived you. Old Man Yang wasn't my father at all."

I was startled and alarmed. My mind went blank.

"Do you still remember that I once said I would show you proof?" Her voice seemed to be coming from far away. "In fact, I couldn't show you any, because it was precisely this proof that made me realize he wasn't my father. All along, he said he had something that would prove our relationship. One day, he finally pulled an old handkerchief out of a dilapidated trunk. On it was an embroidered red eagle spreading its wings to take flight. I understood at a glance: the handkerchief was an old one, but the red eagle had only recently been embroidered. He said that my ma gave him this handkerchief just as he was leaving home and told him to take it along as a keepsake. She said, 'When our daughter grows up, this will help the two of you reunite.' At that moment, I was drenched in cold sweat. I knew he was lying—that he was deceiving me. As you know, when my father left home, I was only one year old and my name was Hongying—Red Cherry. My nickname was Aying—Little Flower. If there'd really been such a handkerchief, a cherry blossom should have been embroidered on it. Or a cluster of red cherries. As for the *ying* meaning eagle, you know that I didn't change my name to Red Eagle until just before I left the city for the countryside."

I stood gazing at her blankly. It was a long time before I could speak. "So you're saying that you've known for ages that Old Man Yang wasn't your father? In that case, why did you embrace him as your father? Why did you have to make it seem true? Didn't this hurt you?"

Yanni bent her head in thought, then said hesitantly, "There wasn't any reason. Emotionally, I simply wanted a father too much. After I saw that handkerchief, I couldn't sleep all night. I thought that with the Great Northern Wilderness being so large, where would I go to find my real father? He had probably died a long time ago. In any case, if I couldn't find my real father, then couldn't anyone be my father? Wasn't it all the same? And besides, Old Man Yang was all alone and so pitiful. He really wanted to have a daughter."

"You could have figured something out back then; you could have mailed a picture of Old Man Yang to Hangzhou to see if your ma recognized him."

"I've never told you—not long after I left for the Great Northern Wilderness, my ma broke off relations with me."

Words failed me. Tardily, I linked arms with Yanni and walked with her toward the house. As we walked, I tried to comfort her. "In all the years you've been here, you've been true to yourself and good to Old Man Yang. Now Old Man Yang has passed on, and you need to consider what you will do with the rest of your life—go back to Hangzhou with your children or remarry and make a new family."

Yanni abruptly stopped me. With a sneer, she said softly, "Don't say anything. I chose my own path, and I can't complain about the blisters on my feet. I will never try to find another father for my children. Just look—these two fatherless children of mine are more sensible than other children. Sometimes, I'm really puzzled. Back then, why was I so foolish as to have to find a father for myself?"

A youngster who'd been tramping along behind caught up with us. In both hands, he was holding a gorgeous red crab apple, which he tried to tuck into my pocket. He said, "Auntie, you must be hungry. Try this fruit: it's soft and sweet." Yanni grabbed it and threw it with all her strength. Smiling, she said, "That's it—leave it for Old Man Yang to eat. Come on, let's go home. I'll slice a watermelon for you."

Like green and red billiard balls, the soft fruit rolled along the ground. To tell the truth, I hated to see it go to waste.

That fall, I traveled to lots of places in the Great Northern Wilderness and never saw another crab apple tree. In the era of the educated city youth, it was the most coveted kind of fruit on the farms where we worked. Small and tart. Nowadays farm families generally don't grow them.

Are Birds Better at Walking or Flying?

Are you ready? —Hong Wei asked himself.
Not yet. —Hong Wei answered himself.
Aren't you ready yet? —Hong Wei asked himself again.
Patience. I need more time to get ready. —Hong Wei answered himself again while also admonishing himself.
Okay, then wait until fall. Set out after the autumn harvest. That's what he decided to do.

The agronomist Hong Wei was close to middle age, and it was an important thing he was getting ready to do. At least from his point-of-view, nothing was more important right then. He'd been preparing for this for—what? Ten years? Twenty years? Actually even longer. Could you say that he'd begun the day that Miss Cai left Hong River Farm to go back to the city? Had he been making his arrangements in secret? No, that wouldn't be quite true. The facts didn't bear this out. The fact was that in the last few years those educated youth from Shanghai and Harbin who had been among the first to return to the cities had begun to go back to the farms to visit. They talked of other educated youth who'd returned to the cities and of what they were doing now. When someone mentioned Miss Cai, Hong Wei's ears began turning like an audiotape. Although no one could say for sure what Miss Cai had been doing since returning to the city, by chance he got hold of a vague address for her in a small city in Liaoning Province.

The wind was blowing so hard that day that chicken feathers and scraps of paper along the road were whirling all over the place. When Hong Wei heard the words "Miss Cai," it was as if he were suddenly clasping a hot water bottle—hot water was swishing around in his heart. He thought back to many years ago—the year he was nine, a third grader, and what it was like the first time Miss Cai taught his class. Back then, she had two long braids, and her cheeks were as white and delicate as eggs that had just been boiled and peeled. She told them about a bird called an ostrich. Thirty years had passed, yet Hong Wei could still hear Miss Cai's pleasant voice—like a skylark in the meadow, rising and falling in the classroom.

"What do you think: are birds better at walking or flying?"

———*Flying.* ———*Naturally birds are better at flying.*

In general, that's right. But there's one exception.

What bird can only walk and not fly?

The ostrich.

It was the first picture of an ostrich that Hong Wei had seen. The big bird wore a suit of black feathers, and its big eyes glared murderously. It was ugly, with its bare bottom and its tightly pinched head, its neck blotched with red fleshy spikes and bare of feathers. Miss Cai said, "In the desert the ostrich darts around as though flying. It can cover sixty kilometers in an hour: it's many times faster than 'East-Red' tractors." Just before class let out that day, looking into Hong Wei's eyes, Miss Cai said, "Of all the birds, the ostrich is the biggest walking bird. Almost any bird in the world can fly. But to be good at walking: that's a tour de force. What does it mean to stand out from the crowd? Precisely this."

Hong Wei subconsciously rubbed his rump, and all at once he blushed.

In fact, the year before Miss Cai taught his class, Hong Wei "recognized" this educated youth from Shanghai. Seven and a half that year, he had just started first grade. The first moment he laid eyes on her, his heart beat so fast that even decades later, whenever he recalled that instant, it seemed like a vivid replay of a riveting movie scene.

A sudden flood smashed the defense perimeter along the riverside and poured through the wall around the barracks of the army farm. With his parents' help, he climbed a poplar tree and then moved from it to an adjacent roof. All the young city people at the camp, as well as the older leaders and their family members, were shouting themselves hoarse and scrambling toward high places. The flood kept rising. On the water's surface, rubber boots, basins—all sorts of debris—bobbed up and down. Hong Wei, agitated, was sitting on the ridge of the red-tiled house when he looked up and saw the large wooden tower in front of the camp. Three stories tall, the tower was used to detect fire or floods in the pastures, as well as any enemy movements. Long ago on a clear day, Hong Wei and Erga had climbed it, and Hong Wei believed he could almost see Beijing from the top. This time, a lot of people were crowded on top. The four chunky legs of the tower were already swollen from the flood, and still the water was rising. Next to the large wooden tower was a cistern the depth of many people standing on one another's shoulders. People said it was left over from the time of the puppet government in Manchuria when the Japanese opened up the wasteland for cultivation. After the arrival of the city youth, they had scraped and smoothed the four sides and turned it into a swimming pool. On summer evenings after knocking off work, the male educated youth swam in it. People could indeed float around on water and move around like fish. Hong Wei was flabbergasted.

Just as Hong Wei was letting his imagination run wild on the rooftop, he suddenly heard the poignant sound of crying coming from the "swimming pool." In the crowd of people who had fled the flood, someone's little girl had fallen into the cistern. The adults were scared out of their wits. Someone shouted, "Save her! Save her!" Someone screamed through her tears, "I can't swim. What should I do? Does anyone here know how to swim?" Just then, a flying fish leapt from the roof of the large wooden tower. It spun around in the air and then—like a rocket—landed right in the middle of the "swimming pool." A light spray splashed up. Before Hong Wei could see what was happening, the little girl had been pulled ashore. Then the silver-colored fish herself leapt ashore, and finally Hong Wei could see distinctly: it was a young woman, her white underwear clinging tightly to her body. She was dripping wet.

What was that called? It was called diving. Open your eyes! After the flood receded, Erga told Hong Wei he had heard that the girl from Shanghai had been on the diving team when she was in the Children's Sports School.

"What's a Children's Sports School?" Hong Wei's mind was spinning. The city youth had brought a lot of words along that he'd never even heard before. "I don't know, either, but anyhow, she can fly down from a really high diving board without even blinking her eyes."

And so, the first time Hong Wei saw Miss Cai, she was in midair. Not exactly a proper place to get to know someone. From then on, for some reason, all of Hong Wei's ideas came when he was in midair. He didn't know how to swim. He could only be like a long-armed ape in the forest, swinging and swaying back and forth among the trees. But his dreams were filled with fish that could fly. These fish were always silver-colored. When they spread their fins, they were like soft little braids rising in the breeze.

Not long after Miss Cai became Hong Wei's homeroom teacher, all the city kids teaching in the primary school began raising a ruckus about restoring the basketball court. So, in their spare time, they leveled off the playground.

They drew lines with white lime and set the backboard up straight. A female teacher unraveled the thread from her embroidered gloves and crocheted a net basket to hang from the bare hoop. Soon the basketball court was just like the real thing. The teachers also said they wanted to erect a horizontal bar, parallel bars, and flying rings. When Hong Wei heard this, he was dumbfounded. Miss Cai bent down and whispered to him, "Hey, get your father to give the school some wooden planks. They need to be straight." Before being transferred to civilian work in 1956, his father had been a lieutenant serving with the National Guard for General Gao Gang. Not long after that, the general was removed from his post, the guard unit disbanded, and all the officers and men sent to the farming battlefront in the Great Northern Wilderness. Now, if you were a company-level leader, you were in charge of more than a hundred educated youth from the cities. It was said that Hong Wei was born in the place where a large-scale battle was under way to open up the wasteland. Still, Hong Wei didn't dare ask his father for wooden planks. He and Erga stole all the poles from the rough barriers of their families' courtyard walls and the logs being saved in the storehouse for making dining tables, and took them to the school. Among them, the city youth had all kinds of talent, including a male teacher skilled at carpentry. He saw to it that the wooden planks were planed and sanded by the teachers and then polished smooth. Then they were set up horizontally and perpendicular to each other, turning into something like cannons and howitzers—these were the "horizontal bars," "parallel bars," and "uneven bars." Miss Cai took a few light running steps, leapt—her body supple as a noodle—and instinctively turned a somersault onto a "bar." Hong Wei's eyes almost spun out of their sockets. A male teacher got a few reinforced bars—thicker even than a finger—from the plowing unit and bent them into rings. Covering them with red rubber, he tied two rings to a fork high in a tree. He said these were the "swinging rings." As Miss Cai grabbed the rings, her whole body began rising gently. She was like a swallow flying back and forth in the air. Suddenly, she let go of the rings and did a somersault in midair, landing like a flower petal. Hong Wei was shaking with fear. She said, "I'll teach you how," but Hong Wei shook his head decisively. He was really afraid. She said, "I'll hold you up until you can do it alone. You'll feel as if you're flying."

The semester was almost over before Hong Wei was able to make one small turn on the "horizontal bar."

What Hong Wei liked doing best was watching the educated youth play basketball. Whenever he heard there would be a game he rushed over, burning with excitement. On Sundays and in the slack farm season, a team of five educated youth played against another team of five. Because they weren't wearing proper uniforms, you couldn't tell who was fighting with whom for the ball. Hong Wei could never tell which was the home team. He wished he could play basketball, but he was too short. No one would ever find him among the other players on the playground, and no one would ever pass the ball to him. The best he could do was to station himself outside the white line of the basketball court, take off his basketball shoes and sit on them, and be a faithful spectator—one of the crowd. Each time, from the beginning of the game to the end, he sat there motionless. Before long, the educated youth entrusted this loyal spectator with an important task: they stacked up their clothes—reeking of hot sweat—next to his feet. Some of them took off their wristwatches: the game was too fast, and the watches might be smashed. One after another, they carefully encircled Hong Wei's thin arm with their watches, as if he were the conveyor belt in a watch factory, or the counter where watches were sold. Most of the watches were the "Shanghai" or the "Jewel Flower" brand, all steel or half-steel. He knew all of the players. He had now become a sort of "goalie" for the game—what a great honor that was! If he tried even harder, he could probably make referee. Erga was jealous, because no one gave him a watch for safekeeping.

Hong Wei watched a lot of games and gradually began playing favorites. No matter who was playing, whichever team that included Miss Cai was the one he rooted for with all his might. He shouted himself hoarse. In his eyes, Miss Cai was the prettiest of all the female city youth. He told Erga that when Miss Cai—carrying her backpack—went out on errands and reached the road, if there was a "Rout" or a "Great Liberation" truck behind her, all she had to do was wave and the driver would never fail to meekly grind to a stop. Even Erga agreed that this was so. When the fall rice was just sprouting, Hong Wei asked his mother to cook it. When the crab apples had just reddened on one side, he asked his father to pick some. Then he would wrap the rice and crab apples in a new, snow-white towel and give them to Miss Cai. The first time, when he had just reached the dorm for the females from the city, he was stopped by a shrill-voiced girl. She stuck one foot out and wouldn't let him in the door. Puckering her mouth, she said, "Hey kid, let me inspect you. Do you have any lice in your hair?" Blushing, he burst into tears. When Miss Cai heard him crying, she walked up with a basin of clean water and washed his face, neck, and filthy little hands with fragrant soap. The water tickled him, tickled as it ran past his ears, and he couldn't keep from sneezing. Hot tears streamed down his face . . .

During summer vacation, Miss Cai started teaching him and Erga how to swim in the "swimming pool." At first he flopped up and down in the water, and his wringing wet hair stuck in tendrils to his head. He couldn't do anything except the "dog paddle." He felt very much like a dog that had fallen into the water. Looking at the white clouds galloping overhead like a herd of horses, Hong Wei was in a trance. He couldn't imagine how many times bigger the world was than the Northern Wilderness.

When summer vacation was almost over, he could swim several laps in the "swimming pool." It was the first time he heard Miss Cai use new words such as "breast stroke" and "free-style swim." The day before school started, Miss Cai took him, Erga, and a few other classmates to swim at the reservoir a few kilometers away from the barracks. It was the first time he saw her wear the thing called a "swimming suit." Elastic sewn at regular intervals on the pale green cloth made the swimming suit bulge shapelessly in several places, like a huge frog. The top and bottom of the "swimming suit" were actually connected. He couldn't figure out how she got into it. Compared with any other clothing he'd ever seen, it seemed very tight and revealed her chest, neck, and thighs—all as white as steamed bread. Only when Miss Cai cut through the dark green waves with her snow-white arms and swam lightheartedly off into the distance did Hong Wei finally dare overtake her with his eyes. The teacher in the water wasn't the teacher who ordinarily taught his class: she was like a white swan that had come from a long way away and had dropped into the lake to amuse herself at leisure. The white swan's crest was black, her hair coiled into a chignon on top of her head. Hong Wei would never forget that afternoon. Under the flaming sun, the lake water was still cool. Miss Cai's laughter flew past like a string of beads: "Swim. Don't be afraid. Let go of your hands and feet. That's it. Swim over to me. Great! Try it again. Lift your head to breathe. Kick your legs. You need to balance your arms and legs. That's it . . ."

The summer that Hong Wei was nine, he found out that there was a kind of clothing called a "swimming suit" and that there was something called "sports." This was what his teen-aged city teachers taught him. When he was gasping for breath after swimming back and forth in the inlet and having trouble standing up because of the underwater silt, his Miss Cai laughingly seized his ears, turned him to one side, and shook him so the water would run out of his ears. She also told him, "Speed is everything in sports! You have to learn to swim even faster!"

Are you ready? —Hong Wei asked himself.
Not yet. —Hong Wei answered himself.
Aren't you ready yet? —Hong Wei asked himself again.
Patience. I need more time to get ready. —Hong Wei answered himself again, admonishing himself.
Okay, then wait until fall. Set out after the autumn harvest. That's what he decided to do.

As a matter of fact, back then Hong Wei let Miss Cai down. In the Great Northern Wilderness, the reservoir was frozen most of the year, and summer was as fleeting as a rabbit going through the brush. Swimming was a rare luxury! Hong Wei also gradually became aware that he wasn't very coordinated. Besides that, whatever sport he attempted, he wasn't fast enough. Even though deep in his heart he was passionate about sports and hoped to show his love for Miss Cai through his passion for sports, he doubted his ability. Time after time, his clumsy performance in gym class disappointed him: he wished he could die. He rushed over to Miss Cai's dorm more often than ever to give her bags of sticky beans, wild duck eggs, or radishes and other vegetables that had just ripened in his family's garden. Every time he went to see Miss Cai, he stood up while they talked; he never sat on her bed. Whenever he went to the city youths' dorm, he scrubbed his face and changed into clean socks that weren't smelly. He told his mother, "The city youth don't like dirty little kids." Once he rubbed a little of his mother's cold cream on his chapped hands. Surprised, his mother tapped his forehead and scolded him good-naturedly, "Huh. The city kids get dirtier by the day, while you little ones act like peacocks!"

It seemed to Hong Wei that his life was changing bit by bit. He didn't know when this began, but through the iced-over windows of the classroom he could see what others couldn't—faraway places at the edge of the horizon. He knew that Shanghai—with its numerous tall buildings—was over there. Shanghai was Miss Cai's hometown. When Miss Cai went home to see her family, she brought back enough "White Rabbit" candies to give several to each student. Because Hong Wei couldn't bear to eat them, he stuffed them into his pockets until they stuck fast to his clothes. There wasn't much homework back then, but he was still busy with his studies. In addition, the students were caught up in the waves of all the political movements. Miss Cai lectured for precisely one hour without repeating one sentence. Hong Wei admired her a lot for this. So Hong Wei frequently got into trouble on purpose. He caught a toad and brought it to the classroom or, at the construction site for the school building, he threw pebbles taken from the sandpile and finally broke the classroom windows. He also blocked up the flue of the classroom stove so that the smell of smoke suffused the classroom. At times like that, Erga always betrayed him, selling Hong Wei out in short order. And so Miss Cai would keep him after school and talk with him. It was always one hour, and naturally she didn't repeat herself even once. Hong Wei felt that he was luckier than everyone else: Miss Cai wasn't giving a lecture to the whole class but to him alone. She got angry just with him, or curled her lips, or glared. Or smiled a little. No matter what Miss Cai said, Hong Wei nodded his head vigorously. Each time, he pledged in all sincerity that he wouldn't do it again, and then he left—feeling on top of the world. He thought it was his good fortune to listen to Miss Cai give him hell: it made him happy. It was as if he had become addicted. Every few weeks, he found an excuse to report to Miss Cai's office. This went on until one day she apparently finally caught onto his little trick. From then on, no matter what mischief he got into, she didn't pay any attention. It was only at this point that Hong Wei decided to "turn over a new leaf." Later, Miss Cai let the children try some entertainment. They would sit together to sing, each one holding a clacking board, and while singing, they would strike the board, which was exciting to listen to. Hong Wei still remembered the skit was called "Relatives Everywhere." It told of the Woman Zhao, who went to the army to see her son. After disembarking from the train, she got lost, and at last a kindly person took her to her son . . . Miss Cai painted several black wrinkles at the corners of her eyes to play the Woman Zhao. Hong Wei laughed so hard his tummy hurt . . .

Hong Wei was now approaching middle age. Vivid tales of his boyhood filled his memory. Just as sharply focused as they'd been at the time, the memories didn't fade. Whenever agronomist Hong Wei recalled the past as he walked around the farm, he snorted with spontaneous laughter—"The Woman Zhao neither ate nor drank. Two streams of hot tears fell from her eyes . . ." Hong Wei hummed the melody. Strange—in the intervening thirty years, he hadn't forgotten a single line of the lyrics. He supposed he had the "city youth complex." Everything he had learned at the beginning of life, the good life habits that his wife often complimented him on, his ideals and his industry: all of it had come from his youthful teachers from the city. If he didn't take the initiative to go to Harbin or Shanghai to see them, he would probably regret it for the rest of his life. Right. All the educated youth had come back to the farm to visit—all except Miss Cai. She never came. Not once. Every year when he heard that an old city youth had come back, he rushed over to the guesthouse with high hopes. Over the years, he saw lots of people, but Miss Cai was never among those city youth who were now growing distinctly old and fat.

A gale could clear away little things like badminton cocks, ping-pong balls, and even volleyballs, but something like a shot put was weighing heavily on his heart.

The year that Miss Cai went back to the city, he was already in junior high school. He hadn't heard that she was leaving; naturally, she couldn't make a special trip to the school to say good-bye to him. When she left, there was no activity at all: it was just like a cloud in the sky over the meadow, silently vanishing over the horizon. It was only after Hong Wei got out of school for winter vacation and went back to the farm that he heard his dad talk of Miss Cai's departure. Dad said that Miss Cai's boyfriend was an educated youth from Tianjin. They weren't allowed to go back to Shanghai, nor could they go back to Tianjin. They could just go to a small city in her father's old stamping grounds of Liaoning. That day, Hong Wei went to the farm's office and pulled down a bunch of abandoned chops from the windowsill. He trampled the chops—made of radishes and soap—with all his might. The radishes were already frozen stiff, and he sprained his ankle when he kicked too hard.

Are birds better at walking or flying? Better at flying? No, one bird is the exception.
What bird is that? The ostrich.

In middle age, every time the agronomist Hong Wei recalled the young teachers from his boyhood, his heart ached a little.

After graduating from high school, Hong Wei didn't get into a university. He supposed it was because Miss Cai had set too much store by physical education and slighted the serious subjects. But he didn't blame her one bit. Even though he wasn't good at phys ed, he still loved it because it was Miss Cai who had first taught him in phys ed. After the city youth left, one company after another, the basketball and volleyball games on the farm continued. Without many spectators, though, they weren't like real games but more like practice. For a while, he was part of the crew showing movies. It wasn't until he started toadying to the Propaganda Chief's family by splitting firewood, carrying coal, and hauling firewood that he got this job. Showing movies was easy work. In the daytime, he just hung around the office, much of the time listening to the radio. This was how he discovered that a man always talked incessantly at every major sports, giving the listeners a play-by-play account, telling them how a goal had just been scored and how a player had missed the basket, how tall and how heavy each player was, and what special skills each player brought to the game. Hong Wei was fascinated: the game appeared vividly before his eyes. The commentary was just like the basketball in a star player's hands. It all poured into his head; none of it seeped out. Somewhat later, he came to know of an announcer named Song Shixiong. His mouth was like a radio: once turned on, it never rested. In the long northern winter, it grew dark before the end of the afternoon. After he finished showing movies in the evening, he still hung around the office. Night after night, he listened to Song Shixiong on the radio. He remembered one night when it was snowing heavily: the coal fire in the stove was roaring like a train going across the snowy fields. The hoarse voice was coming from the radio that he hugged to his chest—each syllable hurried along ahead, not daring to pause even a second. The voice grew faster and faster, more and more emphatic, spinning and flying in midair. No longer a voice, it was a kind of velocity, an unparalleled force. It was like a steam engine desperately dragging him ahead—

Are birds better at walking or flying? Better at flying? No, one bird is the exception.

He saw a large black bird—with its thick-soled claws, it was striding and leaping idiotically through the vast open fields of the Great Northern Wilderness. Its feathers were light, and it was all legs: it sprang three meters in one stride. It wasn't walking, but instead flying with its claws. The ostrich can't fly, but it can reach the speed of flying while it's on the ground. And humans? The human has no wings but can fly with his voice . . .

Hong Wei awakened to a cold room. The fire had gone out; sunshine was streaming through the windowpane. Bits of ice as fragile as cicada wings were like the snowflake-besprinkled wings of the big bird puffing and flapping as it scampered in the wind. He remembered distinctly that on that particular day he started disciplining himself. He wanted to turn his voice into velocity and become a part-time sportscaster.

The training he set for himself lasted even longer than the winter. People frequently saw a lanky youth standing at the intersection of the field and the highway, his gaze like a torch as he stared intently at every car driving past. He was mumbling to himself. He had only an instant to glance at, memorize, and report the car's license number and thus hone his skills of memorization and response time, and even train his mouth. He was satisfied with his invention of this method of discipline. By the time spring came, he could already say a little something without stammering. He ran around all the offices madly grabbing up all the newspapers and then clipping out all the sports reports. If he didn't have enough, he made the tough decision to spend the pin money he'd saved, and in the short vacation during the off-season for farming he rode the train to Jiamusi, where he looked up information in the library. He went in when it opened at nine o'clock and didn't leave until it closed at six o'clock, and then right away took the night train back. The library didn't allow smoking, and that was really hard on a guy; at noon, he ate a slice of bread and was faint from hunger. It wasn't easy to make the trip to Jiamusi; it cost him money and time. But even if it cost more, he would make the sacrifice. You asked for it, didn't you? If you didn't have a lot of data in your head, you wouldn't be able to explain anything about the game. Who wanted to listen to foolish patter? For a few months, his father made a face whenever he saw his furtive comings and goings. People must have been quietly telling his parents: *I bet your son isn't right in the head. Haven't you seen him standing in the snow day after day? Look at the frost on his face. What was he staring at out there? You need to take him in for a check-up.* His father spied on him secretly for a few days. In Hong Wei's room, he found a large pile of old account books with palm-sized newspaper clippings pasted on each page. His father, who used to be the supervisor of the city youths' farm, saw a lot of strangers' names and photos in the newspaper clippings. They all looked muscular and powerful. You could even smell the sweat pouring from their strong bodies. When his father finally found him, Hong Wei was on the bumpy basketball court giving his first play-by-play commentary. Sweat was dripping from his hair, his head was swiveling like a rattle-drum, his eyes were roaming all over like a thief's, his tongue was like a spring with his voice changing into pieces of soft catkins blown in some unknown direction by the wind. When the whistle blew at the end of the game, a lot of people were shouting *Hong Wei! Hong Wei!* In that instant, Hong Wei thought he had really turned into an ostrich, itching as he was to plunge his head into the jubilant applause . . .

And so Hong Wei began his career as a part-time sports commentator. In the brief sports season lasting from spring to fall, he was invited to all of the farms to provide commentary. This new profession opened people's eyes: farmers realized for the first time that if a sports event lacked a commentator, it was as vapid as watching a silent movie. During the dynamic 1980s, he was as popular as blue jeans or pop music. His reputation spread far and wide. In the far-flung farm fields, someone always suggested inviting Hong Wei to be the commentator for their games.

When Hong Wei appeared, his image on the sports field was without peer. His pants were creased smartly—sharp enough to pare a carrot. He often wore a stylish checkered shirt. Someone asked him why he was wearing girl's clothes—thus revealing an incredible ignorance of fashion. His shoes had to be carefully polished the night before. When he rose early in the morning, he polished them again until they shone: you could see your reflection in them. He'd learned how to polish shoes several years before from those young Shanghai guys in the city kids' dormitory. After he started working, he gave his first month's wages to a Shanghai youth who was going home for a visit and asked him to buy a pair of trousers for him—the kind with cuffs at the ankles. The male educated youth from Shanghai all liked to wear pointed "rocket-style" shoes. Over the years, he had bought new shoes several times, always in the "rocket style." This hadn't changed in twenty years. When he began wearing them, whenever Zhou Xiaofei from the PR Section saw his shoes, she curled her lips and spat, "You peacock!" Before many years had passed, Xiaofei became his wife. She permed her hair, and was even more of a show-off than he was. Later on, Hong Wei realized that he had some habits that others once criticized as defects. He had learned most of them little by little from the city kids on the farm: the roots of his "defects" went back to that time. He had kept these habits all the while, until later on, even if he wanted to change, he couldn't.

One year at harvest time, he received a letter from the provincial capital. The return address on the envelope was the Provincial Sports Commission. The envelope alone intimidated him. Even more unimaginably, this letter, sealed with the official stamp of the Provincial Sports Commission, was actually inviting him to be the commentator for the All-Province Sports Meet. All travel expenses would be paid, as would his lost wages. Hong Wei thought: *Maybe the Sports Commission has made a mistake.* Then he thought: *For a few hundred miles all around, who else can handle sports commentary? No one.* He let Xiaofei read the letter. She said enthusiastically, "This is the reward for your efforts. Why not take it as an opportunity to visit the big city for free!"

Hong Wei would never forget his experience in the provincial capital. He sat behind a table next to the swimming pool. In front of him was a mass of microphones, tape recorders, and lots of things he didn't recognize. The music began, along with cheers from the crowd, but the blue pool water and the high diving board were an expanse of darkness in front of him. His body was shaking involuntarily, like a blade of grass in a gale. Under the huge ceiling of the arena, he heard his trembling, incoherent voice bumping up and down like broken feathers. Under the glare of the lights, little by little he began to distinguish countless strange faces swaying in the arena. In that split second, he suddenly thought of Miss Cai. Perhaps, he thought, she was sitting quietly in the crowd. When the competition ended, she would run down the steps. No. Perhaps Miss Cai was standing on the diving board—just like that early morning years ago that was brimming over with water: like a flying silver fish, she would leap from the sky like a bolt of lightning . . . His mind was wandering. His mouth suddenly became nimble, and his tongue galloped like a river, flowing vigorously hundreds of miles straight down from the mountains.

The applause reached a crescendo and then stopped. The lights in the arena dimmed. The loudspeakers grew silent. The competition had ended, and people streamed from the arena. The swimming pool was suddenly empty, the greenish waves of the pool like a concrete megalith. He walked out woodenly, neither happy nor excited. Outside stood a woman alone. His heart leaped; he walked past her, and then in the dim street light, saw that it was a young girl with fresh flowers . . .

It wasn't Miss Cai. His Miss Cai was an ostrich that had disappeared into the depths of the desert.

Just then, Hong Wei thought back to when he was a child in the classroom: Miss Cai had taught them to recite the word "yearning." He realized that he hadn't forgotten Miss Cai for an instant. But why hadn't she ever come back to the farm to take a look around? She'd left more than twenty years ago: why hadn't she sent even one letter? Looking up, Hong Wei saw neon lights filling the sky like the glow of a sunset. The dazzling light hurt his eyes. He thought, *What window of which building in this city is Miss Cai hiding behind?* At any rate, in his imagination, Miss Cai was surely working in a sports-related job.

After he got home, the first thing he said to Xiaofei was, "Since Miss Cai hasn't come back to our farm, I have to think of a way to go and see her."

Are you ready? —Hong Wei asked himself.
Soon, soon. —Hong Wei answered himself.

What else do you have to do to get ready? —Hong Wei asked himself again.

He had his driver's license and had learned to drive quite well. Years ago, after he left the movie crew, the farm had sent him to the Agronomy University. When he returned to the farm, he became an agronomist. His work wasn't outstanding, but still it was up to snuff. He was just waiting for the Tax Bureau, where Erga worked, to buy a car, and then he could borrow the new car and go to see Miss Cai. Only a special trip by car to Liaoning would be good enough. Presumably, the car would be speedy. It was almost thirty years earlier that he had heard Miss Cai say the word "speed." If he drove, that would be faster than the ostrich striding in the desert—many times faster.

Okay. Now, he finally had Miss Cai's address. Everything was ready. Okay, then, he'd better hit the road.

Hong Wei's luggage filled the whole trunk. Besides gifts for Miss Cai—a small amount of choice Northeast rice and high-quality yellow beans, and a small carton of fresh milk—there were also several extremely heavy cardboard boxes packed with his treasures. They constituted his entire "property" from more than twenty years: the boxes held more than a dozen old black leather account books filled with press clippings and photos from his years as commentator for the sports meets at dozens of farms—including a photo of him with Mu Tiezhu, the tallest basketball player back then. There were also countless red velour-covered certificates honoring him, presented to him by all kinds of organizations and bureaus. Xiaofei tied them together into a large bundle with red string. This looked spectacular. As for the hundreds of sports articles he had published in those years, amounting to hundreds of newspaper pages, he filled another cardboard box with them. It was around the time he turned thirty-six that Hong Wei had stopped working as a sports commentator. He felt that to continue with his endless patter at sporting events was like marking time. It lacked any sense of "speed." He had worked so many years as a part-time "reporter" that he knew everyone and everything in the sports world both in China and abroad. Five or six years earlier, he had started writing short blurbs about sports. That was really satisfying. The articles appeared in several newspapers and magazines. Starting out at the local level, he eventually placed his articles in publications distributed nationwide. Each line he wrote was accurate and easy to understand. A few years earlier, he had even won a national prize for good reporting.

But what thrilled him most was the thing he really wanted Miss Cai to see. Hidden at the very bottom of a cardboard box was a thick manuscript that he had written by hand. A real manuscript. The week before, Xiaofei had typed it on the computer, printed it out, and bound it. He'd been working on this manuscript for three years. It was at least three hundred thousand words long: even Hong Wei himself didn't believe that he could have written such a long book.

The title itself was startling: "A Century of the Summer Olympics— Written before the Opening of the Beijing Olympics." It included information about all the major personages in the history of the Olympics. It described the arenas of the Summer Games for the last hundred years, along with historical background and some anecdotes. In his view, it was a book strong in information, interest, theory, and reliability. After it came out some time in the future, readers surely wouldn't be able to put it down. When it came right down to it, he had prepared painstakingly all these years for this manuscript. He wanted to give it to Miss Cai. He wanted her to know that from the time she left the farm, he hadn't slacked off for even a day. It was as though she were still present in his life, gazing at him with her gentle eyes. He wanted to show her all these clippings and data, not to flaunt them, but to let her see that at the starting line of life, she had given him the most important encouragement. No. It was more than that: she had influenced nearly his whole life. At the age of nine, Miss Cai had entered the Children's Sports School. After all her training, she must surely still love sports. Could there be any better gift than this manuscript to express his gratitude to her?

It was a sunny late autumn day with a chill in the air. When Hong Wei started out, his mood was like the light in the white clouds. The straight highway cut through the vast fields, as though it would connect with the other end of the world. He accelerated to 130 kilometers an hour. He hoped to reach that city before dark; he didn't want to stop overnight on the way. The wind was howling outside the windows, and the car was like a big bird spreading its wings and about to fly. Are birds better at walking or flying? Maybe Hong Wei was a bird not good at flying, but he took long strides on the ground, and he could stride at winged velocity.

Hong Wei drove fast for twelve hours. He was dismayed that it was dark when he reached the small city. He thought he would find a hotel for the night and then first thing in the morning go to the address he had for Miss Cai. But he also thought she would have to go to work in the daytime. Most of the time she wouldn't be home. It would be better to look for her home at night: he'd have a much better chance of seeing her. He drove slowly, following the streetlights in the dark city, asking directions all the way. He was imagining Miss Cai's surprise and joy at seeing him. So many years had passed: would she remember him? Still, he was sure—no matter how much Miss Cai might have changed—he would recognize her.

It wasn't hard to find her home: it was a large compound on a small street that housed a lot of people. He found the right address, but the door was locked and it was dark inside. He knocked on the next door. Someone looked out and said politely, "You're looking for Auntie Cai. She isn't off work yet." Hong Wei asked where she worked. The person said, "Not far away. Just turn east when you go out of the alley and you'll see a movie theater. She sells lottery tickets at the stand at the entrance to the theater." He asked, "What kind of lottery tickets?" The person answered, "Sports lottery tickets. As soon as you get there, you'll see." His heart sank. He wanted to ask more, but the person had already closed the door.

Hong Wei drove over to the theater, which was just letting out. There was a large crowd of people. At a glance, he saw the words "Sports Lottery Tickets" at the corner of the newspaper kiosk. A pudgy middle-aged woman, wrapped in a bulky padded jacket, was staring at the stream of people. When he dashed over to the kiosk, her eyes flashed and she asked him anxiously, "Buy a lottery ticket? The winner will be announced tomorrow. Why not try your luck? If you have good luck, two *yuan* will bring you a hundred thousand times as much."

Hong Wei was dumbfounded. Her hoarse, raspy voice was like that of a stranger: it nearly bruised his eardrums. Desperately, he kept his eyes open, crossed his arms, forced himself to stand still, and watched her blankly, hoping to see a little of the way she used to look. In the worn-out face of the woman before him, he seemed to see the familiar expression from years ago—like a meteor rapidly cutting across the sky and then disappearing into darkness.

"Are you going to buy a ticket or not?" she said impatiently. "Just two *yuan*. It won't break you."

He held his breath, and quietly said, "Miss Cai . . ."

He added, "I'm Hong Wei."

The woman shook her head blankly. "What did you say? You're mistaken!"

His chest tightening, Hong Wei let out a "whoosh," then asked abruptly, "Are birds better at walking or flying?"

The woman glared at him, and muttered angrily, "What do you think you're doing? If you aren't going to buy a ticket, then stop blocking the way!"

Hong Wei's brain felt like a pot of paste. He actually couldn't remember a word of what he had prepared for so many years to say. His body turned cold, his face hot, his feet wobbly, and his head dizzy. Distracted for a moment, he subconsciously felt his pocket, pulled out his wallet, and took out all of his money.

Handing her the wad of money, he said, "I'll spend all of this!"

The woman was dumbfounded. She asked, "The numbers—do you want to choose them or do you want the machine to choose?"

"Whatever you like," he answered.

Happy smiles lit the woman's face. She quickly bent her head to count the money, then deftly punched the keys. The machine clattered, and the first little ticket came out. She looked up, intending to give the little numbered ticket to the customer who had suddenly appeared out of nowhere. She rubbed her eyes—the foolish man had disappeared. From a street not far away came the sound of a car's motor starting up.

Hong Wei hurried along the highway. Ice-cold tears trickled down his cheeks. He wanted to get home that night. He didn't want to stay a minute longer in this strange little city. But he had to gas up first. The car was too heavy: he was considering throwing out all the cardboard boxes in the trunk. All of a sudden, it occurred to him that those old educated youths had been drinking too much, and so they must have given him the wrong address. This woman couldn't be his Miss Cai. Next time, he had to get the right address. He had no doubt that he would make the trip again.

꙰

Please Take Me with You

~ 1 ~

It was twenty-eight years before Du Zhong finally returned to China in the last few days of the twentieth century. When he went back to his hometown, he discovered that he recognized almost no one. Nor did many people recognize him. In Hangzhou, he strolled on streets that now were strange to him. He would stand absently at an intersection and look all around. He had to keep asking for directions before he could continue on to an undetermined destination. He thought to himself that this resembled his travel in various parts of the world. In the faces of those he'd rubbed shoulders with, there were no friends. Nor were there any more enemies.

Du Zhong had experienced years of being friendless: this condition was as endless and familiar as a Russian winter. But the sense of having no enemies left him despondent and empty. He felt like a leaf blown down by the wind, drifting randomly. Naturally, people wouldn't give him a second glance. It was the first time that Du Zhong had realized that if a person had neither friends nor enemies, it was like being in a deserted room and unable to find a place to sit.

Thus it was that a bored Du Zhong walked along Hangzhou's noisy downtown streets. The old house where he'd lived as a child, the large courtyard with its autumn scent of cassia flowers, the small brown British-style building with the pitched roof: all had disappeared without a trace. The quiet little lane of former days had been widened into a six-lane thoroughfare. Like two rushing rivers, cars rolled on in opposite directions. Like a little black ant, he circled several times around a large mansion with blue glass walls, assessing the scope of its foundation: it must be the site of the old place where he had lived thirty years earlier. Like a large mountain erected from the ground up, it lay heavily on the carpet of grass from the past. In the gray-blue evening mist, the building looked even more like an immense, expensive tomb that had buried his entire childhood.

He didn't know in what corner of the city those people might now be hiding—the ones who, back in the Cultural Revolution years, had whipped his parents, the ones who had forced him to surrender his red armband. The city had removed its old, tattered clothing and changed into the fashions worn by the rest of the world—new and shimmering. The past was gone. The city was now like an innocent infant with neither thoughts nor memories. Since all the people seemed to have moved, old addresses were useless. But Du Zhong knew that those people lived on in degradation in the cracks of the streets or hidden in the dark spaces of tall buildings. He couldn't find them, nor did he want to find them. Since most of his friends had scattered and he had no way to reach them, he thought that having no enemies was just like having no friends: either made for a boring life.

Unconcerned, Du Zhong walked along doing his utmost to imagine himself a tourist unconnected with this city. He'd left no trace of himself here, just as the city had left no mark on him. But things weren't so simple. A few days later, after getting over the jet lag that had made him sleepy and dizzy, he quickly discovered that he had parked himself in an extremely awkward position. Not only had he brought his eyes back from faraway France, but also his whole body: besides his arms and legs and internal organs, he had his nose and ears.

He seemed to pick up an unusual scent—like a ghost, with no shape, no color—drifting in the air. It was a faint floral scent, like springtime's magnolia, or perhaps a certain cold cream. It carried a slight smell of human perspiration, and then gradually turned into an acidic smell, mixed with the odor of deep-fried stinky tofu or fried fish. It fell onto his sleeves and collar, and clung there. These smells held the indelible marks of time: they chased him or caught up with him as he walked through this city. In these scents, he smelled his long ago self.

Some mostly imperceptible and chaotic sounds began brushing against his ears. In the still of the night, these sounds would suddenly be amplified many times over—as in the summer when typhoons attacked, the huge aromatic camphor trees swayed in the wind, and their leaves clamored as they slapped against the rooftops. On that long ago rainy night, an emaciated man had been tied to a rough tree trunk. His sorrowful wails had come from within the sound of rain, like a soul that had suffered injustice. At daylight, the sound of the rain and the sound of weeping had stopped. The man had died. But his tearful appeal stayed in the sky above the city, always giving Du Zhong the sense that it was raining lightly . . .

Now, these sounds and scents had actually come back with Du Zhong. He couldn't help feeling thrilled.

It seemed his heart also had a problem: a latent ache surprisingly scurried out, settling temporarily in his chest and then rapidly vanishing. It was like a blunt knife silently grinding at him. But no blood could be seen. Each ache was like a lawless sneak attack and was thoroughly exhausting.

He believed that no matter where in the world he went, he could always play the part of the passerby, but alone in this city where he was born and grew up, he could hardly be a tourist.

The twenty-eight years he'd been away from China were half a lifetime. By the time he returned, his parents had died. Only one younger sister was left. When he emerged from the airport, he headed for the middle-aged woman who was holding up a sign with his name. As he hugged her, tears soaked both of their faces. Even though they had written each other for years and had exchanged many photos, he couldn't find even a trace of the little sister from before. She told him of some things that had happened after their parents were politically rehabilitated. Also, just before they died, they expressed everlasting regret about their son who had disappeared years before. The day after Du Zhong returned to Hangzhou, he paid his respects at his parents' graves. He knelt and wailed for a long time. Then he and his sister planted two cypresses in front of the graves. When the roots went into the ground, he suddenly thought, *From now on, my roots in this city will exist like this.*

In France, Du Zhong had persevered for some years in his search and endured setbacks time after time, and finally after contacting a relative in Jiangsu, he had found his sister—his only close relative: this was damned lucky. A close relative, an umbilical cord that couldn't be snipped, linked his past with his future. But actually it wasn't his sister he wanted most to find. He'd been staying for several days now with his sister, secretly hoping that by going through her social connections he might find ways to get in touch with some former classmates and buddies from his days in the Great Northern Wilderness. There were some things he ought to wrap up before the century ended; it was for this reason that he had decided to come back.

Du Zhong didn't know how his sister had managed to find Meng Di for him. When he mentioned Meng Di, he wasn't holding out any great hope. He was afraid the man named Meng Di would probably have long since forgotten there was ever a person named Du Zhong. But over the years, Du Zhong had never forgotten this name—Meng Di. It wasn't because of Meng Di himself that he remembered him, but because of a girl named

Chu Xiaoxi. On that cold winter night, when he went to see Chu Xiaoxi at Wanshan Farm, she had taken him to the men's dorm and arranged for him to share a bed with Meng Di. He guessed that Meng Di and Chu Xiaoxi had a special relationship. Now that he was back, Chu Xiaoxi had disappeared without a trace from today's Hangzhou. Meng Di was the only route to Xiaoxi.

He and Meng Di agreed to meet at the "Willow Shade" Teahouse. From Meng Di's tone over the phone, he was reluctant to see Du Zhong. He didn't express even a particle of enthusiasm.

It was from Meng Di's impassive narration that Du Zhong learned for the first time of things that had happened later. This "later" referred to the winter of 1971, after he left Wanshan Farm. By the time he awakened the next morning in the men's dorm, Meng Di and Chu Xiaoxi had already gone to clean out the livestock stalls. He walked by himself to the highway and hitched a ride on a food delivery truck to the train station. He took the train, and then boarded another truck to go back to Huma, the village where he was stationed. Then, following the route he had carefully worked out long before, on a windy, snowy night, he crossed the border of Heilongjiang and reached the Soviet Union. At the time, he'd had no way to anticipate everything that would constitute the "later." He was utterly ignorant of what had happened in those twenty-eight years.

It had been years since Du Zhong had spent a winter in Hangzhou. He kept trembling from a bone-penetrating cold that was invading his back. The teacup in his hand didn't give off the slightest warmth: he might as well have been clutching a piece of ice. His fingers were frozen numb. After listening to Meng Di's tale, he took a long time to say, "Meng Di, if it had occurred to me back then that I'd be putting others at risk by seeing them before I went across the border, I'd never have gone to Wanshan Farm to see Xiaoxi."

Meng Di sipped his tea and said, "Apparently, you can't handle Hangzhou's dialect anymore. You'd better just use *putonghua*."

Switching to Mandarin, Du Zhong said, "But back then, there was no way I could tell Chu Xiaoxi that the real reason for my visit was to take my leave of her. I couldn't leave without saying good-bye."

Meng Di smiled coldly.

When Du Zhong set his cup down on the table, it rocked a bit and some tea splashed out. He supposed his Mandarin wasn't easy to listen to either, all mixed together as it was with Russian, French, and English endings. It was like a bad cocktail. As he sopped up the tea with a napkin, he asked, "Are you saying that after I left, Chu Xiaoxi was considered an accessory and isolated and interrogated for months and stripped of her party membership and all other responsibilities? Are you saying that she forfeited her future? But I still don't understand. Where I worked, who could have known that before crossing the border I went to Wanshan Farm and saw Chu Xiaoxi?"

"I'm afraid that's a question you have to ask yourself. Maybe you inadvertently told someone? Maybe you left some clues in the things you threw out before leaving? Also, stool pigeons were everywhere then."

Chewing on the tea leaves, Meng Di went on, his face expressionless, "Just before you left, how could you possibly not have known that even if by some fluke you succeeded in crossing the river this would implicate a lot of people and have grave repercussions?"

"I . . . back then, I couldn't think about so many things . . . My head was filled with how I would finally be able to cross the river . . ."

Du Zhong was murmuring, his head drooping. He felt as if a cannonball were exploding in his brain; his body seemed to be splitting into countless fragments, his flesh and blood flying all over.

Only by experiencing that inky black, stormy winter night in 1971 did he learn where hell on earth was. But even then the twenty-year-old Du Zhong knew that the world was a place even more terrifying than hell. He knew that hell was the only way out left for him. If he could make his way alone through hell, a small sliver of light would finally gleam in the future. If he plummeted into hell—the deepest place in hell—well . . . , he couldn't see any difference between hell and hell's deepest place.

In the middle of the night, just before Du Zhong set out, he made up his mind to adopt a casual attitude toward death. When living was worse than being dead, what was so dreadful about death? He even hoped that as he traversed that vast, snowy, unpopulated zone he would meet up with a bullet fired from who knew which direction that would end his life in a split second, thereby ending his agony. Because he realized that he was so sensitive to suffering that he couldn't go on with his present life, choosing this way to die suited his inner yearning for freedom and dignity. His stern, arrogant traits had taken root in his youth, or to be more precise, they had come from the eighteenth and nineteenth century European literature he had read. Too bad you could have only one opponent in a duel. It seemed that everyone was his opponent, and yet that no one was. Too many opponents assumed there were no opponents. Without a definite opponent, one simply assumed that one's "enemy" was "a large invisible abstraction," or something unattainable. After several months of thinking about it, Du Zhong finally assigned himself the role of "opponent."

If Meng Di understood Du Zhong's real situation back then, he should know that Du had no choice but to leave.

It was the fourth year of Du Zhong's parents' interrogation in isolation, and Du Zhong still couldn't see any possibility that his parents would one day be released and allowed to go home. A letter he wrote to a friend also brought unexpected trouble. In the slack farming season of winter he got several days off under the pretext of going to Beian to see a doctor. Dodging ticket takers and clinging to trains, he journeyed from the Sino-Soviet border to Hangzhou. Before he was sent down to the countryside, he had taken his little sister to be cared for by relatives in Jiangsu. Du Zhong stayed with a former classmate, a close friend. Although he searched all over the city for several days, he couldn't get any news of his parents. Another family had moved in on the ground floor of the little house that had given him so much happiness as a child. Each room on the second floor where he and his family lived was now sealed. Already in tatters, the seals were like bats flapping their wings in the cold shadowy draft . . .

The disaster for young Du Zhong began in 1967. In the space of one night, everything turned upside down—the expanding and deepening political movement had finally spread to Du Zhong's family. His parents' connection with the "Soviet revisionists" when they had been in the Soviet Union, as well as the many "questionable parts of their background" that Du Zhong knew nothing about, were all regarded by the Red Guards as a treasured, glittering victory. After the Second World War, his parents had been sent to the Soviet Union on a work-study program. Returning to China in 1953, they had brought back one of the yields of their stay, Du Zhong, who had been born in Moscow. His childhood name was Drooka. After his parents came back to China, they were assigned jobs in Hangzhou as leading cadres for provincial bureaus. The family's life was tranquil before the Cultural Revolution began. Even if shadows hung over his parents' heads early on, happy little Drooka was unaware of them. In 1967, however, his parents disappeared, and everything else was over, too. Du Zhong was forced to give up his Red Guard armband. When he was evicted from the little house, he felt like a sparrow whose feathers had all been pecked off until it was pitched down to earth from the sky.

Du Zhong's only way out was to escape from Hangzhou—the farther, the better. He couldn't remember now why he had chosen to go to Heilongjiang in the first place. At a remove of some decades, he still wanted to plead that it was not premeditated; he could merely say it was preordained. In fact, when he signed up to go to the place called Huma on the frontier, it involved a lot of setbacks. Back then, a person with his kind of "background" wasn't qualified to work on the "anti-Soviet front line." And so he even wrote a loyalty pledge in blood. Luckily, a buddy who'd been in school with him from first grade to tenth grade happened to be the leader for the youth sent down to the Great Northern Wilderness. When the train started moving, Du Zhong was watching all the olive-drab arms waving out the windows. He thought to himself that perhaps he was the only one on this long train who, like a lucky fish, had slipped through the net of political interrogation.

With its pristine snowfields and verdant open country, the vast, fertile Great Northern Wilderness soothed his injured spirit. Sweat couldn't rinse away his shame, but at least it could attest to his determination to be politically reborn. One heavy snow followed another, blocking the roads to the outside world. Time after time, Du Zhong braved the wind and snow to walk miles to the township post office, hoping there'd be a letter from Hangzhou with news of his parents. Maybe, deep in his heart, he hoped even more for letters from Chu Xiaoxi. Since arriving at Huma, he'd started writing to her all the time. In the beginning, he sent the letters to Hangzhou. Later, when Chu Xiaoxi also went to the Great Northern Wilderness, he mailed his long letters to her at Wanshan Farm. He still remembered how he had described life in Heilongjiang when he first arrived in Huma. He had told her that "Huma" was the word in the Daur language for the riptide that was obscured from the sun in the mountains and canyons. In the winter, the temperature could drop to 52 degrees below zero Celsius. Before the Cultural Revolution, the local people could pasture their herds on islands in the middle of the river. In early spring, the local folk took their cattle and sheep to the islands, where the pastureland was fertile and the water abundant. When they brought the herds back in the autumn, they had many dozen more animals. Most of the locals were immigrants from Shandong who had settled in the Northeast in the old days, so the Russian women from the other side of the river who had married them could all speak the Shandong dialect. They all said if you drank the Heilong River water, your hair would turn blonde and your nose would grow bigger, so the people here were all people of mixed blood. Because they looked Russian, they were barred from the party, the military, and the local militia. There were many different kinds of river fish in the Heilong. It was said that these fish were a tender delicacy, but up to then Du Zhong hadn't eaten any. The sturgeon eggs were like black pearls, while the large golden-red salmon roe were like carnelians. In a place called West Ridge, several thousand Soviet Red Army soldiers were buried. Nearby was an active volcano; from which red sparks flickered at night. . . . Too bad all of this was hearsay: he hadn't seen any of it himself. His daily life consisted only of work and study. He really wanted to take a look at the riverside. He'd heard that in the summer you could even make out clearly the hats of the fishermen on the other shore and the spots on the pretty spotted dogs . . .

At first, Chu Xiaoxi wrote back often. Strangely, Xiaoxi didn't seem to have a bit of interest in the fascinating things Du Zhong wrote about. Her letters were always about their fervent work: opening up the wasteland, weeding, harvesting wheat—and how time after time they had completed their missions victoriously. Du Zhong thought Xiaoxi's letters were completely impersonal. Sentences like these even showed up in her letters: "Farm work has changed me from a petty bourgeois intellectual into a down-to-earth worker, but I still haven't revised my worldview thoroughly enough." "What we plant are ordinary crops, but our harvests are great anti-Soviet achievements." . . . Du Zhong thought to himself, *Does a girl who had just finished seventh grade when the Cultural Revolution began dare call herself a petty bourgeois intellectual?* He looked forward to her letters, but he also dreaded receiving them. If he let the slightest hint of depression show in his letters, Xiaoxi's answer would be harshly critical. She wanted him to get back on the correct path, so all he could do was defend himself when he wrote back. During the slack winter season, he spent a lot of his free time writing to her, hoping he could make her understand him. His letters became longer and longer, and more and more vehement. As a result, there were longer intervals between Chu Xiaoxi's letters, and they became shorter and shorter . . .

But Du Zhong still looked forward to Chu Xiaoxi's letters. His only friend among the youth from Hangzhou had transferred to another unit. He had no one to talk to. He needed one person who would listen to him. And Chu Xiaoxi was an angelic girl who had given him warmth and friendship during his most trying times.

Time after time, Du Zhong made the round trip between the village and the township. Like a single artemisia plant wobbling on the vast snowfield, he might be snapped at any time by wind and snow. In the otherwise quiet fields, the commune's high-pitched loudspeaker screamed, but it was as if the whole world had already died.

The waiting was endless. He didn't get the letters he was waiting for from his parents or Chu Xiaoxi, but he did hear the "happy news" that his tenth grade buddy had joined the military. In this distant border region, after his only friend left, Du Zhong began to worry. He read and reread the box of books he'd brought with him from Hangzhou. Their covers were tattered. He had almost memorized the first part of Pushkin's long poem, "Eugene Onegin":

> I linger at the seaside, waiting for good weather.
> I wave at passing boats.
> I greet the storms that smash against the waves and follow the
>   passageway of freedom on the sea.
> When can I begin my own voyage of freedom?

In the 1960s, the Soviet Union withdrew all aid to China, rupturing relations. In 1964, Du Zhong started middle school, where he learned English. He studied Russian purely out of interest. He studied it on his own, with some tutoring from his parents. Before his parents were isolated for interrogation, he could already converse in Russian with simple sentences. In secret, Du Zhong tried translating some Russian poems into Chinese to make time pass more quickly. After a while, he could recite the lines from memory.

The grass greened, then turned yellow again. Snow fell, then melted. Du Zhong ran out of patience.

He started writing letters to his army friend. He poured out his depression, as well as some immature criticisms. The criticisms weren't what his soldier buddy thought they were—"instigated" or "influenced" by others. That wasn't true. They were merely doubts that had arisen from Du Zhong's inner discontent. They were complaints linked to his experience. There were also the incompatible sensibilities that the works of literature had left with him. He raised many of his doubts in his letters. He pleaded with his buddy, who back then had dared to hoist him up onto the train car heading to the front line of anti-Soviet revisionism. He never dreamed that his army buddy wasn't the same now as before; rather, he was rapidly growing up. After reading Du Zhong's letter, his friend felt tremendous misgivings. He felt that Du Zhong's thinking was dangerous—simply too dangerous. He'd better save this buddy who'd lost his bearings after he himself had left. He sent a letter back to the commune, attaching a long note requesting that the party organization help Du Zhong. His language was earnest: he hoped Du Zhong would realize his errors and change his ways. Du Zhong was devastated by this blow—not because of the series of criticism meetings that the commune and production brigade held as a result of this incident, or because Du Zhong was forced to write numerous self-criticisms, but because—after being tossed by dangerous winds and waves for several years—Du Zhong still thought there was a shore ahead of him, or at least that there was a ship beside him all the while. But now, as he lifted his eyes in all directions, he realized that he was alone on the boundless ocean. In the high winds and rough seas, neither birds nor islands were in sight. His cry for help hadn't been answered. The small boat was leaking. One more crest, and the boat would capsize.

For the first time, Du Zhong felt truly alone. And he despaired.

He knew that he'd come to a dead end. This letter was enough to ruin his already slim chances of a future. Now, he had no hope at all for a change in luck or a way out.

Still, he earnestly and painfully wrote profound self-criticisms, one after another, about the absurdities in his letter. Just before New Year's Day a red carbuncle appeared on his back, and then he started running a fever. At that time, all the city youth were getting ready to go back to Hangzhou to visit their families, and no one was in the mood to continue the ferocious attack on him. The commune authorities allowed him to go to Beian to see a doctor. He hitched a ride, first on an oxcart, and then on a truck, and finally on a bus. After having surgery at the hospital and getting authorization for sick leave, he hopped a train to Hangzhou.

One day early in 1971, Du Zhong stood for a long time in front of the sealed door to his old home. He couldn't keep himself from touching the door lightly. To his surprise, he found that the dust-covered lock wasn't very strong anymore. He turned around and left. At an out-of-the-way general store, he bought pliers and a flashlight. That night, he crept toward his old home and broke in easily. In rooms that had long been unoccupied, he choked on the strong smell of mold and dust. He had no idea what he wanted to do: he just wanted to take a look around, that's all. Maybe he could find something useful among the dilapidated furnishings. By the faint light of the flashlight, he moved around silently, like a ghost. The tilting clothes rack, the leaning cupboard, and the scraps of paper all over the floor reminded him again of his loneliness and despair. He sat down wearily on the floor. Looking up, he saw a picture on the wall.

For years now, Du Zhong had thought that it was as if someone had held out a hand in the flickering light and pointed out that spot to him. He had no way to explain it: back then, why had he all of a sudden felt so intensely curious about that picture frame? It was the size of a book. His parents had brought it back with them from the Soviet Union. It had always hung right here. Perhaps because it held a charcoal drawing of Lenin, the frame was in perfect condition, and surprisingly it hadn't been carried off by anyone. As Du Zhong brushed off the surface dust with his sleeve, he thought to himself that maybe this was a memento his parents had left for him. He hid it under his coat and quietly left.

The next morning at his schoolmate's home, after everyone had left for work, he took out the picture frame and looked at it carefully. The picture inside seemed a little askew. Since he had nothing else to do anyway, he pulled the little nails off the back of the frame with the pliers and freed the flimsy cardboard backing. In the instant that he was thinking of straightening the picture, he suddenly started hyperventilating. Between the picture and the cardboard he discovered a stiff, somewhat yellowed piece of paper. When he turned it over to look at it, it seemed to be some kind of form: Russian words were printed on it. Du Zhong held his breath and opened his eyes wide. He began reading the blurry Russian words. His head was bathed in sweat, and his heart was about to jump out of his throat. He simply didn't dare believe it: this was a document having to do with him—a birth certificate stating that in 1951 Du Zhong (Russian name: Drooka) was born in a certain hospital in Moscow.

Why would his parents have wanted to hide his birth certificate in a place like this? As it happened, he discovered this piece of paper that had been so carefully saved just when he was beginning to think he had no way out. Was this perhaps a sign, a direction? Where would it lead him? Into a trap or to an escape?

Du Zhong was stunned. He thought about this all day. By twilight, when his schoolmate's whole family came home, he had already put the frame back the way it was, wrapped it tightly in an undershirt, and stuffed it into his simple suitcase. A momentous decision leapt audaciously into his desperate, confused mind—indeed he was frightened by his own thoughts, but he had no choice. He realized that this was the only path he could take. Without any way to retreat, all he could do was move ahead courageously. Even if precipices or traps lay ahead, he had to pawn his young life, fling caution to the winds, and give it a try.

In the days following—in the brief time Du Zhong was in Hangzhou—he began making careful preparations. Once more, he went secretly into the sealed old house, where, among various things, he actually found a telescope manufactured in the Soviet Union. Perhaps it was providence that in the home of his classmate, who had stayed in the city and was working in a factory, he found a compass that glowed in the dark. Using the excuse that he often got lost on the frontier, he begged his friend to give him the compass. He didn't need much more; he merely needed nerve and courage. He believed that his proficiency in Russian would serve him well.

Years later, when he recalled his almost crazy behavior back then, he thought the motivation for his actions was simply the survival instinct of a desperate cornered beast. It was the adventurous spirit of a smug hot-blooded young man. It was also his madcap idea of wanting to see for himself the true face of the birthplace of Communism. If he could say that a little poetic longing and romance were mixed in with this, then they came from the quiet flowing Don, the boat trackers on the banks of the Volga, the vast grasslands, and the sorrowful *Swan Lake* . . .

Maybe it was just because of this that on the way back from Hangzhou to Huma he made a special point of detouring to Wanshan Farm on the banks of the Songhua River so that he could see Chu Xiaoxi. Their solemn and stirring parting could be processed only in his heart. Only he knew that if he crossed that river successfully he would not be able to return. And if he were killed on the border, then he certainly wouldn't be coming back. So, whether he succeeded or not, when he left this time he was parting forever from Chu Xiaoxi.

After he got back to Huma, his work performance was exceptional. Several times, he hid his telescope and went to a faraway meadow to collect kindling. He knew the sentry outposts on the riverbank like the back of his hand. Between the two banks of the river on a frontier like this with vast land and few people, there would always be a secluded path that escaped detection. You just had to look for it.

Eventually the windy, snowy night that he had been waiting for arrived. In the roaring wind and slanting snow he wrested the iron bar off the shed where the production brigade kept its horses and drove more than a dozen horses out. The horses ran around like crazy all over the fields, providing the best possible cover for what he was about to do. He turned a thick leather jacket inside out and wrapped it tightly around himself. He thought if he froze to death in the fields, he would look like a sheep buried in the snow when morning came.

In fact, there was just one step between life and death. To the twenty-year-old Du Zhong, the national border was the boundary marker between life and death. Everything was in chaos from heaven to earth; an icy shell formed on his face. His eyeballs seemed frozen in place. Over and over, he wiped the frost from his eyelashes. In the distance a faint light glimmered like a desert mirage.

Out of the darkness came the sound of Russian ordering him to stop. A few soldiers seized him and promptly tied him up. He didn't say anything when they took him to a small warm cabin, but—with his hands almost frozen—drew out his birth certificate, as well as a frontier residence card bearing his name.

Meng Di lightly cracked a melon seed and chewed it slowly. "To tell you the truth, I never actually expected to see you in Hangzhou. Back then, when it seemed that you would never be shipped back to China, everyone figured that if you weren't shot as you crossed the river, then you must have frozen to death. That the Russians even accepted you is a miracle in itself, or rather a mystery. But I'm not at all interested in knowing specifically why you weren't sent back here. These days, people our age all know that if you were able to stay there, naturally it was because you were useful to them. But one of your sister's friends told me that it was from France that you came back. I'd really like to know. Did you simply go through France, or did you settle there a long time ago?"

"In the mid-1980s I went from the Soviet Union to France. My wife is Russian and she knows French. She had to wait until the 1990s for an opportunity to leave Russia and join me in France. Now we live together in the southern part of France, where I work in a university library. You probably understand that in the last twenty-some years there was no possibility for me to come home and see my family."

Meng Di muttered to himself for a while, and then asked, "Du Zhong, forgive me for asking: Since you risked your life to reach your destination, why on earth did you leave that spot once more to go to France?" Meng Di emphasized the words "once more."

Du Zhong quickly replied, "Out of despair."

"What made you despair?"

"You should know."

"Can it be that whenever one experiences despair, one simply quits?"

"Right. I wasn't rebellious in any other way. Quitting was my only choice."

"Just like you abandoned Chu Xiaoxi back then?"

". . . No, Chu Xiaoxi and I were simply friends. She wasn't what I needed to rebel against. I did not abandon her."

"Then, what if someday you don't have anything more you can abandon—then what?"

"In fact, now I am all I have left. That's the bottom line."

There was a long silence. Du Zhong took a cigarette from Meng Di's cigarette case. He'd stopped smoking years ago.

Du Zhong really had no desire to tell the story of his years overseas. After all, he and Meng Di weren't close. Someday, if he saw Chu Xiaoxi and if she was interested in listening, then he would tell her how he'd spent these twenty-eight years. After the snowstorm had passed, he'd been escorted to Blagoveshensk and then sent to Chita. After numerous investigations and a lot of waiting, he was finally permitted to stay in the Far Eastern District. First he was sent to a university to study international politics, and then he worked for an institute researching Sino-Soviet relations. Meng Di was right on this point—because of his and his family's special background, he was useful to them. But what Meng Di didn't understand was that he wasn't *very* useful. They had wanted him to broadcast Chinese on the international radio station, but he declined. A few years later, he was sent to another research institute in Moscow. By then, he had begun teaching himself English and French. But at just about the same time, he came down with a serious case of melancholia because of the endless sunless winter, the oppression and nervous tension of his daily life, and a long period of homesickness. He was suddenly fed up with it all. He lost interest in his so-called grand and mysterious work. Sometimes he even hallucinated. He felt that—except for the food and the languages—there was essentially no difference between being here and being on the opposite side of the river back then. He wondered if he had really "gotten away" all those years before? Would it be necessary for him to get away all over again?

That summer, he took the opportunity to go to France for treatment of his melancholia, and didn't return to Moscow. His wife's friends and relatives in France provided him with living expenses. For several years, he was intermittently troubled by this depression. Finally, when the Soviet Union broke apart, his wife joined him in France. It was only then that he gradually recovered his health. After he began to rebound, he settled his family in and found suitable work. Only after several years of putting money aside was it finally possible for him to make his first trip back to China.

Twenty-eight years. Circling around half a world. Such a long, long curve.

Meng Di said, "But I still don't understand; you knew very well that crossing the river would lead to grave repercussions. Why did you have to see Chu Xiaoxi before you left? Do you know how many people you implicated by staying that one night at Wanshan Farm? Everyone who talked with you was repeatedly questioned. As for me, because I let you stay with me in the dorm and shared my quilt with you, my membership in the Communist Youth League was revoked.

"It was even worse for Chu Xiaoxi. If it hadn't been for this incident, the next year she would have had a very good chance to be chosen to study in a university. But, all because of you, she was thrown into limbo. She couldn't leave the Great Northern Wilderness until seven years later—1978, when most of the other students went back to the cities, too. For a while, the other female students at the farm didn't dare talk to her. I tried to console her, but it was useless because she always felt she'd let me down. She kept apologizing to me. Since she was weighed down by so much pressure, I was really afraid she'd go to pieces . . ."

"Yes, as I listen to you talk of all this, I think I was a sinner." Du Zhong let out a long sigh. This sigh had been suppressed in his chest all the while. When it passed through his throat, it was like a smelly, sticky stream of blood spurting out. He was also coughing continuously, so each word he spoke took all of his strength: "In my remaining years, if I can see Chu Xiaoxi just once, I'll beg for her forgiveness. Today, here, please accept my apologies, but I have no way to compensate you for the losses I caused you back then . . ."

Du Zhong's eyes smarted and his breathing became more labored. He really didn't want to think back on the last time he'd seen Chu Xiaoxi. There was also no way to tell Meng Di that such a costly meeting in fact had been very unpleasant. Not only was it unpleasant, it had even been like a sharp sword cutting a permanent wound onto his heart. It was this that had firmed up his resolve to get away. Back then, it was because of Chu Xiaoxi's innocence that the two of them had grown close to one another, but it was also because of her innocence that they had parted. It was with a lost heart and a dazed soul that he had walked toward the snowfields on that inky dark night. Time after time, he'd fallen down in the snow and climbed back up again. He'd felt that only his legs were still risking death to continue moving; his heart was already frozen stiff . . .

Before leaving Willow Shade teahouse, he hesitated several times and then said that he still had some questions about what happened after he crossed the river. For instance, why was Chu Xiaoxi punished so harshly? Chu

Xiaoxi had treated him like a guest and a friend; she had known nothing about his plans to get away. Once she'd explained her situation, she should have been okay. How could it have been handled like this? Had Chu Xiaoxi expressed sympathy and understanding about his leaving? He was speaking carefully: he knew that deep in his heart he still longed for a certain consolation. Meng Di responded quickly, "No, with her orthodox political attitude back then, how could she have sympathized with a . . . She was very cooperative with the investigation." Suddenly, Meng Di's tone turned rather unfriendly as he asked Du Zhong, "Are you really in the dark or are you just pretending to be?"

"What do you mean?" Du Zhong was at a loss.

"What I mean is this. You must know—the crux of the problem was that Chu Xiaoxi was unable to explain herself."

"Why?"

"Because of that scrap of paper."

"What scrap of paper?"

"You really don't remember that piece of paper? A piece of paper with horizontal blue lines, probably torn out of a notebook. Both Chinese and Russian were written on it: one line above, one below—Chinese and Russian juxtaposed. Actually, both sentences said the same thing."

"What?"

"Please take me with you!"

"Please take me with you?"

"Right. Even after more than twenty years, I still can't forget these words: 'Please take me with you.'"

Du Zhong's mind was blank. He couldn't think; he was confused. He thought this sentence seemed to have a little something to do with him. But he couldn't remember how this sentence was related to him.

Meng Di sneered, "How come you can't remember what you wrote your-self? That evening, you and Chu Xiaoxi were chatting in the little room where she was working. In your haste, you dropped the piece of paper there. The piece of paper had Russian on it; in those days, this put people on their guard. So, the next day, when some guy picked it up, he kept it and didn't say a word. Then he turned it over to the supervisors. After you crossed the river, a large-scale investigation began, and this scrap of paper became ironclad evidence. The problem was that no one wanted to believe that it was you who had lost that scrap of paper. One student from Hangzhou said that since Chu Xiaoxi became acquainted with you during the Cultural Revolution, you must have been the one who taught her Russian. The investigators even analyzed her handwriting and finally concluded that the scrap of paper had come from her. It was she who sometime earlier had written 'Please take me with you.' She meant to give it to you. In other words, Chu Xiaoxi wanted to go with you, but you were afraid she'd be in the way and so you didn't agree. At the time, I was the only one who believed Chu Xiaoxi wasn't guilty. It was a shame she had no way to prove that she hadn't written the words on that scrap of paper . . ."

Instantly, Du Zhong remembered. He vaguely recalled that on the way back from Hangzhou to the Great Northern Wilderness, as he transferred from one train to another and waited for trains, he had passed the time by writing some lines with Chinese and Russian juxtaposed. He was practicing his Russian. Of course, this could have included the sentence "Please take me with you"—the sort of sentence that he would need to know after crossing the river. Right. He'd written this in his notebook, and then had torn the page out to throw it away. He didn't know why he hadn't done that; he just knew that later, he couldn't find this scrap of paper. Luckily, he had already memorized the sentence "Please take me with you," and so he had put the incident out of his mind. His oversight back then had actually provoked such a great disaster. How could he have unwittingly harmed the person he treasured the most?

Du Zhong forced a smile. He felt that this was more and more preposterous, even incredible. As he confronted that faraway scrap of paper, he thought that no words of regret or apology could atone for what he had done. There was nothing he could say to Meng Di.

After Du Zhong paid for the tea, he and Meng Di went outside together in silence.

Du Zhong stopped under a large phoenix tree. He thought that no matter what, he had to say one last thing to Meng Di. If he didn't say it now, he'd probably never have another chance. Despite everything, he wanted to give it a try.

"I heard that . . . I heard that in the 1980s Chu Xiaoxi went to America." Du Zhong was nervous. "Meng Di, it doesn't matter what you might think of me, but can you tell me Chu Xiaoxi's address in America?"

"No. I'm seldom in touch with her." Meng Di refused at once.

"Can't you think of some way to find out for me?" Du Zhong was imploring him. He thought he was a little pitiful. "Meng Di, you live in Hangzhou. If you want to find her, surely you can. But in just a few more days I'll go back to France. I just want . . . just hope you can give me a chance to apologize to her and ask for her forgiveness. Even her phone number would help . . . "

Meng Di didn't say anything, but just slowly mounted his bicycle and said good-bye without shaking hands.

From Meng Di's inability to disguise his expression, Du Zhong realized that Meng Di did indeed have ways to get in touch with Chu Xiaoxi.

~ *2* ~

But Du Zhong could never have guessed that at this very moment Chu Xiaoxi was in Hangzhou.

Almost every year, she flew back from America to Hangzhou once or twice—she was like a migratory bird unbound by the laws of the seasons.

On each endless, lonely flight, Chu Xiaoxi always chose a window seat. She would train her attention for a long time on the clouds suspended outside the window and marvel at the mysterious changes in time and space. It was as if the serenely infinite blue and the pure transparent white were drifting in from that long ago sky above the Great Northern Wilderness. Years ago, wearing a shirt soaked with perspiration, she had leaned on a hoe in the fields and looked at the clouds—layer upon layer folded in upon each other, unending. They were silent—like Chu Xiaoxi's worries, it wasn't easy to penetrate them. In the fields, she could see the curvature of the earth's surface. The arced blue sky was like a very large tent wrapped warmly around the lonely Chu Xiaoxi. The blue sky hadn't changed and the white clouds were the same as before, but Chu Xiaoxi had gone to another side of the world.

Chu Xiaoxi liked the sort of travel that was undisturbed. On clear days, from a window seat you could see the boundless ocean below the lofty sky, its silver light shining like snow, its waves rolling, the wind pursuing the deep blue ripples on the water, the magnificent remoteness of the mist and snow-like spray. Yet this beauty also bestowed the chill of great loneliness. All of this called to mind the Great Northern Wilderness, mantled with ice and snow. The thick snow banks had sealed much of the past for safekeeping: only in the wind did they reveal the weakened tips of weeds. Whenever the snow melted, those buried memories would emerge slowly in the sunshine, just like carefully preserved ashes or rotting bones. Although they had lost their life-giving blood, they would never disappear. Now and then, Chu Xiaoxi made a detour and flew back to China via Europe, where uninterrupted mountain ranges stretched below the clear vast sky. In the sunlight, the mountain peaks and the gloomy ravines were all clearly visible. Once, she suddenly thought these undulating rumples were like people's brains. The rocks, trees, and grottoes that couldn't be seen clearly from the sky were like people's feelings, concealed deeply within these twisting, enshrouded folds.

The bygone days were already as remote as this, yet it also seemed you could touch them.

When the university entrance exams were reinstated in 1978, Chu Xiaoxi had already left the Great Northern Wilderness and returned to Hangzhou because of illness. She was working as a miller in a small factory and teaching herself English at the same time. In 1979, she passed the entrance exam and was admitted to a university in her province. It was only when she was a university student that she began dating seriously. After graduating, she married and had a child. Her husband was a classmate majoring in automation. He, too, had gone down to the countryside and returned to the city. They shared the experiences of this generation, and everything went smoothly for them. The bright sunshine of the 1980s dispelled the shadows that had been hanging over her for years and healed the wounds deep in her heart. She began to be vibrant and open, often writing poems and short essays for the school newspaper. People said that she had an elegant style of writing—why not develop the literary part of her herself? Chu Xiaoxi just laughed. People said that the twenty-first century would be biology's century; biology was her major, and she was crazy about her work. She longed to go overseas to enrich her understanding and to see the world. In the mid-1980s, she and her husband enrolled in American universities. After years of effort, they finished up their master's and doctor's degrees and stayed on in Chicago to work for a biotech company. When they were more settled, they brought their child to America. This was common practice among most Chinese studying overseas then.

In recent years, the company she worked for had opened an office in China for all China-related operations. The company sent her to China periodically to deal with things in that office, so she was used to flying back and forth. Once, she flew United to Shanghai, where she wrapped up her business in just half a day, and that very evening she took the same plane back to Chicago.

That's a rather extreme example. Actually, whenever she came to China on business, if time allowed she would try her best to get back to Hangzhou. Her former classmates and friends seldom kept in touch any longer. She went back to Hangzhou mainly to see her aging parents. After staying with them for two or three days, she'd fly off again.

Whenever she returned to Hangzhou, Chu Xiaoxi generally just stayed home and talked with her parents or tidied up the house a little. Now and then she would phone Meng Di and invite him out for tea or coffee. She'd give his child some chocolates or vitamins that she'd brought back with her. Meng Di didn't often ask about her life in America. Nor did she want to hear what her former classmates and friends were doing now. There wasn't much they could talk about, so they just sat together for a while and then went their separate ways again.

In these years of flying back and forth across the ocean, she'd grown accustomed to the changes in Hangzhou. One time when she came back, an alleyway had disappeared into thin air. The next time, a broad avenue cut grandly through the city. In the blink of an eye, she was seeing large buildings with imposing spires break out of the ground like spring bamboo. Elevated roads formed cloverleafs. They were constructed as swiftly as outdoor sets for movies. Hangzhou was merely one part of a grand movie being produced all over China. When she took a quick glance, Chu Xiaoxi felt that Hangzhou had become a stranger, yet when she looked more carefully, it was still the same familiar city. No matter how much it changed, its flavor was still the same—like a bowl of wonton soup. Now and then, she would hazard some odd ideas: she wished Hangzhou could be like a large heap of toy blocks—all pushed over and then set up again. Hangzhou's streets of the future would go past large broad lawns, each house would be built beneath dense shade trees, and each store would be landscaped with borders of fresh flowers growing in profusion. Concerts and plays would be performed on the riverbank, lamplight would reflect on the river at night, the sound of music would come from the water . . . After Chu Xiaoxi had daydreams like this, she chided herself for being ridiculous. She hadn't been a romantic idealist for a long time. For more than ten years, she had been exacting in her work, cautious and conscientious. She would no longer tax her nerves and trouble herself with things that couldn't be actualized . . .

Chu Xiaoxi suddenly thought that perhaps she was the only one with notions about toy blocks. In her subconscious, wasn't she looking forward to a new beginning for everything? Hoping that the reconstruction following demolition could help rid her mind of her stack of memories? Although the sequel to the story hadn't occurred in this city, almost everything that had happened was connected with Hangzhou. Although she'd been away from Hangzhou for more than a decade, this city kept surprising her with its scattered remnants. Each time she reached Hangzhou, the fragrance of the roadside camphor trees blew against her face. Emanating from those glaze-green leaves was a scent difficult to forget. It always left her light-headed and giddy.

All the while, someone was standing beneath a huge camphor tree, his face hidden by the tree's shade.

Chu Xiaoxi knew that as long as Hangzhou existed, that person wouldn't vanish from the city, although ultimately she had no way of knowing whether or not he was still alive.

That long ago summer evening, the cicadas in the camphor trees had grown quiet. From the small courtyard next door came the sound of scrambling footsteps, followed by the crashing sound of furniture being broken. The sonorous war cry was like the piercing cries of cicadas.

The camphor tree in the courtyard was so big that two people together could just barely encircle it with their arms. Two nights before, an old man had been tied to the tree and a crowd of people had whipped him with leather belts. His sad, shrill weeping and shouting could be heard all night long.

Chu Xiaoxi leaned against the kitchen window, and from between its iron bars she watched what was going on in the courtyard next door. She saw several students, both male and female, wearing red armbands, untie the old man from the tree and press him down on the ground. She saw a white dunce cap made of paper. Humiliating words were written on it in black. A lot of things had been moved out of the house and loaded onto a truck. A female student slipped a small brocaded box into her pants pocket. Several people were stomping on a lot of thick books and rolled-up scrolls that were scattered on the ground. A male student picked up some books. Chu Xiaoxi couldn't see his face, hidden as it was by the shade of the tree. He had a strange way of walking: standing on tiptoe, he carefully walked past the books scattered on the ground, as though afraid he would destroy them if he stepped on them. Chu Xiaoxi could scarcely keep from laughing: he was acting like a girl. After he piled up the scattered books and paintings, he sat on the doorsill guarding these things. After a while, he took off his glasses and wiped the sweat from them. Chu Xiaoxi thought his expression was apathetic. At first, she wondered if he was the son of the person whose house had been ransacked, but she quickly dismissed this notion. When it grew dark, he left along with the other male students wearing red armbands. At the gate, he turned around for another look at the heaped up things, and Chu Xiaoxi noticed that his forehead was broad and shiny.

That evening, Chu Xiaoxi was alone in the kitchen, hoping the family cat, which had been missing for quite a few days, would return. Xiaoxi made a special point of setting his favorite food—a little fish—out on the windowsill. She hoped the big cat would smell it and come around. She didn't turn the lights on: she thought without the lights on, the cat could return a little more gracefully. After a while, something stirred in the inky black courtyard next door. A black shadow vaulted over the wall and made a beeline for the pile of books at the door of that house. In the darkness, Xiaoxi's heart thumped and she opened her eyes wide. The person turned on a flashlight, and under its weak beam began looking through the books. Just then, another black shadow silently jumped up to the windowsill, and a soft tail whisked Xiaoxi's face. Xiaoxi couldn't keep from crying out. She held the cat with one hand, and as Xiaoxi murmured to it, the cat impatiently snatched the fish. The other black shadow stood up at the sound, looked into the kitchen window for a while, and then walked over toward Chu Xiaoxi.

"Hi there, did you see everything?" He said softly, "I'm not a bad guy."

"What would I have seen? I didn't see anything." Muttering, Chu Xiaoxi turned on the kitchen light. A ray of light shone on his face outside the window. Xiaoxi was surprised to discover that it was the boy student who had earlier picked up some books.

He held up a book, and lowering his voice, said, "Just a few books. I just took a few books. You won't tell anyone, will you?"

Chu Xiaoxi stared at him with big eyes: "How can books be so mysterious? Let me see, okay?"

He hesitated, retreated a step, and then held a book up: "Look, this isn't an evil book."

At a glance, Chu Xiaoxi saw the title, *And Quiet Flows the Don*. With a straight face, she said, "Who knows if it's an evil book? You show up in the middle of the night to steal books. You can't be a good person."

Beads of sweat seeped from his broad forehead. Stuttering, he said, "How can . . . you . . . just make an arbitrary . . . judgment like this? How can you? Without reading it, how can you know if it's evil?"

"Okay, okay," Chu Xiaoxi said impatiently. "Hey, how about this—after you finish reading it, you lend it to me. This will be our secret, and I won't tell a soul."

"But . . ." He was hesitating. "You're too young to read this kind of book . . ."

"I've finished seventh grade. I've read a lot. Really."

He stood there thinking for a while, and then reluctantly nodded his head. Then he warned her not to let anyone else see it. "Don't let even your family know, okay?" Chu Xiaoxi told him her house number and also told him that from the small courtyard where he was standing, he had to make a large loop to reach her home.

Much later, Du Zhong told Chu Xiaoxi that after he went home that evening, he thought and thought. He thought this girl was either asking out of curiosity or out of ignorance: she had actually volunteered to be his confederate. She'd been quick to come up with this idea to extricate him from an awkward situation. If it had been he, he wouldn't have known what to do. So, she was at least bright. Girls who were ignorant yet bright often were rather appealing to smug boys.

Classes had already been suspended. Chu Xiaoxi sat around with nothing to do at home. Her parents were both ordinary white-collar workers with neither questionable backgrounds nor questionable behavior. Her life was too quiet—she was really hoping that something would happen to break up the monotony. After this, for about a year, she intermittently borrowed books from Du Zhong, returned them, borrowed again, returned them again. This went on in secrecy. Now she still remembered the books Du Zhong had lent her: *Marx's Youth, 1793, The Hunchback of Notre Dame, Crime and Punishment,* and *War and Peace.* Generally, it was during the day that Du Zhong brought books over. He put them under a layer of fresh vegetables in his shopping basket. Thus, on days that Du Zhong brought books over, Xiaoxi's family had fresh vegetables to eat. Actually, Xiaoxi understood almost nothing in these books: the characters had long names, and the stories were as far removed from her present life as heaven from earth. She often just turned the pages and then put the book down. But she really loved the feeling of being an "undercover agent." When you knocked on a door, you had to use a secret signal—she found this exciting. It didn't matter much which books she read. But one book—*Robinson Crusoe*—she read more than ten times. It fascinated her so much that she felt as if morning and evening were reversed. One time, Du Zhong told her that his family actually had a set of the Russian edition of *And Quiet Flows the Don,* but it wasn't until he read the Chinese translation that he understood why his parents hadn't given him access to the book. Du Zhong told Chu Xiaoxi that the hero, Gregor Melekhov, sought freedom all his life, and a true free spirit could never settle down. At that time, Du Zhong's enthusiasm was so high that he talked for more than half an hour. Too bad that the fourteen-year-old Chu Xiaoxi remembered only this much.

In 1967, things changed so abruptly that there was no time to prepare. It was a deadly blow for Du Zhong. Almost simultaneously, both of his parents were isolated for interrogation, and it was only then that Chu Xiaoxi learned about his family background. In those few days, Du Zhong's face turned pale and drawn. His shiny forehead seemed covered with a layer of ash. His eyes were gloomy, his spectacles dusty. Xiaoxi's parents immediately forbade her to have anything more to do with Du Zhong. Xiaoxi responded by finding all kinds of excuses to sneak out and run off to meet Du Zhong in a park. She knew that almost none of his relatives, friends, or classmates dared have anything to do with him now, and so in this lonely, helpless time, the arrogant Du Zhong especially needed to be comforted. As Xiaoxi saw it, Du Zhong had steeled himself to reject sympathy. But in truth, inwardly he thirsted for sympathy more than anyone else. Xiaoxi, though, didn't offer him sympathy: she simply enjoyed his company the same as always. Du Zhong could tell her a lot of things that were new to her. A lot of admiration was factored into her fondness for Du Zhong. Even though his family was doomed, he was still the same Du Zhong. When she was with him, Xiaoxi always felt her eyes brightening. Before she left for the Great Northern Wilderness, she received a letter from him. From one sentence in that letter, she understood why he was good to her: "In my most difficult times, you never made me feel that your friendship was a kind of charity." Xiaoxi was moved, but she also felt he was praising her too much because, in fact, girls were born wanting to comfort others. At the time, Xiaoxi often "stole" a few tangerines, dumplings, or water chestnuts for Du Zhong. While he downed them like a hungry wolf, Xiaoxi racked her brains for jokes to tell him. She wanted to make him happy.

In their hurried meetings, they no longer held books in their hands; they weren't in the mood to talk about books. The stories in the books were splendid, but real life was grim. Du Zhong said they had no today, because today was filled with dangers. Nor did they have a tomorrow, for tomorrow was like an inland river that had dried up on the desert. More and more inappropriate words sprang from Du Zhong's mouth, making Chu Xiaoxi tremble with fear. Several years later, after he had vanished from her life, she recalled that back then sixteen-year-old Du Zhong had lectured to an audience of only one person. All of a sudden, she realized that the later scene with him was actually foreshadowed at this earlier time.

Soon, they couldn't continue with even this sort of meeting. After Xiaoxi's parents learned that she was still seeing Du Zhong, they promptly packed her off to her grandmother's home in another county. At fifteen, Chu Xiaoxi didn't know how she could refuse or weasel out of this. And too, she had begun realizing that Du Zhong was becoming too sensitive and that it was harder and harder to get along with him. Chu Xiaoxi was a little afraid to be with him. When she talked with him, he always upset her and made her think that her mind was inferior to his. At Xiaoxi's age, she always believed everything she was told. Why did she unfortunately have to believe whatever Du Zhong told her?

It was years before Chu Xiaoxi realized that while a camphor tree was living, you couldn't smell its scent. It was only after the wood was made into boxes that the fragrance of the wood lasted year after year.

She stayed in the small town for more than six months. Even though they were all a muddle to her, she read the four Confucian classics. She also learned to use a treadle sewing machine and cut out clothing. Once in a while she thought about Du Zhong, but she didn't write to him. Even if she had, he wouldn't have received the letters. She didn't know what he was doing during this time. When she went back to Hangzhou, it was the end of 1968: one batch after another of students was getting ready to leave for Heilongjiang to join the anti-Soviet front line in the Great Northern Wilderness. When she finally heard some news about Du Zhong, it was already the night before he would board the train.

She found him in a classroom at his school. Lots of luggage was spread out haphazardly on a row of desks, and Du Zhong was in the midst of packing books into one wooden box. Her sudden arrival didn't especially surprise him. Clapping the dust off his hands, he said with a smile, "Hey, why have you shown up only now? Why not come along with us?"

"Are you really going to go?"

"You bet. I've had it up to here with Hangzhou."

"Why do you have to go so far away?"

"As long as I'm going, I might as well go far away," he said. "The farther, the better."

Chu Xiaoxi sat down on a stool in the deserted classroom and began crying. She was grief-stricken; she couldn't say a word. Not until that moment did she realize that she actually cared about Du Zhong. He was like a borrowed book: only after you finished reading it and returned it did you realize that you hadn't had time to examine it carefully. With Du Zhong's departure, it would seem as though a corner of this city had collapsed. Without him, the city would be empty.

She wept for a long time. Du Zhong was making quite a racket with his baggage and books. Inwardly, Chu Xiaoxi was perhaps waiting for him to comfort her: maybe walk over and pull her braids, stroke the top of her head, or . . . pull her into his arms and pat her back. But not for a minute did Du Zhong stop what he was doing. Without saying a word, he kept walking back and forth, but he didn't approach Chu Xiaoxi. Disappointed, she looked up and tore off her two new blue sleeve protectors, and handed them to him angrily.

"I don't have anything to give you. I made these sleeve protectors myself. Take them with you; they might be useful."

In the moment that he accepted them, his hand touched her fingertips. Her hands were like ice, but his were hot and sweaty. For a brief moment, his hand covered hers, seemed to hesitate, and then he quickly withdrew it. With a gruff thank-you, he donned the sleeve protectors, rummaged in his baggage, and said, "Then I'd better give you this book. To tell you the truth, I really don't want to give it up. You must take good care of it."

Once, Xiaoxi had wanted to borrow this flimsy book, *Golden Rose*, from him, but he had made all kinds of excuses to get out of lending it to her.

As she took the book in both hands, her palms suddenly swelled a little, and she grew warm all over. She said, "Du Zhong, when you get there, you must write to me. Just mail your letters to me at school; I'll go to the mailroom every day to look for them." With that, she rushed out of the classroom. In the dark corridor, she heard Du Zhong shouting, "You have to write back to me!—"

Chu Xiaoxi never dreamed that the very next spring she would also sign up to go the Great Northern Wilderness; she would be at Wanshan Farm. At that time, all of Hangzhou was filled with red flags and the noise of gongs and drums; she was caught up in the red flags blowing in the wind and driven by the gongs and drums shaking heaven and earth. In an exultant mood, she felt inspired and stimulated. In the instant that the special train for students got underway, Chu Xiaoxi—a big red flower on her chest—felt that all of a sudden she had changed into another Chu Xiaoxi, a new Chu Xiaoxi—Chu Xiaoxi the heroic valiant soldier. In the songs that rocked the train car, she suddenly remembered something Du Zhong had said: *As long as I'm going, I might as well go far away. The farther, the better.* And now she was really going far away. She didn't know why, but she could summon up only a blurry image of Du Zhong's face. That distant place wasn't far from him, but it seemed that he was farther and farther away from her.

Not long after Chu Xiaoxi arrived at Wanshan Farm, she wrote to Du Zhong. His letters were always long, so thick that they often were bursting out of the envelope. His handwriting was also quite illegible, as though—if he didn't write quickly—the words would get stuck in his throat. At the beginning, he talked of the history and customs of Huma, but not about frontier defense. Some days later, the closely written words filling the pages, he began talking of the French Revolution, the British Industrial Revolution, and Japan's Meiji Restoration. Whenever Chu Xiaoxi saw that she had a letter from Du Zhong, she tensed up. Reading his letters had become a hardship. Sometimes, she wondered in a trance where these letters had come from: it was as though Du Zhong wasn't on the anti-Soviet front line but in a library cut off from the world. Finally Xiaoxi ran out of patience. When she wrote back, she told him tactfully that discipline at the farm was strict, the work was difficult, and in addition every evening they had to study Mao's works. She didn't have enough time to read his letters and write back. Could he shorten his letters?

Sometime later, Du Zhong suddenly sent her a song, "Song of the Students in the Countryside," written by a student from Nanjing. Solemn and stirring, it gave voice to all his feelings. Xiaoxi gave her fellow students the lyrics. When someone whispered to her that this song was being condemned and told her to tear it up immediately, Xiaoxi grew cold all over. Keeping this incident in mind, she wrote less and less frequently to Du Zhong, and her letters grew shorter and shorter. Those were good days for Chu Xiaoxi: she was named a model soldier and a model worker. She was also promoted to lead a research unit and had even been allowed to apply for party membership. There was no comparison between her fiery, spirited life and the gloom, pessimism, and depression expressed in Du Zhong's letters. Xiaoxi felt that she and Du Zhong were riding carts dashing in opposite directions. They met for a moment in the dust raised by the carts, and then went their separate ways.

She was annoyed and distressed whenever she wrote back to Du Zhong, because she really couldn't come up with anything to say. One time he wrote that most of her letters were rubbish. He went on to say that if the Chu Xiaoxi of 1970 were compared with the Chu Xiaoxi of 1966, one could tell that her brain had atrophied in those four years. These words wounded her so deeply that she didn't write to him for several months. She still hadn't written back when he worked up the courage to go to Wanshan Farm and suddenly appeared at her dormitory door that cold day . . .

It's unbearable to look back on the past. In all those years, Chu Xiaoxi had done a lot of things; the only thing she'd been unable to accomplish was forgetting.

This time when Chu Xiaoxi came back to Hangzhou she could stay only two days and then had to go on to Beijing on business. After she got home and saw her parents, she was just wondering whether or not to call Meng Di when he phoned her. She was quite surprised, because he had never taken the initiative to phone her.

She said, "Meng Di, you're amazing: I just got in. How did you know I was here?"

Meng Di sounded a little strange: "I didn't know you were here; I just thought I'd try . . ."

She asked him what was up. After muttering to himself, he asked if she could meet him that evening. She agreed at once. She couldn't turn him down, because he'd never made any request before.

Meng Di told the story calmly: when he brought up Du Zhong's name, it was as if he were talking about someone he had just parted from the day before. His detached tone made it impossible for Chu Xiaoxi to react with any surprise, doubt, or panic. He told about his meeting with Du Zhong and about Du Zhong's recent request of him. He talked very fast, as if he didn't want to be interrupted by any questions from her. It was as though if he paused for a moment he wouldn't be able to go on. It gradually dawned on Chu Xiaoxi that Meng Di wasn't criticizing Du Zhong. He evidently had made up his mind that Chu Xiaoxi should evaluate it all for herself.

Chu Xiaoxi felt a little dizzy; everything seemed fuzzy.

Just as he was about to finish, Meng Di startled her. "When I called you, I actually hoped you wouldn't be there. It would have been best if you weren't in Hangzhou; that way, you wouldn't know. But I had to phone, because I know that after all these years, in your heart, things between you and Du Zhong have never truly ended."

All at once, the rims of her eyes reddened.

She said quickly, "No. Let's forget it. I don't want to get in touch with him. So many years have gone by. There's so much to say and no way to say it clearly in a short time. The more that's said, the less clear it would be. Also, there's no *need* to clear it up." She turned the idea down with no further ado. She knew if she detected any doubt in her tone, she would waver.

"... But I still think that his guilt and regret are genuinely sincere," Meng Di added cautiously.

"That's exactly what I'm afraid of." Chu Xiaoxi sighed gently. "I don't want him to apologize to me, because he didn't do it on purpose. Back then, I went through so much deliberate hurt. Finally, I realized that Du Zhong had always tried to save me."

Smiling, Meng Di said, "Maybe this is precisely the point of dislocation between the two of you. Think it over. Du Zhong said that he would go back to France in two days. It's hard to say when you and he will have another chance to meet ..."

Chu Xiaoxi interrupted him. "Day after tomorrow, I'll be on the early flight to Beijing. And all day tomorrow, I have things to do with my family. I have no free time."

Meng Di rose and said, "It's up to you. Call me if anything comes up." And with that, he took his leave.

Facing her half-empty coffee cup, Chu Xiaoxi was sitting alone at the table in a daze, not having fully digested Meng Di's news. She thought Du Zhong was truly a strange person: he was always like a paratrooper mysteriously showing up without warning. It was really annoying. He'd never been heard of since he dropped out of sight more than twenty years ago. Now, like a reincarnation, he'd reentered the world. It seemed this was Du Zhong's style—suddenly vanish, then suddenly reappear. It was all so many years ago, and yet everything was as clearly in focus as though it were only yesterday. In the darkness of that winter twilight, Du Zhong had been like a wooden stake, standing motionless in front of Chu Xiaoxi's dormitory door and shouting gruffly at her. When she saw that it was Du Zhong, Chu Xiaoxi was happy, yet at the same time alarmed, her heart throbbing wildly. The first thought that flashed through her mind was: was something wrong in Du Zhong's home? But he said nothing was wrong; he was just on his way back from Hangzhou and had stopped off to see her. They hadn't seen each other for nearly two years, and he thought maybe they should. They just saw each other through their letters, and he was about to forget what she looked like. When she heard this, Xiaoxi sighed with relief and began laughing. Du Zhong looked her over from head to toe. Frowning, he said, "Xiaoxi, why are you dressed this way? You look more like a guy than a girl. Just now, I almost didn't recognize you."

There was frost all over Xiaoxi's eyelashes. She rubbed her eyes and looked down at herself: she was wearing a padded khaki jacket and padded khaki pants, so overstuffed that she looked like a big bear. Her black cotton shoes were dirty from being splattered with the turds she'd collected. Her thick cotton gloves were like huge bear paws: black cotton batting was coming out of a hole in one fingertip. She subconsciously reached for her hair, but she couldn't feel her braids. Her head was tightly wrapped in a fur hat. Around her neck was a dark red scarf. She groaned unhappily, "What's wrong? What's so bad about the way I'm dressed? Men and women should be equal. Just look at you: Your ears are frozen red. Won't you roll the flaps down even on such a cold day? What a cocky guy you are!"

At her words, Du Zhong swallowed what he'd been about to say, and instead, feeling hungry, asked what time dinner was served. That's when Xiaoxi realized that his sudden arrival meant trouble. Everyone had just knocked off work for the day, and the female students had to do some cleaning in the dorm. She couldn't take him to her dorm, but on such a cold day she couldn't just leave him outside to freeze, either. To openly take him to the mess hall for dinner would be unseemly, too. The next day, others would ask her what he was to her. If others thought she had a boyfriend, that would certainly make it difficult for her to advance. Xiaoxi was in a rather awkward position. Inwardly, she was annoyed with Du Zhong for showing up suddenly without letting her know first. As she thought it over she suddenly remembered the research office where an experiment was underway at that very moment. With a fire banked there, it wouldn't be cold, and she had a key to the room: she'd better take him there and bring him some food. They could chat as they ate.

Xiaoxi opened the door and turned on the light. Du Zhong went in, set his heavy suitcase down, and took off his hat and army coat. Hands behind his back, he looked all around. He paced and nodded his head as if he were inspecting the place. He said, "Not bad." Xiaoxi noticed his sleeve protectors: they'd been laundered until they'd faded to white. They were the ones she'd given him before he went down to the countryside, and he had actually worn them from that time until now. Suddenly, she felt warm inside and her resentment evaporated.

Du Zhong's gaze stopped at the wall. A sneer appeared on his face, as he said, "Huh, what's this? What's all this?"

Xiaoxi was adding coals to the fire. Looking up, she saw the large piece of red paper pasted to the wall. On it were poems written by the female students for the poetry contest:

With a concerted effort, we greet the spring sowing.
We sow the seeds, and sow the songs.
When autumn comes, we'll have a great harvest.
The commissariat's quota will be met, and joy will fill our hearts.

Du Zhong said harshly, "Is this a poem? What a joke. It's a slogan."
Xiaoxi was a little disappointed, but she didn't have time to argue with
him. She said, "Wait here and rest a while. I'll pick up the food. If I wait any
longer, the mess hall will be closed." "Go ahead." He waved his hand and
turned his attention to the bottles and boxes holding the experiments.

When Xiaoxi came back with the food, she saw that Du Zhong was digging in the dirt with his hands. She said, "Hey, what are you doing? We're testing the seedlings' rate of growth in wintertime. Don't mess with them."

Without looking up, Du Zhong said, "Where are the seedlings? None of
them has sprouted yet; I don't see anything going on here."

After setting the rice box down, Xiaoxi rushed to put the soil back. As
she pressed it into place, she said, "Just look at you. You've loosened my soil—
just the wrong thing to do. The most important thing in the first stage of
raising seedlings is that the soil needs to be tamped down. The firmer it is, the
more open the seedlings' capillaries are. Then they absorb water quickly and
sprout quickly. It doesn't work without the pressure. Get it?"

Du Zhong's expression turned serious. He snorted, "Tamped down? Is
such a popular term used even in the scientific field?!"

Ignoring him, Xiaoxi tapped the rice box with a spoon and said, "It's
getting cold. Let's hurry up and eat." Glancing at the rice box, Du Zhong
said, "Anything to go with the rice?" She said, "Yes, of course, but just some
pickled stuff." She opened the rice box: inside were a few dark steamed buns,
a fistful of pickled vegetables without oil, and two pieces of pickled beancurd. She smiled and said, "When you put the pickled beancurd in a bun,
it's really tasty. I saved them for a long time. Today I'm treating you, so let's
share them." Du Zhong had no sooner sat down than he suddenly stood up
again, took a wrinkled package out of his bag, and said, "I almost forgot to
give you this."

When Xiaoxi opened the package, she saw a few fresh sausages, a bag
of small dried shrimp, and a bag of bamboo shoots, as well as a pile of dark-
colored things—some smashed gray shells and sticky soy sauce pressed together into the shape of a cake and giving off a familiar, awful odor. She said,
"What's this?" After staring for a while, Du Zhong remembered what they

were. "They're preserved eggs. That's right, preserved eggs. How the hell did they get like this?" Xiaoxi laughed and said, "Let's eat them." They ate them with spoons, and spat out the shells. Xiaoxi felt hungry: they stopped talking and dug into the food. With neither soy sauce nor salt, she and Du Zhong mixed the pickled vegetables with the rest of the preserved eggs, and then ate the mixture with the steamed bread. The other rice box was filled with soy sauce soup. Du Zhong sipped his soup: he didn't make a sound. After a while, he suddenly said "Hey!" and stood up and rushed outside. He shouted that he had to get some water so he could gargle. He said there was sand in the bread, and it had gotten into his teeth.

"You're just too picky." Xiaoxi glared at him. "We eat this every day. Here on the farm, we think it's great that we can have bread made from flour. I haven't even given you any corn bread yet. I'm only now realizing how many diehard capitalist habits you've always had. You've been in the countryside for more than two years—hasn't the reeducation done you any good?"

Du Zhong didn't answer. He rinsed his mouth with some of the water from the bucket used to water the seeds. He was staring at Xiaoxi, looking at her carefully. "Hey, Xiaoxi, what's wrong with your eyes? It seems . . . How come one eyelid has a single fold and the other a double fold? I remember that your eyes always both had single folds . . ."

Xiaoxi subconsciously rubbed her eyes and explained, "Last winter during the big campaign to cut willow twigs in the marsh, the oxcart full of willow twigs fell over, and I was pinned under them. A twig punctured one eyelid, and it bled. But the big campaign was so intense then that I insisted it wasn't serious enough to keep me from the front line. I simply bandaged it; I didn't go to the farm's clinic for treatment. By the time I recovered, that eyelid had a double fold." She stressed, "Actually it doesn't interfere one bit with my work."

Du Zhong taunted her, "Great! Now you've got a pair of different eyes just like a Persian cat. Sort of a valuable breed." He stood up and took a small black box out of his bag. "I almost forgot, we should have music to dine by. Let's listen to music together to celebrate our reunion." His face was all smiles.

Music? This was a strange word to Xiaoxi. In her present environment, there were merely songs, not music. Music: didn't that sound too much like a luxury? And anyway, where would the music come from even if you did feel like listening to it? As Du Zhong fiddled with the black box, Xiaoxi saw that it was a tiny radio. Du Zhong twirled the on-off button and kept adjusting it. The radio made a terrible scratchy noise: there was nothing musical about it. "It seems there's too much jamming here; the signal is bad." He was a little dejected. "Where we are, we can hear music anytime, and it's extremely clear—just as clear as CCB."

She wasn't paying much attention to what he was saying. She was anxious to ask him about things in Hangzhou, and she also had to talk with him about everything here on the farm, including her own progress and achievements. Since she felt uncomfortable bringing this up in letters, now she could tell him face to face. She asked about his parents, and asked if he had gone to see the winter sweet shrubs in Hangzhou. Du Zhong muttered to himself and then said that probably his parents would never be able to come back; he could no longer concern himself with this. He hadn't gone to see the winter sweet shrubs, because he wasn't much interested in them. He answered her questions briefly and then went back to fiddling with the radio.

Xiaoxi was annoyed: "You don't care about this and you don't care about that. What *do* you care about?"

Du Zhong held up the radio and said, "This!"

"Then why did you come so far to see me? You could have just stayed with your radio."

"It's not exactly the same. You're a live person."

As Xiaoxi tidied up the rice boxes, she said, "Then why aren't you talking with me?"

Du Zhong didn't bother looking up. "I came to see you simply because I wanted to see you. I wrote so many letters that you never answered, so I thought I'd come and find out what had happened to you. What's the point of talking a lot? I wanted to play this radio for you, so you could hear some sounds you can't ordinarily hear." Full of complaints, Xiaoxi shouted, "If you have nothing to say, just leave."

He finally put the radio down and said with a soft sigh, "This radio was my parents' present to me on my fifteenth birthday. Luckily, I had it on me the day our home was searched, so it wasn't confiscated. I took it with me when I went down to the countryside, never dreaming that it could be put to such good use. Oh, okay. Let's just talk. What do you want to talk about?"

Still out of sorts, Xiaoxi said, "Talk to me about what you've been thinking these last two years. I didn't have time to read those long confusing tirades in your letters. Not that I would understand them, anyway."

Du Zhong suddenly lowered his voice. "What have I been thinking about? Do you really want to know? Here's what I've been thinking about.

Since the textbooks say that capitalism is feudalism's natural enemy, then why do we still have to use pesticides?"

"Pesticides? What are you talking about?"

"Just like natural enemies, hasn't socialism become a pesticide?"

"Your . . . this kind of metaphor is absurd."

"What's wrong with it?" Du Zhong said, "Natural enemies have the natural ability to kill. It's the law of nature. But pesticides are made by man to kill."

Xiaoxi interrupted angrily, "How can you think this way? You're too . . . too . . ." For the moment, she couldn't think of the right words. She wanted to say "reactionary," but she felt that was too cruel. If she said he was "going too far," that wouldn't be strong enough. There was simply no way to reason with him. Had he come to see her just to hawk his insecticides? Xiaoxi was speechless with anger.

Suddenly the lights went out and they couldn't see each other. On the farm, power outages were common. Darkness rose like dense clouds. She felt like a submarine sinking to the bottom of the dark water. She heard Du Zhong's heavy breathing. He said, "Don't worry, I have a flashlight." She heard him bumping into things and turning his bag inside out, but the flashlight didn't materialize. Xiaoxi groped her way over to the windowsill in the corner, where she felt for matches and a small candle. She struck a match and the flame gradually brightened, the golden yellow flame flickering in the dark, and Du Zhong's pale face floated up out of the darkness. Suddenly, Xiaoxi thought that Du Zhong was now like a plaster statue with stiff, frozen lines.

The candle was almost the length of a small firecracker. People called it "kowtow"—meaning that in the time it took to kowtow the candle would burn out. Hyperbole though that was, it was true that this kind of candle didn't burn very long. Still, this stub of a candle was all that the quota system allowed them. Xiaoxi thought, *Dinner is over, the power is out, and if I get back to the dorm too late, people are going to get the wrong idea. I'd better find him a place to stay soon.* Just as she was trying to figure out who Du Zhong could spend the night with, the radio suddenly began making a sound. Xiaoxi trembled with fright. The candle flame also began swaying. Xiaoxi heard a woman's low, tender voice, like threads of dust hanging from the rafters, swinging gently in the air. Her Chinese pronunciation was rather odd; she was using the wrong tones. It was completely different from the CCB announcers' pronunciation. Although the sound was blurry and vague, Xiaoxi was finally able to understand her. The woman's voice said: "You must be familiar with the name of China's greatest violinist. From the time the Cultural Revolution began, he saw with his own eyes the tragic fate of China's intellectuals. He, too, was interrogated, persecuted, and humiliated. A few years ago, he finally risked his life to go into exile in a western country. Now, my dear friends, we will play his well-known 'Thinking of Home.'"

In that moment, Xiaoxi almost forgot to breathe. The desolate, sorrowful tune was like the folk songs from the highlands of the yellow earth. It broke your heart. It was also like the gurgling springs in the forests and the white clouds drifting in the blue sky, like a breeze passing through a canyon, like the light dance of snowflakes. It had been a long, long time since she'd heard such sweet violin music: it was like a bevy of fairies whirling around in this crude room. The weak candle flame was moving to the music's rhythm. The small dark room suddenly became bright and warm . . . The flame dimmed, flickered a few times, and went out. The room was dark again. Xiaoxi groped in the dark for another candle, but just got dust on her fingers. Then she remembered that there was only this one spare candle in the room. The music continued playing in the dark night, its rhythm gradually turning heavy and oppressive. Light suddenly shone from a flashlight: it cut through the sound of the music and landed on her padded jacket. The red Mao badge on her chest glistened a blackish red. She came to with a start. "Du Zhong, what are you doing?" She shouted: "You're listening to . . . listening to . . . Turn your radio off right now!" She covered her ears. "I don't want to listen, I don't want to listen. It's too dangerous. Have you gone crazy? Do you hear me? Turn it off right now!" She was almost in tears as she rushed over and grabbed for the radio. Du Zhong tucked the radio in at his chest. Xiaoxi heard a "*po*," and then the sound vanished. Suddenly, the room was quiet again, like a tightly sealed root cellar.

"How come you're so scared?" Du Zhong asked coldly. "Is this a sin?"

Xiaoxi was back to normal, but she was furious. She couldn't figure out how Du Zhong could have changed so much in the two years that she hadn't seen him. Actually, his letters had already shown signs of ideological backsliding. Because of her sympathy and gentleness, she tried to appease him. She couldn't watch helplessly as he continued this way. No matter how he scorned or ridiculed her, because of their unforgettable friendship two years earlier, she had to hold a hand out to him. Xiaoxi thought she had never before been so determined and firm. She stood up and vehemently told Du Zhong off. She would never forget what she said. Over the years, she repeatedly reviewed and examined every word, and each time her heart ached. What she said was: "Du Zhong, you listen to me. Every one of your present agonies and grievances comes from the changes in your life. Before the Cultural Revolution, your life was too easy; you didn't understand one whit about the ordinary people's suffering and dreams. Because of your parents' political problems, you became fiercely discontented. This is the trouble that comes from selfish thoughts. I understand, but I cannot condone it. You really have to wake up and see the danger!"

Little by little, the flashlight dimmed, and Du Zhong's face blurred. He didn't say anything but just bit his lips. He kept changing positions; the wooden stool he was sitting on kept creaking. A long time went by, and still he didn't say a word. "Say something." Xiaoxi finally couldn't stand it any longer. "Is it possible that you really haven't thought through this simple point?"

"Right. I haven't. And unless a bullet passes through my brain, I guess I won't." His determined tone left no room for contradiction. Xiaoxi couldn't help but shiver. Du Zhong stood up, stretched lazily, grabbed the flashlight, and said, "Okay. Let me trouble you to find a place for me to spend the night. Tomorrow morning, I'll go back to Huma."

As they were about to leave, Xiaoxi added coal to the stove and stoked the fire. She closed the door. Her heart thumped, as if something were locked inside. It was more than a month before she discovered that Du Zhong had inadvertently left behind a time bomb. In the moment that it detonated, the beautiful ideals that she embraced were blasted into fragments.

There was a bright moon that night. Hanging over the snowy land was a melancholy, sanctified moon color. In the moonlight, the peaceful fields were like a silvery lake, and snowflakes blown by a cold wind created a misty mirage. Xiaoxi felt that she was going to sink into the icy lake—she was very cold. As they walked along the path to the dorm, neither of them said a word. She heard only the squeaking sound of heavy overshoes trampling in the snow. They were walking one ahead of the other, their steps out of sync. She escorted Du Zhong to the male students' dorm, rapped on the door, and shouted for Meng Di. She told Meng Di that a friend had come to see her and asked if he could spend the night. He'd be leaving the next day. Without asking any questions, Meng Di let Du Zhong in. When Xiaoxi and Du Zhong parted, Du Zhong's expression was solemn as he held out his hand and politely touched Xiaoxi's fingertips. The last impression left in Xiaoxi's memory was that his hand was soft and icy cold—like a snowball.

Xiaoxi walked back to the female students' dorm by herself. A knife-like wind chiseled her neck: she was shaking with cold. Her heart felt frozen. In that split second, these words suddenly leapt to mind: "You cannot confuse personal friendship with political problems. You are not allowed to put personal friendship ahead of the good of the cause." This was a quotation from Stalin that she had recently copied from her study materials. It hadn't occurred to her that on this cold winter night, these words would bolster her courage and comfort her. In the moonlight, she saw the shadows of her long strides. Her rough, strong arms were swinging forcefully. On the white snow, the dark shadows of her arms were like the wings of an eagle flying up from the snow-covered field.

But before Chu Xiaoxi could fly, her wings were suddenly clipped. Not long after Spring Festival, she was called in for a talk. The room was packed with people with ominous looks on their faces. Several higher-ups were there, as well as several people from Farm Security. Xiaoxi was bewildered. As if interrogating a criminal, they mentioned Du Zhong's name. They demanded that Chu Xiaoxi tell the truth in answering all their questions about Du Zhong. Chu Xiaoxi was told that on New Year's Eve, Du Zhong had "crossed the river" and so far hadn't been sent back. From scraps of correspondence that he hadn't completely burned when he was about to leave, they had learned of his connection with Chu Xiaoxi. Her mind exploded, and cold sweat ran down her back. Her sweat-soaked underwear was like iron armor tightened around her body.

Du Zhong had indeed come to Wanshan, but his leave-taking was merely symbolic: he'd dropped no hint of what he planned to do.

If she'd known that he intended to cross the river, Xiaoxi would have risked her life to stop him. But she'd been clueless. She hadn't known anything, nor had she discovered anything. In their three hours alone that evening, he had revealed nothing about his criminal intentions. She'd been kept in the dark: she was too childish and innocent, too paralyzed, too imbecilic. She had underestimated the enemy. As a revolutionary youth who had let her guard slip in the class struggle, she felt ashamed, remorseful, and conscience-stricken. Indeed, she despised herself. But no one believed her. Someone said, "When Du Zhong suddenly showed up at Wanshan Farm, why didn't you chat with him openly in the dormitory? Why did you sneak him into the research station? What's more, you talked with him for quite a few hours. If you weren't plotting something, then what were you doing?" Xiaoxi stammered, "Plotting? We were just talking about things at home, of people we know in Hangzhou, of what each of us has learned since coming down to the countryside." They said, "Can anyone here vouch for what you talked about?" Xiaoxi said, "No." They said, "Without someone to vouch for you, how can you prove your innocence? How can you prove you weren't in this with him? How can you prove you didn't help him flee? How can you prove you didn't help him? Otherwise, why did he come to see you?"

Xiaoxi was like a mute. She had no proof with which to defend herself. None at all. For several days in a row, she was locked up in the "little shed," where she reflected on the "historical origins," as well as the present circumstances, of her relationship with Du Zhong. In the dark stillness, she remembered that night in detail: in fact, she remembered a lot of subtle things indicating that Du Zhong had made up his mind to "cross the river." Too bad she'd been too unsophisticated to notice. For example, that damned radio; for example his pesticide metaphor; for example . . . but Xiaoxi couldn't say anything. A certain instinct told her that whatever she said would lead to even more trouble. Making every effort to review everything, she bitterly acknowledged her mistake, saying that she was resolved to distance herself from Du Zhong; at the same time, she kept her mouth shut and feigned ignorance about certain things. For years afterward, Xiaoxi periodically recalled the interrogation that she'd undergone for several months at Wanshan Farm. Her stubborn silence back then didn't stem from her conscience, but from basic common sense—the need for self-protection. And perhaps in her subconscious she still felt a little friendship for Du Zhong. He had talked to her of so many things he shouldn't have spoken of, things he hadn't dared say to others, and so most probably he had trusted her. Maybe she was the only person he trusted. She had to respect this trust. Xiaoxi was hoping that she could avoid her fate, but in the end she couldn't. The first part of the special interrogation came up with nothing. But one quiet night, her interrogators exultantly produced a tiny scrap of crumpled paper. The Chinese writing on it was as clear as ever:

"Please take me with you!"
Below it was a line of Russian:
"Please take me with you!"

Xiaoxi's heart was pounding like crazy, and she felt she would choke on her own breath. She felt as if she would soon keel over. She recognized Du Zhong's handwriting: he'd written her so many letters, she couldn't be wrong about this. This wasn't a frame-up: it was something Du Zhong had written himself. But Xiaoxi had never seen this scrap of paper. Where had it come from? And how had the special investigative team gotten its hands on it? Even if Du Zhong had written this, what did it have to do with her? Xiaoxi's brain was as mixed up as a pot of porridge. She felt that she would never be able to explain her innocence even if she had a thousand mouths.

—*Please take me with you!* "It's absolutely clear: you wanted Du Zhong to take you with him, and cross the river with him! But Du Zhong was very cunning: he was afraid you'd be excess baggage; he didn't want to take you along. You say you've never seen this scrap of paper: that's a lie! It was found in the research station. That night, you and Du Zhong were the only ones there. If you didn't write this, who did? We've already investigated: before the Cultural Revolution, Du Zhong began learning Russian. While he was still in Hangzhou, he must have tutored you in Russian for years. It's easy to see that the two of you have been in touch with foreign countries for a long time, secretly planning to flee . . ." "But I . . . my behavior ever since I came to the Great Northern Wilderness has been above reproach. Recently, my application for party membership was accepted. Why on earth would I flee?" "That's all a sham! Just a cover for your real purpose."

"If I had really wanted to go, I could have said so directly to him. Why on earth would I want to write it down?" Xiaoxi felt this was as absurd as it could get. "That's . . . That's because . . . because if you said it directly to him, you were afraid the walls had ears, and you'd be overheard. This piece of paper exposes your intentions . . ."

It was useless to argue; nothing could be changed now. After Chu Xiaoxi was formally accused of an abortive attempt to rebel and flee, she was quickly stripped of her party membership. She also lost all her positions and titles. Unable to recover from these blows, Chu Xiaoxi sank into depression. It wasn't until the night before she left Wanshan Farm that she unwittingly learned that her "interrogation" and punishments had been manipulated by one of her peers who at the time was on a fast track to the top. He had to get rid of Chu Xiaoxi, who might have been a threat to his getting ahead in the future. He and Chu Xiaoxi were always at loggerheads, so he couldn't be softhearted toward her. For years afterward, lonely and depressed, Chu Xiaoxi had thought back countless times to the winter night when she and Du Zhong had seen each other. Her recollections were like a fine-toothed comb combing through every detail of their meeting in the experimental station. Sometimes she felt that everything had been determined by fate: because of the power failure, Du Zhong had rummaged around in his bag to find a flashlight. And that was precisely when the scrap of paper had fallen out, but neither of them had noticed it.

Chu Xiaoxi had hated Du Zhong for a long time. She felt that he had always treated her as if she were an ignorant audience. He just needed someone to listen to him, but he didn't care about the other person's feelings. He didn't stop to consider that his quiet leave-taking would harm those he'd interacted with. One of the reasons Chu Xiaoxi had never been able to forgive him was that he had never thought of her as an equal or as a friend sharing secrets. If he had, then maybe even if her interrogation and punishments had been even worse, she might have thought it was all worthwhile.

The beautiful future Chu Xiaoxi had yearned for was abruptly destroyed the year she was nineteen. Ruthlessly cut off, without even a sliver of a space to turn it around. It was like a high-speed steam engine, forced to slam on the brakes when an obstacle suddenly appeared on the tracks. In those days when she was discriminated against and isolated from others, she felt as if her young life had been cracked into two parts. All she could do was plunge into hard work in order to anesthetize herself and protect herself with silence. She started reading voraciously; taking advantage of the chance to go home to Hangzhou to see her family, she brought back high school textbooks, as well as any other books she could lay her hands on. For years, it was books that comforted her lonely soul. This went on until 1978 when she, like most of the other students, returned to the city.

After that incident, when she went back to Hangzhou to see her family for Spring Festival, she received a note from Meng Di asking her to forget the past and start over. And in a vague tone, he asked if he could be her "best friend." Chu Xiaoxi didn't answer him. She didn't want to live forever in the midst of her regret about Meng Di, for he had also been punished because he'd put Du Zhong up for the night. She felt she couldn't use her feelings to compensate for having embroiled him in trouble.

Nineteen is so young. Everything could start all over. Du Zhong's sudden departure had made Chu Xiaoxi grow up in a hurry. But from her nineteen-year-old vantage point, her future had been blocked. What could she do? All she could do was begin endless self-examination. So now, Xiaoxi couldn't see Du Zhong. She was near the end of her self-examination and was afraid a new round might begin if she saw him.

~ 3 ~

Chu Xiaoxi got out of the cab and, pulling her luggage, hurried into the airport. She'd arisen a little late that morning, and it was almost time to board the plane. She rushed through the empty corridor to the large electronic display board to find out which counter she should go to. Just then, she heard someone call her name softly. Following the sound, she looked ahead and saw a middle-aged stranger smiling a little as he looked at her. She didn't recognize him, but it seemed to her that his broad forehead was a little familiar: she had a hazy recollection that maybe they'd known each other in the past.

"I'm Du Zhong. You don't recognize me, do you?"

Chu Xiaoxi looked at him blankly with her big eyes.

"Meng Di told me which flight you'd be taking. I wanted to catch up with you and see you once more," Du Zhong said courteously. "Actually, it isn't really like seeing you off, because I'm also going home today. As it happens, I'll be on the ten o'clock flight to Shanghai and then transfer to a flight to France. I thought about it all last night: if I missed this chance to see you, I didn't know when there'd be another chance."

In that split second, Du Zhong's appearance as he stood at the door of the dormitory flashed through Chu Xiaoxi's mind. He'd always suddenly appeared and then just as suddenly disappeared. This was exactly what he always did.

Du Zhong smiled and said, "It's been more than twenty years. No wonder you don't recognize me. But I can still recognize you at a glance. Really. It seems as though you haven't changed much at all. Anyhow, you seem the same as always."

"No, I'm not the same. Actually, I've changed a lot. Inside." Chu Xiaoxi extended her hand to Du Zhong.

"I hear you come back to Hangzhou often." Du Zhong shook her hand firmly. The smooth skin of her hand was like pliable camphor leaves.

"True. I've come back more than usual the last few years." Xiaoxi gently extricated her hand.

"But I can't come back often, so it was really important to me to see you now."

"I'd never have thought that you could go through so many hardships, and still be so strong and healthy. I'm . . . so happy to see that," Xiaoxi said.

"Actually, I came today simply to say something to you. All those years ago, when I was so ignorant and rash, I involved you and also hurt you in ways that I can't make up for. I really regret this," Du Zhong said earnestly. "After I left, I didn't know anything about what happened to all of you. It was only after I came back this time that Meng Di told me. I had to see you to beg your forgiveness face to face. Otherwise, my conscience would bother me until the day I die. That scrap of paper . . ."

Chu Xiaoxi looked irritated as she interrupted him: "Too bad so many years have gone by, and not one of the people who should have apologized to me, not one of the people who should have felt regret, has expressed any regret to me. *Ai*, you said . . . What do you have to apologize for?" Noticing his embarrassment, Chu Xiaoxi added, "But now that we're face to face, actually I want to take the opportunity to thank you."

Du Zhong spread his hands out in surprise. "Why?"

"What do you think?" Xiaoxi smiled a little.

"I don't know how you can talk of gratitude. You aren't mocking me by saying this, are you?"

"No, I'm not joking. Look, if it hadn't been for all the trouble you caused me after you crossed the river, I would have continued on the same trajectory. Oh, I think you know what that would have meant." Chu Xiaoxi had calmed down. Suddenly, she felt a lot of words gushing up from her heart—words that had been lingering in her mind for years, deposited there drop by drop. Now they were densely massed in her chest and she was yearning to release them.

"If it hadn't been for what happened back then, I don't know how I might have changed. Maybe I would have become an exquisite tool, a model for those times, or a clumsy parrot. But you unwittingly placed a rock on that path, suddenly upsetting the applecart. My smooth trajectory was forcibly blocked, thrusting me off course. Although that wasn't what I wanted then and it wasn't what I chose for myself, when all is said and done, I was shoved toward a new door: I had no choice but to go through it and walk into another room. People say all roads lead to Rome. So many years have gone by: maybe we've reached the same goal by taking different paths. When I was studying for my doctorate in America, it occurred to me now and then that you actually saved me. After you left, I was forced to become the person I am now. Why shouldn't I thank you? To be able to say this to you face to face today is also good for my conscience. You don't need to feel any guilt for what you did back then . . ."

Du Zhong was stunned. Xiaoxi's face went out of focus. In a kind of misty hallucination, he almost doubted whether this was really Chu Xiaoxi. Could it be another woman with the same name?

"Actually . . . actually, back then we were all too young . . ." Du Zhong was talking a little incoherently.

Chu Xiaoxi laughed out loud, and so did he.

Chu Xiaoxi's flight was announced. With a glance at her watch, she said apologetically to Du Zhong that if she didn't board the flight now, she'd miss it, and her schedule in Beijing was completely filled. There wasn't any way to change it.

Du Zhong nodded his head. "Then I'll walk over there with you. Sort of like seeing you off."

After Chu Xiaoxi went through security, she looked back and waved at Du Zhong and then disappeared around a corner. Du Zhong stood there for a while. He sighed as he realized he'd forgotten to get Chu Xiaoxi's phone number in America. He heard the roar of the plane taking off; his eyes following the sound, he thought he and Chu Xiaoxi would be flying in different directions and would touch down in different hemispheres, separated by vast oceans.

A little later, when his airplane left the ground, Du Zhong looked down from the window: he could see the newly planted camphor trees on both sides of the highway in the suburbs. Tender green leaves were already forming, but last year's dark-colored leaves hadn't yet fallen. He regretted the gnawing feeling he had for Hangzhou. In fact, Hangzhou was just one stop, just one small step on life's journey: leaving, landing, and then flying away.

In a trance, Du Zhong felt a void-like absurdity—like an illusion—about this trip to Hangzhou. Even Chu Xiaoxi had become blurry. If he held out his hand, he could touch the clear blue cloudless sky. It was as if he were flying straight ahead toward the arced heavenly vault: no matter which flight path he was on, maybe he and Chu Xiaoxi would meet again somewhere in the world.

The earth is round. His years of travel experience had given him an unwavering belief in this much.

⋟♭↷

Zhima

When Guo Zhima dashed into the building next to the Big Bell Temple, the lobby was already filled with women. She was scolding herself, *Too late, too late—late again!* She had had to take three buses to get here and so had been on the road for more than an hour. She was dismayed at the sight of so many people ahead of her. They were supposed to stand in line, but where the hell was the line? Everyone was simply crowded together in a sticky clump outside the door. A young nurse in a pointed white cap called out a woman's name in a long, drawn-out voice. A woman came out of the door blushing, and another woman squeezed in right away. A man shoved through the crowd as if he meant to go in with her, but the young nurse had closed the door as someone shouted from within, "Hey, you! Look at the sign on the door! Keep out!"

Zhima thought to herself, *When you're here away from your village, every city person wants to teach you a lesson.*

The blue words on the door were as big as straw hats: PREGNANCY TESTS.

What was the big deal? You had the test, the form was punched, and it went from the Women's Association to your hometown to prove that you weren't breaking the population-control laws while working in the city. PREGNANCY TESTS—Zhima had seen this sign every three months since she'd arrived in Beijing five years ago. Even if the words were written upside down, she'd know them. She didn't care for these pregnancy tests at all. Each time, she had to pay fifty *yuan*—three days' wages—all for nothing. Nevertheless, she looked forward to going to the place where the tests were conducted. From the fourth to the tenth of each month, by orders of the Women's Association, it was as though a party was being held especially for the women of Henan Province who were working in Beijing. Everyone in the room was from Henan, and their chattering filled your ears. Zhima was familiar with that lively sound—the voices crisp and light and high, as if the women were actors in a play. Between tests, she didn't hear it and she missed the sound. Aside from the doctor's soft-spoken manner and the shiny, bright machine in the room, pregnancy tests done in Beijing were no different from the ones managed by Population Control in the countryside. The women were the same kind of women. Their clothes were a little neater than those worn at home, and maybe they permed their hair, but as soon as they opened their mouths, you knew they were from Henan.

Zhima paid the fee and joined the crowd of women, each pressing against the woman in front of her and taking a step forward every once in a while. Tightly grasping her identity card, her temporary residence card, and the card allowing her to work away from home, her hands began sweating. She didn't dare lose these credentials, for without them she couldn't be tested, and if she couldn't have the pregnancy test, the village would fine her several hundred *yuan*—way too much! Just thinking of the fine made Zhima angry. Because the local government had too many people on its payroll, it looked for any excuse to fine someone to make up the budget shortfall. What was the pregnancy test for? She'd worked in Beijing all these years, always sleeping alone. No seed could be sown. Could any seedling grow from an empty belly?

The sleeping situation for her man at home, Xishu, wasn't any better. Besides farming the land, he raised a brood of piglets that he slept with night after night. Instead of cuddling up with his wife, he could sleep only with the piglets. The nine piglets were Xishu's whole life, and that's why he had to watch over them, especially at night. When a pig weighed 150 or 200 kilograms, it could be sold for several thousand *yuan*.

Last year, Zhima's mother-in-law had raised seven sheep. When they were fully fattened, each one weighed thirty-five or forty kilograms. Soon they should leave the pen, but you didn't dare take chances. The flock of sheep was kept in the kitchen, where Father-in-law unrolled a carpet and slept close to them. One morning, he opened his eyes and was dumbstruck at what he saw. Shivering, he yelled for Mother-in-law, "The sheep are gone!" "How can that be?" she asked, her eyes blurry. "They've been stolen," he replied. "In the middle of the night when I stretched out my hand, I felt a handful of soft fleece. How could they have been stolen?" As she ran to the kitchen, Mother-in-law cursed her husband, "Why didn't the thief steal you, too? If I'd been sleeping with you, I'd have sold you before midnight and run off with someone else! By the time you woke up, I'd have already been in Zhumadian!" It wasn't bad enough that Father-in-law had lost the sheep; he also had to put up with his wife's curses. He wished he could die. Seven sheep. Ah, seven of them: the family had depended on them for a year's livelihood. Mother-in-law wept. Father-in-law wept.

Xishu telephoned Zhima, and asked her to send some money home. Zhima also wept. When she first arrived in Beijing, she was homesick every day. Sometimes, she had asked herself how she could miss her hometown so much. In the village, thieves stole almost everything they laid their eyes on. They never bothered to steal from people in other villages; they just stole from the ones they knew well. Zhima's family had never stolen from other people, but other people coveted what her family had: when they raised chickens, they lost chickens; when they raised ducks, they lost ducks. They took every precaution against theft. Would Xishu have dared not sleep with the piglets? No one would believe it if you said that Zhima and Xishu hadn't been married even three days when Xishu moved to the kitchen to keep watch over the cattle. It was the same in every household that had a cow. It was as though the man and the cow were husband and wife. Every night, Xishu slept with the cattle, and Zhima slept with the poultry. In their ten years of marriage, Zhima hadn't slept with Xishu the whole night more than a few times. It would be so easy for Zhima and Xishu to wait until the chickens, ducks, pigs, and sheep were all slaughtered and sold, and then sleep together one night . . . and—oops!—make another baby by accident.

Looking at the sign "PREGNANCY TESTS," Zhima's eyes hurt. As she thought of Xishu sleeping with the piglets every night, she felt angry. Still, she couldn't blame Beijing people for disliking Henan people. When Zhima was looking for work at the Housekeeper Placement Center, someone would eventually show up and ask her something. But as soon as she opened her mouth, the person's expression would change, and she would shake her head and start to leave. Annoyed, the auntie working at the Placement Center would say, "What's wrong with people from Henan? Henan people aren't all bad. Try her out for a week; if she doesn't work out, then bring her back here." When Liu Danni took her home for a few days, Auntie Li followed Zhima around like a tail. Zhima knew that Auntie was afraid that she would . . . Zhima couldn't even say the word "steal." She thought, *If you can tolerate it, you can watch me night after night just like Xishu watches the pigs. If a thief really comes, the seven sheep would be stolen anyway.* A week passed. One evening, Auntie Li was watching TV. She let out a long sigh and said, "You can stay. You silly Guo."

Zhima knew that she was a little thickheaded. In school, she had always been satisfied with barely passing the exams. But she was diligent and quick, and not afraid of work. She took Auntie Li's "Silly Guo" as a compliment. A silly person would never take other people's things.

"*Guo—Zhi—ma!*" the young nurse at the pregnancy-test center called out, as if singing. The nurse was amused. "*Zhima*. How did you get a name like that? How funny! It's your turn. Hurry and go in."

Zhima didn't smile. She didn't think there was anything funny about her name. The day her mother gave birth to her, the *zhima*—sesame—blossomed at the front door. The colorful little petals were just like the baby's little earlobes. Her mother had said, "Let's name her Zhima, and she will grow and blossom like sesame." This nurse was still young and hadn't seen much of the world. She didn't know that village boys were given names like Urinal, Brick, Donkey Baby, and Dog's Egg. Those names, not Zhima's, were the ones that were "how funny." Zhima didn't like it one bit that Uncle Liu and Auntie Li called her "Xiao Guo." *Guo* had the same sound as the word for pot—little pots, big pots, iron pots, clay pots. Even the word for hunchback had the same sound. She would much prefer to be called Zhima: sesame could be made into sesame oil, and no family—rich or poor—could be without sesame.

Zhima lay down on a cot covered with a white sheet. She quickly unfastened her pants and slipped them down over her round little belly. An instrument like a TV set was positioned above her head. A female doctor with a respirator squeezed "toothpaste" onto her belly, and then moved a stiff brush back and forth over the ice-cold "toothpaste." The machine was creaking, like the sound of a mouse gnawing on something. Zhima knew this instrument was called an "ultrasound." She had been "ultrasounded" for years, yet each time, she was terrified that the brush would gnaw through her tummy. She didn't move. Suddenly, she felt sorry for Xishu: he couldn't get close to her body, but this machine nibbled at it every three months. Who invented this damn pregnancy test? It was just like searching pockets and arresting a sneak thief—telling women one by one to open up their tummies to check to see if you were sneakily carrying a child. Zhima felt unspeakably wronged.

Before Zhima's indignation reached her face, the sound of the gnawing mouse abruptly stopped "All done. You can get up now." The female doctor covered her tummy with a tissue. The nurse said, "We'll send the form to your province's Women's Association. You can go."

Zhima sat up and said, "Punch the card for me." The nurse punched the card in front of her.

Zhima was relieved. She rubbed the "toothpaste" off her tummy, fastened her pants, said thank you, and left.

Hurrying off, Zhima felt a little injured: at home, fifty *yuan* could do a lot of things: it could buy a quilt for the bed, or make a chest. It could buy a shirt and trousers for Father, and there would still be quite a lot left. You had to sell more than a hundred pounds of eggs to earn fifty *yuan*. And that's not counting the cost of feed and the vet's fees. For that, selling more than two hundred pounds of eggs wasn't enough. But if you didn't leave home to work, you wouldn't be able to earn 500 *yuan* a month, and if you couldn't earn that, you wouldn't have even this fifty *yuan*. And if you didn't have this, you wouldn't be able to pay off the debt you owed for having more children than allowed. Then no one in the family would have a good life. No matter how you looked at it, it was still better to come to the city to work than to stay at home. Forget the fifty. Just think of it as a brood of chickens you'd raised which all died from the chicken pest.

Each time she had the pregnancy test, Zhima had to reconsider these things before feeling a little better about it. Now, she looked up at the clock in the lobby, realizing that she must hurry back to the house and cook. All of a sudden, someone in the line shouted, "Zhima! Zhima!" It had been a long time since she'd heard anyone call her by name, and the sound warmed her heart. The voice was clear and brisk: it had to be someone from her hometown. As Zhima's eyes swept over the crowd, someone's warm arms encircled her.

Was it Feng? Zhima couldn't quite believe that she had really run into a fellow villager! Feng was a lot thinner than before, so thin that her eyes were sunken. The two women were the same age. Last year, after Zhima had gone home to help harvest the wheat, she had brought Feng back with her to Beijing to find work. Each time Zhima went home, lots of young women—married and single—always pleaded with her to bring them to Beijing to look for work. Zhima hated these requests. But last year, gritting her teeth, she had brought seven or eight village women with her and turned them all over to the Housekeeper Placement Center. After several months she had phoned the Center only to learn that all but one of these women had taken off. Some had been fired because they were lazy and dirty. Others had bought train tickets and left on their own, unaccustomed to the city and unable to earn much—and besides, they were homesick. The only one who stayed was the woman named Feng. She took care of a rich family's child. Zhima knew that Feng couldn't leave Beijing: back in the village, her husband beat her up whenever he got drunk. Feng wanted a divorce, but her man wouldn't let her go. So she hid in the city and didn't look back. This situation was called "flight from the marriage."

Looking at Zhima, Feng said, "Zhima, your face has filled out. You're pale and plump. Everything must be going well for you."

Zhima just said uh-huh. Only she knew the hardships she faced. She thought for a moment, then swallowed her thoughts and didn't speak of them.

Feng was drawing her enthusiastically along by the hand, asking about this and that. How much did Zhima earn every month, did she eat rice or noodles, did she have a TV to watch, how did her employers treat her, and so on. Zhima answered the questions one by one. Then Feng looked her up and down and said, "Zhima, when you left your house today, why didn't you wear something a little more attractive?" Zhima laughed and said, "Where would I get pretty clothes? I'm a weasel always wearing the same fur." Feng also laughed. Just then it occurred to Zhima that she hadn't asked how things were going for Feng. "Feng—ah, you're doing great. You made it after all! Actually, it isn't too hard as long as you can adjust."

Zhima hadn't finished speaking when Feng's eyes reddened. She began talking aimlessly. Only by listening closely could Zhima pick up the gist of what she was saying: "If I'd known how stingy people are in the city, I'd never have come here. Shut up in a tall building the whole day, my feet never touching the earth. I can't go out—it's almost like being a pig in a pen. Taking care of the child, I'm afraid she'll bump into something, or fall, or choke on her food. I haven't had a good night's sleep for months. It isn't that the job is difficult. I've gotten used to it. I don't mind being wronged or seeing the expressions on my employers' faces. It's just that I don't have enough to eat. A family that is so rich that every two or three days they buy their child toys costing several hundred *yuan*—why won't they let me eat enough? Each meal is a small bowl of rice—sure, there are vegetables and meat, too, but so little rice. You take one bite and there's nothing left. I'm terribly hungry all day long. I drink so much water that I'm peeing all day . . ."

Tired of listening, Zhima interrupted, "I'm not afraid of not having enough to eat. I'm just afraid of being wronged."

Feng curled her lip. "Ah. Have you tried going hungry for months? When you're hungry, you don't have any strength. How can you do anything?"

The line moved forward. Zhima was being dragged along by Feng. As she talked, she walked along with Feng. Zhima thought, *I can't keep Feng company for her pregnancy test. It's time to go home and cook dinner.* But Feng didn't let her go. She said, "I'm so glad to see you. Your family is doing well. Down the road, you have to help me out." Zhima said, "What makes you think my family is doing so well? We still haven't paid off the fine for violating the population-control policy. And the year before last, we built a house that we still owe several thousand *yuan* on." Feng said, "Who are you kidding? The villagers say that your family bought a tractor a few days ago. Xishu is driving the tractor all over. He's in seventh heaven!"

All at once, a buzzing exploded in Zhima's head. "*What?!*" Her eyes popped. "Xishu bought a tractor?! Why wasn't I told?" Glancing at her, Feng said, "Don't act so innocent. You might pull the wool over other people's eyes, but not mine!" Zhima blushed in irritation. "Who's pulling the wool over your eyes? That asshole Xishu—if he really bought a tractor, he didn't tell me. He's pulling the wool over *my* eyes!"

Zhima said she had to leave. Her head felt swollen, and the soles of her feet were burning up. She wanted desperately to get to the public phone outside the lobby and call Xishu and clear this up immediately. Feng saw that Zhima appeared agitated, but because it was almost her turn, she clutched at Zhima's arm and said, "Do what you have to do, but give me your phone number so that the two of us can take a day off and get together to talk some more. Oh, and if you hear of a somewhat better household needing a hand, let me know."

Zhima didn't want to gossip any longer with Feng, and in her agitation she forgot what Auntie Li had said: *Don't give out our phone number.* Borrowing a ballpoint pen from the person behind her, Zhima scribbled the Liu family's phone number on a one-*yuan* note that Feng pulled out of her pocket. She didn't forget to warn her, "You mustn't phone at lunch time. The old couple take their naps then. Will you remember?" With that, she broke away from Feng and walked out the door.

Xishu, you skunk! You asshole! You didn't say one word to me about such an important thing as buying a tractor. I'm not through with you! If you hit me, I'll fight back! You have your fist, but I have my rolling pin and broom. Auntie Li said, That's called . . . that's called self-defense. It isn't against the law! If you dare to hit me again, I'll leave you. I'll stay in the city and never go back. You can keep Gang with you. I'll take Yan with me, and send her to school in the city. I'll support her by myself. I earn several hundred yuan a month. That's enough to support Yan, isn't it? In all these years, isn't it only because I earn money by working away from home that we've been able to pay off most of our debt? Could you have done as well as this? You couldn't be a coal miner because you'd be afraid of cave-ins. You couldn't work as a mason in the city because you couldn't earn enough to make it worth your while. Sure, you raise a few pigs, but you're always afraid someone will steal them. You're a big man, but can you earn even a little money for the family? And now you're so headstrong that you've bought a tractor! You loser! If you aren't a skunk, then what are you?

Zhima stood in line in front of the phone booth. She hated this. She was silently cursing Xishu. She had used up all the usual swear words, but the line in front of the phone booth wasn't getting any shorter. Zhima began to feel impatient. How could so many people be making phone calls? She could tell from their accents that they were all from Henan. It seemed that nowadays no one from Henan was staying at home; they had all fled to Beijing to find work. She decided not to wait any longer. She would hurry back to Uncle Liu's home, and in the evening, after finishing her chores, she would tell Auntie Li that something was wrong at home and that she needed to use the phone. Auntie Li would surely agree.

Zhima boarded the bus. People were getting off work and were packed together like corncobs at the autumn harvest. Cars filled the road. People were everywhere, on both sides of the street, and judging by the way they were rubbernecking, most were also from the countryside. If Zhima hadn't come to Beijing, she'd never have known that China contained so many people. They were like bugs in the cotton fields, like wriggling worms in the loblollies on a rainy day—more than you could ever catch. It was hard to know how many of them came because of the fine for violating the population-control policy. Zhima felt slightly ashamed. It wasn't hard to give birth; it was pretty much like laying an egg. But if you promised to have only one child and then had another, you had to pay a large fine. Yan, for example. To give birth to Yan, Zhima had had to pawn the last half of her life.

Xishu, listen to me: if you don't take the tractor back, I'll take Yan away. As she was shouting to herself, Zhima held the handrail tightly. *Back then, you and your mother insisted that I have another child, and so now this is the way we live—so poor that three people share one quilt. So poor that we can't install windows in the house we built. All year long, we hear the swishing sound of the plastic sheets flapping in the window frames . . .*

Suddenly, tears of distress gushed from Zhima's eyes. Bowing her head, she wiped them away with the back of her hand. She was gazing blankly at the slowly receding street scenes. She thought of Yan and felt as if a needle were pricking her heart. Actually, she couldn't blame just Xishu for Yan; she had to blame his mother. The first time around, Zhima had given birth to a sturdy son whom they named Gang. When he was barely a month old, the village's party secretary came to look for Father-in-law. He said, "After all, you're a party member. Why not set an example? Get a one-child certificate for your son and daughter-in-law. That'll make it easier for me to deal with the higher-ups." Before three days had passed, Father-in-law regretted this because Mother-in-law cursed him out roundly. And then for three years she was after Zhima every day to have another child. Zhima said, "You arranged for the certificate; it's against the law for me to have another child." Mother-in-law said, "Are you brain dead? You see these people in our village. Where did they come from? Who has only one child?" Zhima ignored Mother-in-law. She could see with her own eyes that families with more than one child were fined to the point of ruin by the village government. She was scared stiff.

A year went by, and then, with no warning, she came down with a painful stomachache. Each month when she had her period, the blood flowed like urine. When she went to the hospital for an examination, she was told that she had an inflammation, and the doctor removed her IUD. In less than two months, Zhima's inflammation became much better, and she didn't have a period. When she went in for another examination, she learned she was pregnant. When the hospital told Zhima to get an abortion, Mother-in-law and Father-in-law, along with two brothers, rushed to the hospital, snatched her away, and took her home. Zhima said, "Then we have to hurry up and get a certificate allowing me to have this child." Mother-in-law said, "That's easy for you to say. A permission certificate costs five hundred *yuan*. We can't come up with even fifty. I've never heard of anyone having to spend money for a certificate in order to have a child. Fuck the certificate!"

The child was born. A girl. Mother-in-law's face was longer than a donkey's. She made egg soup for Zhima, scooped out a spoonful of brown sugar to add to it, and then on second thought put half back in the jar. Noticing this, Zhima lost her appetite. She felt as if a block of iron were attached to her heart, and she couldn't breathe normally.

Sure enough, when Yan was just a month old, Yang Baoguo and some others turned up. Yang Baoguo was a somebody—the one in charge of Population Control for the whole village. Whoever he said should be fined was fined. He was even more inflexible than Judge Bao of old, and more overbearing than the village head. One year, when her neighbor Cao-er was seven or eight months along with her third child, Zhima heard the sound of a car, and then saw Yang Baoguo and three other men jump out. Just like kidnappers in the movies, they dragged the big-bellied Cao-er into the car and took her to the village clinic. One cut of the knife was enough to slaughter the unborn child. Cao-er wanted to jump into the river, and Yang Baoguo told his henchmen not to stop her. After that, Cao-er shivered whenever she heard Yang Baoguo's name, and whenever a child cried, the adults scared it into utter silence by saying that Yang Baoguo was on the way.

When Yang Baoguo and others came to Zhima's door, without a word they began stripping the doors and windows from their home. After that, they moved their belongings out—hemp bags of grain, cupboards, chests, stools, tables, shelves. The house couldn't be moved, but they loaded everything they could carry onto their truck. They even took the cows and pigs out of their pens. The ratty truck was completely filled. Father-in-law pleaded in a small voice, "Anyhow, why not leave behind a little something? You can see that we don't have anything. How will we live?" As he tied things onto the truck with a rope, Yang Baoguo shouted, "Why do you have so many children? Don't you know that Henan's population is exploding? What's the country supposed to do?" Wringing her hands, Mother-in-law was moaning that the baby had already been born. "Do you dare take the child by the throat?!" Yang Baoguo answered, "No, but I'll fine you to death. If you want these things back, then get thirty thousand *yuan* and buy them back." Looking on helplessly, Mother-in-law watched Yang Baoguo's wreck of a truck make off with all their household goods. She followed the truck and shouted, "You bastard Yang Baoguo! Damn your ancestors! Damn you—I hope you die without sons!" The dust raised by the truck turned the tears on her face into little mud balls. Mother-in-law . . .

All at once, Zhima shrieked: "Stop the bus! Stop! I've missed my stop!" She frantically squeezed her way forward, but no one paid any attention to her, and the bus moved even faster. She was so upset that she considered jumping out a window. Finally, when the bus pulled up at the next stop, Zhima hustled off and ran back to the one she had missed. After a while, another bus came, and this time Zhima didn't dare get wrapped up in her thoughts again. She just peered at one stop after another. It would be dark soon, and Zhima was afraid of the dark, for the darkness turned the city into a maze. Every place looked the same, and she was completely confused. When she had first come to Beijing, she had gotten lost. It was like getting lost in the graveyard next to the village. Eventually, she ran into a cop, who took her back to the home where she was working. Zhima understood then why so many policemen were on the streets: since all the buildings in the city were alike, they were afraid people wouldn't be able to find their own homes after dark.

Zhima wasn't afraid after she got off this bus, for she knew where she was now. She could see her building in the distance—a large matchbox standing on end. It housed so many people that if you weren't careful and forgot just one number, you'd walk into someone else's apartment. This would never happen at home in Zhao Village. If you built a house there, it would always be your home.

After Yang Baoguo and the men with him had taken everything, they'd heaped it up in the village government's courtyard. The furnishings were rotting in the wind and rain. Xishu borrowed a few thousand *yuan* from a moneylender. Then, since that wasn't enough, he persuaded a cousin who drove for the village head to intercede for him. Thus, he was finally able to retrieve a load of their furnishings, but now they had a debt as well as a fine. Although Xishu raised even more pigs and sheep and grew even more foodstuff, still he would be lucky if he could pay the interest on the usurious loan. Did Zhima have any way out? No. The debt was a noose around her neck that Zhima thought would soon strangle her. She walked in the cornfields: the ears of yellow corn were growing perfectly, but nothing could turn them into gold. More than half of the money they earned went to pay for the fertilizer and pesticides they'd bought on credit. And then there were the taxes. Zhima walked alongside the broad Ru River. The turbid water was dyed black by run-off from the mines at the upper reaches. Not even a fish could be seen. On the other side of the river was her mother's home. Her mother was ill, her father old. Zhima was empty-handed. What could she take to her parents? She couldn't even pay the boatman to get across. At noontime, she walked around the village in a big circle until her legs hurt, and then she went home. She said straight to Xishu's face, "Shu—oh, I've thought it through. I have to leave the village to work."

"You work?" Xishu raised his eyebrows. "What can you do? Can you build walls or foundations? If you go to the city, will you shuck corn or pick cotton? Someone like you doesn't have any street smarts. If things don't go well, you'll be done for."

"I can wash clothes and cook, can't I? Can't I be a housekeeper? I've made some inquiries. If you're a housekeeper, you don't have to worry about food or lodging, and you get paid besides. After the harvest, Apricot's sister-in-law is going, and I'll go with her. What can she do to me? Sell me?!" Zhima spoke forcefully. Xishu stood there looking idiotic.

Three years after Zhima went to the city, her earnings were almost enough to pay off the fine Yang Baoguo had imposed. Then, when Zhima went back to see her family the year before last, she discovered that their old house was wobbling so much that it might collapse at any moment. In desperation, Xishu built a new house. And now they owed tens of thousands more. Zhima really didn't know when in this lifetime they would be free of debt. But who could be blamed? Xishu didn't gamble or drink. All he did all day long was work. If he couldn't make money from the earth, could she blame him? Blame Mother-in-law? She had to admit that she couldn't blame Mother-in-law, either. When Zhima went to Beijing, she left two-year-old Yan behind for Mother-in-law to bring up, so the situation was hard on Mother-in-law, too. Zhima didn't dare blame the government, either. The government had been upfront about everything. How could you not get a permission certificate? But in this world, everything had to have a cause and effect.

Having mulled this over for years, Zhima had decided that the one to blame was that damn Yang Baoguo. It was Yang Baoguo who had fined them so much that Zhima's family was driven from pillar to post, and family members had to live apart. Why didn't Yang Baoguo do something else for a living? In his administration of this cold-blooded population control, who knew where the money from the fines went? Maybe straight into his wallet. Zhima had thought about her family's situation from every angle. Auntie Li, her employer, said no one was to blame but Zhima herself. Zhima wasn't convinced. She hadn't gotten pregnant on purpose. She was careless once: should she take the blame for that? After five years, Zhima still couldn't get rid of the resentment in her heart. But Xishu didn't seem worried. Where had he borrowed money to buy a tractor? Did he *want* to piss Zhima off?!

Zhima jogged the rest of the way home and went into the building. The elevator operator Xiaolan smiled at her and said, "Did you go out to see your fellow villagers?" Zhima nodded carelessly. Looking her up and down, Xiaolan said, "After this, when you go out, you need to be give some thought to your image." At a loss, Zhima asked, "What do you mean by image?" Xiaolan clicked her tongue and said, "You don't even understand what 'image' is? Just take a look at yourself."

Zhima looked down at herself. Her pants were all right, and so was her coat. They weren't buttoned wrong, and there weren't any grease spots on her clothes. She couldn't figure out what part of her "image" looked wrong. Xiaolan was from Sichuan: it was because of her good "image" that she had been hired for the elevator job. At the ninth floor, Zhima twisted away from Xiaolan, smoothed the sweaty hair on her forehead, and rang the Liu family's doorbell.

Zhima went in. With no time to drink any water, she just went to the toilet and then washed her hands. This was Auntie Li's rule. Auntie Li had "rules" for everything. She also had a lot of "pay-attention-to" procedures. Even though Zhima had been with the Liu family for more than three years, she still couldn't remember all of them. Noticing the quiet in the living room, Zhima remembered that it was the weekend. Liu Danni had gone shopping with her family and wasn't back yet. Breathing a sigh of relief, Zhima called out, "Auntie, I'm back." Then she put on an apron, rolled up her sleeves, and went into the kitchen. Before going out, she had washed the vegetables for dinner and mixed the dough for noodles. After rolling the noodles out, she could put them into a pot—and dinner would be ready. Zhima didn't ever worry about cooking noodles. And as far as cooking dumplings and pancakes was concerned, she'd have no problem opening a breakfast diner. But to do this, you had to have assistants and "capital." Zhima didn't have either, so she had to settle for being a housekeeper.

Uncle Liu and Auntie Li had four children. Two were overseas, and one was in Shenzhen. Liu Danni was the fourth child and the mother of little Tiantian. Danni, Tiantian's father, and Tiantian all lived with the old couple, and ordinarily they went to work or school as soon as it was daylight. In the daytime, the only ones home were Uncle Liu and Auntie Li. A few years earlier, Uncle Liu had had a stroke, and he was still unsteady on one of his legs. The family was small, yet the home had five or six rooms. It took two hours to dust and sweep. You couldn't skip even one piece of furniture.

One of the Liu sons was doing post-doctoral work in the United States. At first, Zhima didn't know what post-doctoral work meant. Did it mean following the PhD and carrying his briefcase, or did it mean serving as a guard for the PhD? Uncle Liu said that a post-doc was simply a scholar and that now many post-docs came from poverty-stricken regions. Zhima was just hoping that Gang and Yan would be good at their studies. She didn't dare think that they might be post-docs one day. She would be satisfied if they were good enough to get into a community college and receive even a little higher education. She certainly didn't want them to be like her: she had graduated only from primary school. Instead of going to junior high, she'd stayed home and helped her mother take care of her little brother and sister. She also helped her father with the farming. From the time she was a child, she had never been afraid of work. Before Zhima came to Beijing, her family was always the first in Zhao Village to finish harvesting the wheat. So now, Father-in-law and Mother-in-law always looked forward to Zhima returning for the wheat harvest.

Bursting into the kitchen, Auntie Li said, "Make soft noodles this time, and the chicken soup has to be bland today. Your uncle has a stomachache."

Zhima said, "Oh," and plunged into kneading the dough. Then, dividing it into three parts, she started rolling it out.

To be fair, Zhima felt that Uncle Liu and Auntie Li treated her quite well. Every month, they paid her wages on time—and down to the last penny. Danni gave her sweaters, coats, trousers, shoes, and even socks. Although they were a little used, Zhima never had to buy any clothes, thus saving a good bit of money. And she also had plenty to eat: Auntie Li always gave her a large plateful, so Zhima was often full to the point of bursting. Uncle Liu told Danni that Guo Zhima's job wasn't called "nursemaid," but "housekeeping assistant." When guests came to the house, Uncle Liu introduced her as "Comrade Guo." The guest would extend a hand to Zhima, but Zhima would hide her hand behind her back and blush shyly. Uncle Liu was an old cadre, proper in speech and manner. He never said anything about the villages, but rather about the "grass roots." Zhima thought that "grass roots" was a strange term that was usually said in an offensive way, but it sounded fine when Uncle Liu said it. In her more than three years with the Liu household she had learned a lot and grown pale and plump. When she had gone home the previous year, even Xishu had said, "You have a good life in the city. Why do you keep thinking about coming back here?"

In Zhima's hands, the white dough turned into a thin pancake—as thin as the paper Yan wrote on. She dusted the surface with flour, folded it over several times, and then cut it into thin noodles. Zhima put the pot for boiling noodles on top of the stove and turned on the gas. She was intent only on cooking dinner a little faster than usual so that she would have more time for phoning Xishu. How much did he have to spend for that tractor? It must have been at least a year's wages for Zhima. *Such a big purchase,* she thought, *and you didn't even talk it over with me, Xishu. You just decided on your own and bought it?* If Zhima stood next to the tractor's tires, and compared herself with it, she would really turn into a sesame seed that had fallen to the ground and disappeared. As the old saying went, there's no place like home. *Xishu, do you know how hard it is to be away from home?* Just take eating as an example: when people at home ate, they sauntered all through the village with their bowls of food, or else squatted at the foot of the wall to chat and eat with a large group of people. But when city people ate, they all sat around a table. It had felt so unnatural for her to sit on a stool and put her bowl on the table that in the beginning she had trouble eating enough. She felt like standing up, or squatting, but she was afraid people would laugh at her. The first family she worked for were southerners. Every day, they ate two meals of rice and one meal of rice porridge. Zhima couldn't get even one mouthful of rice down. She changed employers. The next family she worked for didn't eat rice: they loved corn mush, steamed corn bread, braised sweet potatoes, boiled sweet potatoes, sweet potato porridge, and millet. They said coarse grains were healthful—lowering your cholesterol and blood pressure. But the grains turned Zhima's face green, and the sour aftertaste lasted all day. As a child, she'd eaten corn and sweet potatoes because there was nothing else to eat then. She hated food like this. Even though the villagers often had no money, everyone ate food made from wheat flour at every meal. They fed corn and sweet potatoes to the pigs. Before leaving home, Zhima had imagined all kinds of hardships in the city, but she had never dreamed that she'd have to eat pig fodder. *Can you believe it, Xishu?* Zhima went back to the Housekeeper Placement Center and waited for a long time. Then Liu Danni showed up there, and asked right away, "Can you make noodles and other flour-based dishes?" Zhima knew then that she'd finally found the right household.

No sooner had she plucked the noodles from the pot than Danni and her family came home. Zhima brought the food to the table and called Uncle Liu and Auntie Li to dinner. Then everything started going wrong: she spilled the soup and dropped the chopsticks; and when Auntie Li tasted the noodles, she frowned. "Zhima, didn't I tell you that today I wanted you to cook soft, thin noodles? Just look at this. And the salads are too salty . . ."

Zhima was dazed as she looked at the noodles in the bowl. She didn't know, either, why she'd rolled out such poor noodles.

Auntie Li said, "Guo, when you went for the pregnancy test today, did you meet up with some problem?" Surprised, Zhima asked, "How did you know?" Auntie Li smiled. "I know you well, you silly Guo. If any little thing distracts you, you grow careless in your work."

Zhima bent her head and didn't say anything. After gulping down some of the noodles, she couldn't bear to be silent any longer. She told the family about running into Feng and hearing her news that Xishu had bought a tractor. Before she'd finished talking, Danni began shouting, "This Xishu is just too unreasonable! When a family makes a major purchase, they have to discuss it first. How could he decide this on his own?"

Zhima asked, "What did you say? What is . . . 'dis . . . cuss'?"

"'Discuss:' that means that everyone gets together and talks about it," Uncle Liu answered. "When things involve the whole family, they have to be discussed first."

"And what's more, the money is money that Young Guo has earned through hard work in the city. The debt incurred for building the house hasn't been paid off, and now her husband has borrowed money to buy a tractor. Xishu has spent much too much; he might as well be an American." Danni went on, "Oh, Xiao Guo, you earn money to support the family, but you don't have even a little control over money matters. Are you just a moneymaking machine for your family? . . ."

"Hey, try to be fair," Tiantian's father interrupted. "Xishu probably had his reasons. Young Guo, don't be angry. Call him and clear it up before you say any more."

Zhima felt that this meal was tasteless, flavorless. She didn't know what she was eating. *Moneymaking machine?* Danni's words were like a knife cutting into Zhima's heart. In past years, Zhima kept house but didn't make the decisions. Nobody would listen to her. Xishu was a good man, but he had a violent temper. If Zhima didn't do as he said, he would beat her with whatever tool he had in his hand. Once, when Zhima had a painful toothache, Father-in-law went to the village clinic and brought back some pills. Zhima had never taken medicine. She drank a large jar of water, but the pill wouldn't go down. Angry, Zhima surreptitiously tossed the pill under the bed. A few days later, Xishu was looking for his shoes under the bed; that white pill was stuck to the top of his shoe. Xishu swore at Zhima for wasting medicine, and then he took his fists to her. It's not that Zhima took it lying down. She scratched his face, and the two of them fought until Mother-in-law pulled them apart.

After Zhima came to Beijing and started sending money home, Xishu seemed to change. When she went home once a year, his whole face was wreathed in smiles at seeing her. He never again lifted a finger against her. She really thought that he had started respecting her. But now this tractor incident had cooled part of her heart. After all, Xishu was still the same Xishu and Zhima was still the same Zhima. Their life was still the same. Even if Zhima won a million-*yuan* lottery, Xishu would still be the boss.

Zhima started to wash the dishes and broke a plate right away. Auntie Li didn't say anything, but Zhima felt bad. "Auntie Li, please let me pay for this—just take it out of my wages." Auntie Li said, "Okay, okay, finish up your work quickly and go to my room and make your phone call. Don't forget to dial 17931 first."

When she had finished, Zhima hurried to Auntie Li's room. She didn't much like to telephone Xishu. The village homes shared party lines, so when you dialed a number, several people picked up the phone at once. Their voices would all be jumbled together, so no one could hear anyone else distinctly. Once, Brick, a man who was working elsewhere, made a phone call to his wife Ye-er. He said, "Ye-er, I miss you so much." Ye-er said, "I miss you, too." Not until they suddenly heard wicked giggles did they realize that others were listening in on their phone call. After that, whenever Brick came back to the village, people would laugh at him and say, "I miss you so much!" Brick was too embarrassed to look anyone in the eye.

Zhima remembered this lesson. Every time she phoned Xishu, she came straight to the point. Actually, what could you say to someone like Xishu that you'd be afraid to have others hear? Zhima would ask him, "Is everything okay at home?" Xishu would answer, "Everything's fine." Xishu would ask, "How are you?" Zhima would say, "Fine." Zhima would think for a moment. "How is everyone at home?" Xishu would reply, "The same as always." Zhima didn't know what else to say. What was the point of this kind of phone call? It just wasted money. But talking with Yan was different. Zhima still recalled what Yan had said to her on the phone a few years ago, when her daughter was four years old. When Xishu got on the line, he held the phone so Yan could hear Zhima's voice. Zhima kept saying into the receiver, "Yan, Yan." Yan hugged the phone and said, "Oh, Ma. Why can't I see you? Where are you hiding?" That silly girl could really make Zhima laugh.

Now, Zhima heard the *du-du* sound of a busy signal. She dialed again, and still got the incessant *du-du* sound. After a while, she tried again, but she was so flustered that she dialed a wrong number. She dialed again, and still the call didn't go through. With a sigh, she replaced the receiver. She thought, *Why didn't Xishu phone me? He could spend several thousand yuan on a tractor, but he begrudged the few yuan for a phone call.* Zhima was annoyed. Maybe she wouldn't call Xishu, but wait to see how he explained himself later!

She went into the living room, where the whole family was watching soccer on TV. She looked at the clock on the wall. The news was already over. So was the weather report. She'd missed the weather report: she didn't know why she felt so empty and desolate. Just then she remembered that she had to wash Tiantian's face and feet, but Danni beckoned her into the kitchen.

Danni said, "I've told you I don't know how many times. Every evening, you have to throw out all of the leftover food. Why are you saving it again? Especially vegetables: unhealthful elements will grow on them overnight. Do you understand?"

Zhima was a little embarrassed. She said with a smile, "The noodles I made tonight weren't very good, and a lot were left over. I was sorry to see that and thought I'd save them for my lunch tomorrow."

Danni said, "You're incredible! Your money isn't paying for the food. This is my home, and while you're living in it, I don't want you eating left-overs, either. You have to get over this bad habit. Haven't I said that you are too farmerish? . . . Okay, okay. Throw the food out, okay?" With that, she left the kitchen. Zhima picked up the bowl, took the lid off the garbage pail, and was about to throw the leftovers into the garbage when she paused.

Danni was only a few years younger than she was, but Zhima frequently felt that they came from two entirely different worlds. Danni and her husband earned ten thousand *yuan* a month, yet they were always complaining that they couldn't make ends meet. Growing up in the city, how could Danni know how precious food was? Zhima felt she had been working for food ever since she was born. Cultivating the land. Threshing the grain. All year, the villagers worried about food. And every year, there was either a drought or a flood. When she was a child, the Production Brigade never distributed enough food. When she was three, an uncle tending cattle stuffed a handful of fodder from the Production Brigade into his mouth. For this, the villagers beat him to death. Auntie Li sometimes joked with her, saying, *Young Guo, you're a little thickheaded. Teaching you something really takes a lot of effort.* Zhima thought to herself, *My head grew up on corn mush, how could I not be thickheaded.* Zhima recalled that when she was eleven—probably around 1981—the Production Brigade divided the land among the households. The whole family worked in the fields from morning to night, hoping to reap a little more grain. The harvest that year was good. In June, the wheat on the drying field flowed like a river. In the fall, they harvested corn, each kernel like gold. Zhima had never seen so much grain before. The grain was stacked up to the rafters in the storehouse, and her parents were smiling from ear to ear. With her little brother and sister in tow, Zhima spent the whole day rolling around and playing on the heaps of grain. At mealtime, she sat on a pile of corn to eat. At bedtime, she didn't go back to the house, but slept on a stack of wheat. The dried grain had the fragrance of the sun. When you inhaled its scent, you felt you'd eaten a meal. When you exhaled, you felt hungry. Zhima and her little brother and sister sang and bounced around on the heaps of grain. When their feet sank into the grain, they jumped again, and bounced again, burrowing into the grain. The stored-up grain was like a quilt, for it was even warmer than the land that had just been plowed. When Zhima's mother plucked them one by one from the stack of grain, Zhima's hair, neck, and shoes were all filled with kernels of grain.

Auntie Li always said that Zhima's memory was bad, but even if it were worse, she would still distinctly remember that when the Production Brigade collective was still operating, it distributed only three or four hundred *jin* of wheat a year to Zhima's family. But after the land was divided, each family could reap three or four thousand *jin* of wheat—more than ten times as much. In the years after the land was divided, Zhima's family enjoyed the best life ever. Even in the barren springtime, they didn't have to borrow food. They ate dried sweet potatoes, and two days out of three, large white *mantou* were steaming in the pot. Nothing was more delicious than a bite of white-flour *mantou* that had just come out of the steamer. It was so soft that before you realized it, you had gulped it all down. It would never scratch your throat as cornbread did. Polishing off one *mantou* left a sweet taste in your mouth for the rest of the day. Zhima had eaten a lot of chicken, duck, fish, and meat in Uncle Liu's home, but she still felt that the most delicious thing in the world was *mantou*.

Zhima still couldn't figure out why village life became harder and harder after she married into Xishu's family. Even though they grew more grain, after selling some and deducting their costs, it was only enough for the family. When they bought things, they had to use the food as barter. When Zhima gave birth to Gang, she nursed him and still worked the land. How could she hold up if she didn't eat? Zhima had a good appetite, but her mother-in-law wasn't happy about this. Each time Zhima lifted a bowl to her mouth and slurped her porridge, Mother-in-law muttered, "How can she eat so much?" Upset, Zhima set her bowl aside. A few years later, Zhima made up her mind to leave. After she left, the family had more than enough food. They bartered Zhima's portion for the most essential daily necessities, such as salt, oil, soy sauce, and vinegar.

Auntie Li looked up from watching TV and asked, "Did you phone Xishu?" Zhima said she couldn't get through. "He goes to bed early. I'll try again tomorrow." Auntie Li said, "Then come and watch TV for a while. Rest a little." Zhima said, "I'm not tired. How could I be tired? I don't do any farming here." She yawned as she said this but still stood in front of the TV. Uncle Liu was changing channels. As a weather report suddenly jumped out from the screen, Zhima felt instantly refreshed.

It was only then that she realized she'd been waiting for the weather report all along. Zhima thought it was strange: she could never remember all of the housework that Auntie Li assigned to her each day, but she never forgot to watch the weather forecast. In the years that Zhima had been in the city, she might have gotten rid of other habits, but watching the weather remained second nature. To tell the truth, she had no reason to care about Beijing's weather. When it was windy or rainy, she stayed inside. On snowy days, there was always the heater. Even hail couldn't hurt her. Wasn't it just a waste of time for Zhima to watch the weather report? Everyone in the Liu family knew that Zhima didn't watch the Beijing weather. What she watched was the Henan weather. On a perfectly clear TV set half the size of a table, the whole of China was on the screen. The weatherman was genial, the weather-girl pretty. They knew everything: they told you where the clouds were coming from, where the wind was going, where it was raining, and where there was a sandstorm. They told you the highest temperature and the lowest temperature. They didn't leave anything out. Henan Province was a little below the central part of China, like a bellybutton. It was easy to locate. Even though those people reported only Zhengzhou's temperature, still Zhengzhou was just three hours from Zhumadian by train. When it was windy in Zhengzhou, the wind would come to Zhumadian. Zhima stared unblinkingly at the TV. She saw that rain was falling in half of China. It was raining all over Henan. Not even a crack showed through. For the last three days, the thick clouds over Henan hadn't moved. Zhima was a little worried: this was the time when the wheat blossomed. If the rain kept falling, the pollen for the wheat would be swept away, and the kernels of wheat couldn't grow. The harvest would be smaller. Distracted for a while as she watched Henan, Hebei, Shandong, and Shanxi disappear one by one, Zhima was finally back to her old self.

When the weather report was over, the day really had come to an end. After watching the weather, Zhima was even more uneasy than before. Why didn't it rain in Beijing? Why did all the rain fall in Henan? The land couldn't stand either drought or being waterlogged. If this went on for another few days, they wouldn't have any *mantou* to eat this year. Later, as she took off her socks, Zhima was still thinking. *Would the Ru River flood?* If it flooded, the crops of the whole village would be destroyed. Zhima burrowed into the quilt, feeling her heart suddenly sink. Her room faced the street. After turning off the light, she heard cars roaring in the distance—like the sound of the Ru River torrents rushing down the mountain. Every night at this time, the trucks coming from other places all took the third ring road, and all night long the sound of cars never ceased. Even though Zhima had been in Beijing for five years, she couldn't get used to this. As soon as she lay down, she began trembling. It was as if that weird tooting sound was roaring into her ears. It was like being pounced on by wild animals that were almost whisking Zhima away . . .

The year the Ru River's reservoir collapsed, Zhima was only six. The rain that had been falling for seven days straight turned the foundation of the wall spongy. At a little after ten o'clock that night, her father shook her awake from her dreams. She heard the roaring sound outside, like thunder falling from heaven to earth. Father and Mother shouted in quavering voices that the water was coming. They ran, taking Zhima, her little brother, and her little sister along. The sky was as black as the bottom of a pot. Zhima was ankle-deep in ice-cold water. Water was everywhere. Father said, "Let's go to the party secretary's house. Since his house is made of tile, it should withstand the water." Soon, the water reached their knees. When they arrived, the party secretary's four-room tile house was filled with people—so many that they blocked the door. The party secretary said, "Hurry up to the roof. If you wait, you won't make it." The men scurried about placing stools on a table so people could reach the roof. Breaking the ceiling tiles with clubs, the men created a large hole. One by one, they helped the women and children up to the roof. When Zhima's mother pulled her up, the table they'd just stood on began floating on the water. *"Father!"* Zhima shouted with all her might. But Father didn't respond. The rope being used to pull up Father and Zhima's little brother snapped, and they had both disappeared. Zhima was sobbing, sitting on the ridge of the roof. Mother said, "Don't move. If you fall into the water, you won't see me again." Zhima held her little sister tightly, not daring to move. Her legs tingled so much that they weren't like her own legs. When she peed down her pantlegs, you couldn't tell the difference between the urine and the rain. That night, Zhima was cold and hungry. Eyes wide open, she watched the dazzling white flood rising inch by inch. Near dawn, her feet were in water. Her mother said, "Don't be afraid. This tile house can't cave in." When she told her mother she was hungry, her mother took one shoe off and scooped up some water from under the eaves for Zhima to drink.

At dawn, the rain stopped. Zhima saw that the village was submerged—it had become one large expanse of water. She couldn't see even the tops of the thatched huts. The adults took hold of a large piece of wood floating on the water, and when the flood began to recede around noon, they propped it against the wall for everyone to slide down. Zhima was cut by the rough wood, and even now, a centipede-like scar remains on her arm. When the water receded, Mother took her and her little sister to look for their home. They couldn't find it. Instead, they saw Father squatting on a muddy mound of thatch, weeping. When Mother saw him, she cried, too. Father put little brother into her arms and said that after the rope had broken, the water washed over him and the child. He bumped into a tree of heaven and climbed it. The water rose a little. He climbed up to a fork in the tree, but the water attacked with a vengeance. All at once, the child fell into the water and disappeared. Father was crying and shouting, but no one came. After a long time, lightning flashed and he saw something sinking in the water. He caught hold of a corner of clothing, and when he pulled it up, he saw that it was their child. He held the boy upside down on his shoulder, and their son vomited out all of the water he'd taken in. As he was being held upside down, the child revived. Mother said, "If the child had died, I couldn't have gone on living."

The next day, the weather was fine. Everywhere in the village were bodies of those who had drowned. Zhima didn't dare look. She covered her eyes with her hands, carefully peeking between her fingers so that she could see the street. Even through the cracks, she saw dead people. In the remains of the thatched hut were a few sacks of corn flour that hadn't been washed away. As soon as the sun came out, the corn flour fermented. The flour gave off a musty smell, and fur was growing on it. It couldn't be eaten. Airplanes flew over, dropping bags of rice, flour, and salt, which the villagers snatched up. The firewood and standing grain were wet and couldn't catch fire. People just mixed some salt into the food and ate it without cooking it. Since Zhima's family hadn't been told that emergency rations were being dropped, they were too late to get any. And no one shared with them. Father and Mother, along with the children, walked many miles to an auntie's home. There, they stayed for half a month—waiting for more relief food to be distributed. Although Auntie Li said that Zhima's memory was bad, even after so many years, the sound of the roaring water still echoed in her ears. It was just like the sound of the vehicles on the road. Zhima didn't like tractors. The moment she heard a tractor, she remembered the night of the flood. She saw herself sitting legs apart on the ridge of the house, her body stiff as wood, not daring to move. . . .

Zhima couldn't sleep. Turning over, she covered her ears with the quilt. The noise of what sounded like a tractor shook the bed. *Just you wait, Xishu, until I go home for the wheat harvest, and then I'll have it out with you!* Zhima shouted at the tractor-like sound outside. *Do you seriously think I'm in the city to enjoy myself? Hunh! All these years, I've endured so many hardships that I've never dared tell you about for fear you wouldn't let me come back here again. You say that the city has towering buildings and asphalt streets. What you say isn't wrong. And in city homes, the floor is cleaned every day: it's even cleaner than our dinner table. And their toilets are shinier than our rice pot. But as nice as it is, it isn't the same as being in our own home. To tell you the truth, when villagers leave home to work in the city, we're all much the same as beggars.*

When Zhima first reached Beijing, she stood on the sidewalk every day, waiting for work. She bought a cold *mantou* for two *jiao*, and asked for some drinking water at a small restaurant. She stood there all day. If a man showed up, and his manner or words didn't seem right, Zhima would go hungry for three days rather than go with him. She was afraid he'd sell her to be a cripple's wife in a remote mountainous area. Her first employers wouldn't let her take a bath or wash her clothes even on scorching hot days. They were afraid she'd waste water and electricity. She had to wait and wash her clothes in the water that the whole family had used for its laundry. They treated her as if she had some contagious disease. At the second household, all of the cupboards were locked. And whenever they ate any treats, they kept their backs to her. They'd rather see basket after basket of fruit rot than let Zhima have some. At the third household, the old woman was even worse. If you said anything to her husband, she would tell her grown children that the old man was having an "affair" or that Zhima was carrying on with her old man. Zhima hated this kind of talk. Later, someone from her hometown told her to go to the Housekeeper Placement Center. It was only then that she met up with reasonable people.

Working in the city, someone like her had to get up in the morning before anyone else did. You were busy every minute. You didn't even have time to wipe away your sweat. It wasn't like being at home; in the village, if you wanted to drop by someone else's house after you were done with the cooking and feeding the poultry, you just picked up your feet and went. If you wanted to pass the time of day with someone, you picked up your bowl of piping hot noodles and took off. From morning until night, you could find people relaxing under the big willow tree and waiting for you to chat with them. At home, except for spring and autumn harvest times, you could generally go to bed whenever you wanted. As for the little housework there was, you could do it whenever you felt like it. True, you had no money in your pocket, but you had a free and easy life.

Xishu, you don't know what it's like to live in someone else's house and see the looks on their faces. With your temper, you wouldn't last three days. In Auntie Li's building, a young housekeeper from the twentieth floor grabbed my hand one day and wept, saying that she was homesick, and that the family she worked for didn't treat her like a human being. When they were sitting around the table eating watermelon, no one offered her any. And after she'd cleared away the dishes, and was about to wipe the table, the old woman berated her: "Besides the dishes, don't you have anything more to do? Go swat the flies!"

Aren't city people and rural people all people? Why are they high and we're low? Xishu, tell me that.

But on the other hand, if I hadn't made up my mind to come to the city to work, how would we ever pay back our debt? Would we have been able to build a new house? No matter how hard it was back then, I got through it. Forget the hardships. As long as I can make money in the city, I can take anything. Do you still remember Gang's primary-school teacher—the young woman named Dai? Well, she also came to Beijing to work. Once when she was sick she ran a very high fever, but she didn't want to spend money on going to the doctor. Finally, she was burning up with the fever and was taken to the hospital. But it was too late. Her husband rushed here from home to bring her a change of clothes, and discovered that she had three thousand yuan in her pocket. She'd saved three thousand yuan, but she didn't want to spend one penny on getting well . . . .

The teacher died. People come into this world—but for what? Look at city people. Take Tiantian's father, mother, and grandparents—they all have jobs, careers. They saved money to travel overseas to whatchamacallit—Bali . . . I don't even know where it is. When they came back, they showed me the pictures. Wow! I haven't been to paradise, but looking at that scenery, I know paradise must be like that. They haven't lived for nothing. Do you think our Gang and Yan will be able to keep going to school? When they grow up, they mustn't live the way we do. For better or worse, they should have real careers. . .

The roaring-water sound of traffic faded, and Zhima's anger and depression began to subside. Her eyelids felt heavy, her head muddled. She dreamed that she was sitting in the courtyard at home, cutting dried sweet potatoes.

As usual, Zhima got up early the next day, still feeling a little dazed and unwell. She impatiently boiled congee in the rice cooker, and boiled some eggs. Then she straightened up the living room by putting away the newspapers and magazines that were scattered around, swept the floor, and wiped the table. Not until everything was in order did she go off to comb her hair and wash her face. Today was Saturday, so Danni and her family were all sleeping in. Uncle Liu and Auntie Li had gone out to exercise. She could wait until Danni and her family got up before heating the milk and toasting the bread. Uncle Liu didn't drink milk, and Auntie Li didn't eat eggs. Tiantian didn't eat congee, and Danni ate her eggs fried. For one family, she had to fix all kinds of dishes. Zhima was plenty busy getting breakfast ready.

At home, Zhima could have just steamed a pot of *mantou* and the family would have eaten them for several days. She could have boiled a pot of soft-noodle soup to feed the whole family. Whatever they ate, they ate their fill. City people had to eat something different at every meal, and they didn't mind the trouble it took to prepare it all. Danni said this was called quality of life. Zhima asked what "quality" meant. Tiantian's father said, "Let me think about how to explain it to you. For example, wheat comes in different varieties, some with large, full kernels, and others with small, shriveled kernels. Wheat with high moisture content isn't high quality. When you sell grain, you can't get much for an inferior grade." Zhima said, "Oh, I see. The life of people in the city is like good wheat." The Lius were amused.

In the city, Zhima had learned quite a lot of other new words and phrases. When people mentioned such things as "information," "high-tech," "discrimination," "domestic violence," and so forth, all she had to do was open her mouth and ask, and Uncle Liu was glad to explain. He talked until it seemed she understood, but sometimes she also seemed even more confused. Auntie Li often said, "Zhima, you're only thirty years old. You have a lot of living ahead of you. You need to try harder to learn more. Read some newspapers in your spare time." So Zhima did. She read and read, but she just grew more confused.

She recalled that when she was a child, every year her father always chose the best wheat to turn over to the commune. When she married Xishu, her father-in-law didn't do things this way. He always took the second-best grain to the commune. And he took the vegetables that had been loaded with chemical fertilizers and pesticides to the market to sell to the town dwellers. He kept the uncontaminated vegetables and grain for his own family to eat. He was a party member, and in the past he had also served as head of the Production Brigade. How come he was so deficient in "quality"? He had also arranged for the one-child certificate and then had gone back on his word, making Zhima's life difficult for several years.

At the sound of a key in the lock, Zhima knew that Uncle Liu and Auntie Li had come back. Zhima hurried into the kitchen to check on the porridge. But the rice cooker—usually bursting with steam by this time—wasn't making any sound at all. Puzzled, she touched the rice cooker. To her astonishment, it was ice-cold, as if it had just been taken out of the snow. What was going on? She turned the rice cooker around and around. She patted it and hit it, and suddenly remembered. When she had covered it a while ago, she must have forgotten to press the little on-off button. If she pressed it now, the porridge wouldn't be ready for at least half an hour. She was glum when she told Auntie Li about this, and Auntie Li wasn't happy. Auntie Li said, "Young Guo, you can't blame me for saying that you're always so negligent. You make at least one mistake a day. After breakfast, Uncle Liu and I have to go out again to hear a lecture on health. Don't you see that your mistakes are affecting our lives?"

Zhima smacked her own head resentfully and said, "What a stupid head I have. Why isn't it in good working condition?"

"It isn't that your head doesn't work well. It's because—from childhood to adulthood—you people don't use your heads. All of you lack training in this," Auntie Li said. "The last time I asked you to wax the floors, the old wax was used up and I gave you another kind of floor wax. You didn't ask any questions, nor did you read the directions. You just carelessly sprayed it on the floor. You have to realize that different brands have different directions. As a result, the wax congealed into little blobs that stuck to the floor. The wax remover that I ordered from Shanghai couldn't get rid of it. So it's still there now. You talk of yourself. But in these last seven or eight years, I've had five housekeepers. Every one of them was just like you. Not one of them used her head. Why? Simply because, ever since you were little, you've never used your heads. But, on the other hand, if someone smart were working for me, I'd be even more uneasy. One time . . ."

It seemed that Auntie Li was going to talk forever. Zhima interrupted timidly, "Shall I go out and buy some jellied tofu? That way, breakfast will be ready in five minutes . . ."

"Good. Let's have jellied tofu," Uncle Liu chimed in. "I haven't had it in ages, and it would hit the spot."

Pot in hand, Zhima went down to buy the jellied tofu. She was a little annoyed with herself. All night long, she'd had confusing dreams. When she got up this morning, her head had felt pretty much like a pot of jellied tofu. She was also still pissed off at Xishu—that skunk. He was always making trouble. Zhima made up her mind not to telephone Xishu; she was afraid she'd start arguing with him. If she got angry, she'd probably make even more mistakes when she used the electrical appliances. The electric rice cooker alone was really annoying. As for the electric bolt, you had to press the little lever down for it to fit right. With so many electrical gadgets, who could remember how to operate all of them? The microwave, for example: after you put something in it, you still had to set the time, choose high or low heat, and finally turn it on. Otherwise, the tray in the box wouldn't turn. If you didn't microwave something long enough, it wasn't hot; if you microwaved something too long, it burned. Nothing could be even a tiny bit off. And then there was the washing machine. Sure, it was computer controlled, but if you set just one of the little buttons wrong, it sat there like a dead cat. One time, no matter what she did, the water wouldn't drain out. Then, all of a sudden, the machine shook violently, almost scaring the wits out of her. Last year, Tiantian's father bought a thirty-five-inch TV set for the family, and put the old, obsolete twenty-inch set in Zhima's little room. Auntie Li said it was for her to watch TV in the evening and widen her horizons. Zhima trembled as she held the remote. She was afraid that if she touched the wrong buttons, the set would explode. After Tiantian's father gave her several lessons, she finally was able to get the picture and the sound. The last few days, Zhima had no idea what button she had touched, but in any case, those TV "channels" all disappeared. The Henan station also disappeared. The only one left was the Beijing station. Zhima couldn't see the Henan opera that she liked so much. She stamped her feet in anger. Tiantian's father said she had discombobulated the remote's "system." When he had time, he would fix it, but when did he ever have time? When he did have a little free time, he had to "go on the net." What did that mean? Where was the net hanging?

From then on, whenever Zhima got anywhere close to a household appliance, her heart started thumping. She didn't dare touch it. She was afraid if she wasn't careful, it would talk back and play tricks on her . . .

It was really true that city people's lives were tiring—not physically but mentally. Zhima felt a surge of sympathy for them. With so many electric appliances, people were becoming just like machines. Zhima would soon turn into a machine, too. But her own home had no electric appliances. And what was life like there? They didn't know about anything going on in the outside world. They ate and slept, slept and ate. If they had nothing to eat, they stole. Though they weren't machines, they were not a whole lot different from animals. If someone could afford a TV set, then the room was crowded with young people at night—just the way it used to be when the Production Brigade showed a movie. Poor Xishu: he didn't dare buy a TV set for his pleasure; his first priority was to buy a tractor. And that was for his work . . .

Zhima sighed. If she had to choose between being a machine and being an animal, she really didn't know what she would decide.

Carrying the pot, Zhima took the elevator to the ground floor. She had no sooner gone out the door than she ran into Chun-e, a young housekeeper from Hunan who was working for a family in the next building. Chun-e had left home not long before. She was a sweet girl, warmly greeting everyone she ran into. It appeared that she was going out to buy groceries, for she had a woven plastic basket in her hand. Taking hold of Zhima's arm, Chun-e whispered, "Zhima, I want to ask you something. You've been in Beijing a long time. You must understand the Beijing language."

Laughing, Zhima said, "Oh, don't bring that up! For a while after I first got here, I couldn't understand a thing. I'd answer the phone, and if the person said he was calling from the Science and Technology University, what I wrote down was 'Kentucky University.' And no one could understand what I said, either. It made for a lot of jokes."

Chun-e's voice was thin as she said, "Do you understand them now? Let me ask you, what does it mean if someone says 'this person is thief-smart'? Does it mean I'm a thief? If they dare say I'm a thief, I'll take them to court!"

Zhima was confused. "Who said you're a thief? If they say this, they have to have proof. Without proof, it's slander . . ."

Chun-e was gasping. "My employer's family said this behind my back in the living room, and I happened to overhear it. They said, 'this girl is thief-smart.'"

Zhima didn't have a clue as to what "thief-smart" meant. She was worrying about Auntie Li waiting to eat jellied tofu, so she said, "Ask someone else, but in the meantime, don't worry about it. I'll ask around for you." As luck would have it, at the breakfast diner, she ran into a housekeeper from Anhui. Zhima asked, "In the Beijing language does 'thief-smart' mean the person is a thief?" The Anhui housekeeper said that in her hometown, that's exactly what it meant. But she didn't know about the Beijing language. After buying the jellied tofu, Zhima hurried back to her building.

When she walked in, Danni was already up. As she served Auntie Li the tofu, Zhima greeted Danni and asked, "Why are you up so early today? It's Sunday—don't you want to sleep in?" Looking unhappy, Danni said, "You're asking me? A phone call early this morning woke me up." Zhima chimed in, "What sort of unreasonable person would call at this hour of the morning?" Danni said, "It was someone looking for you!" Zhima was stunned. "Was it Xishu?" she asked in a small voice. "Naaaah—," Danni drew out her answer. "It was a . . . woman. Someone from Henan, judging by the accent. Didn't I tell you ages ago not to give out our phone number to people from your hometown?"

Zhima put the ladle down, and the jellied tofu spilled over the edge of the bowl. Danni said, "She said she was in Beijing, and would call back after a while. You can tell her that in the future she shouldn't call unless it's urgent." Auntie Li added, "Right. This is a matter of safety. You can't be too careful."

Who could it have been? Of those in Beijing from Zhima's hometown, hardly anyone knew her phone number. Besides, if it weren't something urgent, who would waste money on a phone call? So something must have happened. But who would call Zhima about something urgent? Zhima wasn't in business or anything like that. If somebody really wanted to ask a favor of her, the only other possibility was that somebody wanted to borrow money. Zhima wouldn't lend money—no way! Next month when she went home for the harvest, she would take her savings and apply it toward her family's debt. To ask Zhima a favor was all well and good, but she couldn't lend money. People who borrowed money didn't return it for years.

The morning seemed to drag on. Zhima thought that the batteries in the wall clock must be almost dead because the hands were moving so slowly. When she vacuumed the floor, she couldn't find the electrical outlets. When she washed the clothes, she poured too much detergent into the machine. When she cleaned the vegetables, she kept the rotten parts and threw out the good parts. When Zhima scooped rice out of the container, she forgot whether she had ladled out two scoops or three . . . Zhima thought something terrible, really terrible, must have happened. If her mother or father was sick, or if disaster had befallen her brother or sister, even if she grew wings she couldn't fly back so far . . .

Coming into the kitchen, Danni glanced at Zhima. "Guo, it was just a phone call. Aren't you overreacting? I think that you . . ." She dropped the subject.

"I'm what?" Zhima asked distractedly.

"If I don't tell you, you'll keep wondering about it. I think that you—let me put it this way . . ." Danni's delicate eyebrows were like two willow leaves waving in the breeze. "I think that you're like a person divided into two halves: half is here in our home; the other half stayed in Zhumadian in Henan. Your body and your thoughts are divided. Physically, you're in Beijing, but your mind has never left home. Right?"

Zhima didn't utter a word. In just one moment, Danni had read her mind. Danni was right. She was physically in Beijing, but where was her mind? Not even half of it was present. Where was it? In Zhao Village in Henan.

Zhima agreed in a hurry, and then abruptly digressed. "Let me ask you something. When Beijing people say somebody is 'thief-smart,' are they saying that the person is a thief?" Danni threw back her head and started laughing. She laughed so hard she almost cried. In the midst of her laughter, she said, "My God, where in the world did you get this? When Beijing people say that someone is 'thief-smart,' it's an analogy. It means the person is very shrewd—clever and quick as a thief. It doesn't mean the person is a thief. Definitely not. Do you get it now?"

Zhima also began laughing. As she was laughing, a one-*yuan* note flashed through her mind. Of course. It must be Feng who had telephoned. At the pregnancy testing place, Zhima had written her phone number on a one-*yuan* note for Feng. That was really stupid—couldn't she just have said she couldn't remember it? But Zhima was born slow-witted. She was unable to tell a fib. If it was Feng who had phoned, if Feng was looking for Zhima, then for sure something was up. From the time she was a child, Feng had been a little thief-smart . . .

Just as she was thinking this, the phone rang. She snatched it up: sure enough, it was Feng. Feng's voice was oddly warm. She kept repeating Zhima's name. After a while, Zhima said, "Feng, if you have something to say, just say it. I still have to cook lunch." Feng giggled, as if holding in a secret, and then paused. Finally, she mumbled as she came to the point. It took a lot of effort for Zhima to hear her. She pressed the receiver to her ear so hard that her ear hurt, and still she couldn't hear Feng. When she finally could hear her clearly, she couldn't believe her ears. She asked Feng to repeat herself. Suddenly, a shiver went through Zhima, and the hand holding the receiver froze in midair. She was speechless.

Feng was saying something along these lines:

Apricot, the adopted daughter of Xishu's uncle—who was also the daughter-in-law of Feng's adoptive father—was five months pregnant. A few years ago, she'd given birth to a daughter. The next year, she'd had another child—also a daughter. Apricot's husband wouldn't let her get her tubes tied; worse yet, he told her to have a third child. But Population Control in the villages made strict inspections. Every woman of childbearing age had to produce proof of a pregnancy test every three months, but if Apricot took the test, the cat would soon be out of the bag. Apricot's husband had come up with a way around this. He told the village cadre that he was taking Apricot away to get a job. In fact, he had taken Apricot to a relative's home in Anyang.

He wanted her to have the child there and then return to the village. This was called "the rice is already cooked." After the child was born, could Yang Baoguo stuff the child back into its mother's belly? As long as they had a son, they were willing to pay any fine and take any punishment. A few days ago, Apricot's husband had called Feng, and asked her to think of a way for Apricot to get proof of having taken a pregnancy test, so the village cadres wouldn't become suspicious and make trouble for the family. If Apricot could get over this hurdle, she would just have to wait a few more months. After she gave birth to the child, they wouldn't be afraid of anything . . .

Zhima said, "So what's the point of telling me all this?" Feng said, "That's the very point. Without you, it can't be done." Zhima said, "I'm not a midwife." Feng persisted, "Who asked you to deliver the baby? I want you to get a pregnancy test for Apricot." Zhima stammered, "What? How can I do that? That takes a doctor." Feng began shouting, "How can you be so dumb? I want you to take Apricot's ID card—to pretend to be Apricot. You'll be Apricot, and go for a pregnancy test. Then everything will go smoothly for her."

It was a long time before Zhima finally understood what Feng was suggesting. She said, "Are you asking me to lie?" "What are you saying? So what if it's a lie? It's helping someone. When you were in school, didn't you ever learn about taking pleasure in helping people?"

Zhima countered, "Then . . . Feng, why don't you pretend to be Apricot? You can just do it yourself." "Aiya . . . Aren't I too thin? We don't look anything alike. I'm not at all like the photo on Apricot's ID card. Any doctor would see through this at a glance. But, when I caught sight of you the other day, I thought for a moment that you were Apricot. You're the spittin' image of her. You're the only one who's an exact double."

Zhima was getting a little pissed. "Just forget it. I'm not Apricot—how can I pretend to be?" But Feng wouldn't give up. "You numbskull. If you help someone with something this important, won't she find a way to show her gratitude?" Zhima refused again. "If you want to do it, go ahead. I won't. I'm afraid." Feng was still trying to wear her down. "Didn't I just tell you? I don't look like her. Ah. Just think of it as helping me out. He asked me. I have to do something." "No, I won't do it." Zhima refused again. "I'm really afraid." "I'll go with you, okay?" Feng was almost begging now. "No, that won't make it any better. I've gotta go. Gotta cook lunch." Feng was on the verge of tears. "Give it some more thought. If someone's in trouble, and they haven't asked you for anything in ages, if you don't help out, later on when you go back home, you'll see them around. How will you get along with them? Just tell me that . . ."

After Zhima put the phone down, she leaned against the sofa in a daze. Danni walked over. "What's wrong? Has something happened? I know that if you get a phone call from home, eight or nine times out of ten, it isn't good news."

Zhima thought to herself. She'd been on the phone so long, and Danni was so quick that she probably had already figured it out. It would be better to just tell her and let her suggest something. So she told Danni what was going on with Apricot. Before she'd finished, Danni interrupted, "Oh, I know. They plan to act first and report it later. These days, people are more and more accomplished in hiding illegal pregnancies. Impersonating someone, colluding to conceal a pregnancy. Collective offenses. My God!"

Head lowered, Zhima said, "Don't use words I don't understand. Just tell me what I should do."

"What can I say? Didn't you tell her you didn't want to do it? You said the right thing. Don't look so woebegone. All right, all right, off you go. Get lunch ready." With that, Danni went to check on Tiantian's homework.

Over lunch and in front of Zhima, Danni told Auntie Li about the situation. Auntie Li's face darkened. Composing herself, she said to Zhima, "This won't do. It's against the law to use a fake ID!" Uncle Liu tried to soften her words. "Take it easy. Nothing's been done yet, but we have to cut this off at the pass." Zhima couldn't swallow even one mouthful of food.

That afternoon, as she was cleaning the windowpanes, Zhima saw her reflection in the glass—round face, narrow eyes, wide mouth, short hair with bangs cut straight across her forehead. Zhima was startled. Wasn't this Apricot? Even the timid smile at the corners of her mouth was just like Apricot's. If Zhima really did take a pregnancy test in place of Apricot, the doctor would never catch on. Feng was clever to choose Zhima, but Zhima was sure she would not do it. Auntie Li had said this was against the law. Zhima understood this principle. The tough part was how to tell Feng. Behind Feng was Apricot, and behind Apricot was Xishu's uncle's family, and behind the uncle's family were Father-in-law and Mother-in-law. Behind them? A whole village of men and women, old and young. On top of all this, when Zhima first came to Beijing to work, it was Apricot's sister-in-law who had brought her along . . .

Zhima's feelings were as jumbled as a clump of dry grass. She turned her face away from the glass and stood sideways to clean the windows. She didn't want to look at her face. In the blink of an eye, her face had changed into Apricot's.

Apricot, how could you be so weak-willed: your man told you to have a child and so you're having one? Zhima cursed her. *So, if you have the child and it's another daughter, then what? Anyway, how will you pay the fine of several tens of thousands of* yuan? *The child will have to have food and clothing, and later on will have to go to school. Supporting three children—won't you be the one having a rough time? Birth, birth, birth: all farmers know is giving birth. What's the point? Look at Uncle Liu and Auntie Li—they raised four children, all with good prospects. They all left—went abroad to struggle for their futures. Who stayed with the father and mother to take care of them in old age? When people reach old age, they can't be without caregivers in the family for even one day. And they also have to hire a housekeeper to help out. Suppose you do have one child with you—for example, Danni and her husband. They're so busy all day long, how can they take care of their parents? They struggle to keep their jobs; they worry about being laid off. If they lose their jobs and incomes, how can they bring up their child? Tuition alone at good schools in the city is enough to scare the hell out of you; the average person can't afford it. Danni and her husband have the filial piety to take care of her parents, but they lack the time.*

In Zhima's five years in the city, she'd seen a lot. Articles about unemployment appeared in the newspapers every day—waiting for jobs, getting jobs, but Zhima knew that in the city only one kind of job would always be available, no matter what. That was being a housekeeper, because no urban parent wanted to take care of children, and no urban children had time to take care of the elderly.

For the moment, while she was grumbling about Apricot, Zhima had forgotten that she herself had had one child too many. Zhima thought of the village children. No one watched them or taught them. All day, they played wildly at the side of the road, rolling around until they were like muddy monkeys. Ever since Zhima had left home, Gang had never had grades higher than seventy percent. Yan had just started first grade, so Zhima couldn't tell yet if she had the right stuff to be a student. And she didn't know, either, if the problem was that the village teacher wasn't very good or if Gang and Yan weren't diligent students. In her years away from home, Zhima hadn't supervised the children. How could she tell other people what was right? All year long, Xishu worked the land and raised pigs. When he got home, there wasn't even anyone there to cook dinner. Gang was only seven years old: he could carry firewood and start the fire. He also had to water the garden and feed the poultry. How could he study hard? That's the way all the village children grew up. Zhima had been the same. When they grew up, what could they do?

The men left to work, but they lacked the education to be electricians, so they could work only as bricklayers building walls, foundations, or houses. Or they worked for moving companies, and all the money they earned went into their bellies. It was just those sixteen- and seventeen-year-old girls who could find lighter work—as waitresses or hairdressers. They didn't need an education to scare up work like this. But how would they get along in the future? They'd get married and have children, and in the blink of an eye, they'd be more than thirty years old. When they were as old as Zhima, what would they be able to do except work as housekeepers? These days, even that wasn't easy. *If you could barely read the directions for electric appliances, could you expect a raise from your employer? All the villagers lead their lives in this muddleheaded way, and still they want to have more children. Fuck!*

Zhima recalled that the first time she went home an old woman had asked her, "Where did you go?" Zhima answered that she'd gone to Beijing. Where is Beijing? In the north, far away. How did you get there? By train. What's a train? How can people ride in it? Is it pulled by oxen or horses? No matter how Zhima explained it, she couldn't make the woman understand. Zhima laughed so hard that she had to rub away tears. When Zhima went home last year, it was the farmers' off-season, so the men and women were all squatting at the foot of the wall and gabbing as they took in the sun—which daughters-in-law were filial, which ones were sharp as knives, which household had a three-legged calf, which household's hen was sitting on her nest. On cloudy days, they went inside to play poker. When the women invited Zhima to play cards with them, she said, "Let's just play for fun, not for money." They said, "What's the point in playing if we don't play for money?" Zhima said, "I don't have any money." Someone said, "If you don't, who does? You've been in the city so many years that you must have plenty of money by now." Zhima was both annoyed and amused. She played one evening, and was really upset when she lost four *yuan*, eight *jiao*. She didn't dare play again.

But if she didn't play cards and there wasn't a TV, what could she do after dark? One couldn't go to bed right after dinner every day. Zhima said, "Let's just talk. If you want to know something, just ask me." Someone said, "I heard that Old Wang's daughter went into the city and became a housekeeper. It's said that she lives in a villa. What's a villa? Is it a place especially for growing trees?" Zhima said, "No. A villa is a house, a house like ours—with its own entrance and yard." The woman said, "If a villa is a house like ours, why go to the city to work?" Zhima was stumped.

Someone asked, "I've heard it's easy to earn money as a housekeeper. Are housekeepers bullied?" Zhima said, "It all depends. If the employers are nice people, they won't bully you." Someone else asked, "I've heard that being a housekeeper is like being a long-term hired hand on a farm—you're not asked to eat at the same table with your employers. Does the family you work for ask you to eat with them?" Zhima answered, "Ever since I went to Beijing, I've eaten with whatever family I was working for." Someone said, "I don't care how things are going. Even if I were poorer, I couldn't let my daughter-in-law work as a housekeeper for someone else. For example, if you work as a housekeeper in the hospital, you have to wash the old people's . . . wash their bottoms. Just look at Goudan, who lives on the south side of the village. He built a new house all right, but the money for it was all earned by his daughter-in-law washing people's bottoms every day . . ." They all laughed so hard that they couldn't catch their breath. Zhima felt unhappy.

Aside from farming their small plots of land, people like this either played cards or squatted next to the wall all day. They were too lazy to even listen to the radio. *It serves them right that they are poor,* Zhima thought resentfully. *And still they keep right on having babies. They give birth to people like themselves, who—in a lifetime—won't get any education, won't have any prospects, won't have good lives. A person comes into this world—and for what?* In the past, when she was still at home, Zhima didn't think of these things. But it was different now. Even if she didn't want to think, her brain spun on its own. If she were reincarnated, she certainly wouldn't live like this. At least, she wouldn't live the way these villagers did. She suddenly thought, what Danni had said a few days ago wasn't completely right. Danni had said that Zhima was divided in half—her body in Beijing, her mind at home. This was only half right. When Zhima thought of her home, it was her own children she thought of. She thought of Gang and Yan—that they wouldn't grow up to have lives like hers. But Zhima didn't think about the other villagers—not at all. She sort of looked down on them. They told her to use a fake ID on Apricot's behalf, but if she did that, wouldn't she simply be like them?

Zhima was on tenterhooks the whole day—afraid the phone would ring. She was worried about what to say if Feng phoned again: what could she say that would put an end to Feng's idea?

By the following day, Zhima's face had become much thinner. It was Danni who made a fuss as she called her attention to this. But Zhima was happy about it. She began going into the bathroom three times a day to look in the mirror. She reduced her *mantou* intake from two to just half of one. She thought if she lost weight she would no longer resemble Apricot. And if she didn't look like Apricot, she wouldn't have to take the pregnancy test for her.

In the morning, the entire family had gone out except Uncle Liu. When the phone rang, it was like the squawking of a crow. Zhima purposely ignored it. It rang for a long time before Uncle Liu shouted from the bathroom: "Zhima, answer the phone. Maybe Auntie Li ran into some problem."

No sooner had Zhima picked up the phone than she heard Feng's voice. For a moment, she wanted to throw the receiver down, but she didn't dare. As she stood there in silence, the receiver grew as heavy as a brick.

Feng said, "Zhima, I heard you. Listen to me. Last night, Apricot's husband phoned again. He asked me to tell you that if you take the pregnancy test for Apricot, he won't let you do it for nothing. He said he's already mailed Apricot's ID card. After you send him proof that you took the pregnancy test, he'll give you five hundred *yuan*. He'll give it personally to Xishu."

"So much?!" Zhima blurted out.

"Quite a lot, isn't it? As much as we earn in a month, isn't it?" All of a sudden, Feng's voice turned merry. "The last few years, Apricot's husband has collected trash in Zhengzhou. He's made a lot of money. He's willing to part with some of it because he wants Apricot to bear a son for him. You don't have to worry: when the time comes, if he doesn't give you the money, I'll go after him!"

Zhima said, "If he wants to give me money, then for sure I can't do it. What kind of person would that make me?"

"Ah, just look at yourself." Feng tut-tutted. "You're brain-dead. Why is it that the longer you stay in Beijing, the denser you get? What kind of person would that make you? A good person, a warm-hearted person, a person who knows the meaning of friendship. If villagers see someone dying and don't save him, then their consciences must have been eaten by dogs. He wants to give you the money; it isn't you who demanded it. These days everyone talks of fair trade. This is fair enough . . ."

Zhima thought Feng seemed to have all the arguments. She herself couldn't say anything.

"Zhima, we're all women. Can't you look at it from Apricot's standpoint?" Feng said, "This has to be done in a hurry. Apricot's belly is sticking out more and more every day. If Yang Baoguo finds out and ties her up and takes her in for an abortion, just think about what she'll have to go through. Zhima, why aren't you saying anything? Are you so hard-hearted? . . . Give me your address. When I get Apricot's ID, I'll come by and style your hair the way it is in Apricot's photo. We can't let anyone find out . . ."

"Don't you dare!" Zhima glanced over at Uncle Liu's room. "I don't want that money, and I don't want to be Apricot, either. Don't call me again." Zhima put the phone down. She'd been holding the receiver so tightly that it was damp and sticky. The palm of her hand was sweaty.

She had no sooner hung up than Uncle Liu emerged from his room, a newspaper in his hand. With a smile, he said, "Come, I'll show you an article. It's about something in Miyang in Henan." Uncle Liu spread the newspaper out on the tea table and pointed to a big headline. "Look. 'Ambition Beats Poverty: A Farm Girl Has Passed the Entrance Exam for the Aerospace University.' Come, read it for yourself."

Zhima took the newspaper, but she was embarrassed to read it aloud. She had long since forgotten most of the words she'd learned in school. She read haltingly, and people joked about this. Placing the newspaper on her knees, she buried her head in it. The newspaper said that a farm girl whose parents were both sick and whose family was so poor that they couldn't afford tuition had gone all over on Sundays and vacations, collecting plastic bottles, cardboard, and other discarded things. She had sold them and saved the money for tuition. She had begun doing this in primary school and had continued until she graduated from high school. She had always been first in her class. Then she had passed the entrance exam to the Aerospace University in Beijing. The article gave her name and village, and a photo showed her smiling broadly. She was so poor she had to collect garbage, but she had made her way to the university! As Zhima read this, tears ran down her face.

"Why are you crying? Silly child." Uncle Liu sat down across from Zhima, clipped out the article, and gave it to her. He told her to keep the article and take it with her for Gang and Yan to read when she went home for the harvest. Maybe it would encourage them to study hard. Wiping away tears, Zhima promised to do this. She folded the article carefully into four parts, went to her room, opened the cupboard, wrapped it in a handkerchief, and placed it under her clothes.

In the cupboard there was also a yellow cloth wrapper in which she kept other things to take home. Noticing it, she had to unwrap it and lightly stroke the things inside. Inside the bag were a durable fall shirt and pants in a date-red color that wouldn't show the dirt: they were for Xishu. Zhima had bought them ages ago—before Spring Festival—when she'd gone with Auntie Li to a commodities fair. She'd spent a lot on them. There was also a pink dress, trimmed with white lace on the sleeves and neckline; it was dazzlingly pretty. Danni had given it to her for Yan because it was too small for Tiantian. If Yan put this dress on, all the villagers would come to see her. Tiantian's father had given Zhima a stack of hard-covered notebooks and a box of colored pens for Gang to use in school. In the evening when no one was around, Zhima frequently took these things out. She looked at them under the light, touching them one by one. They were so smooth, so warm, so bright and neat. Every time she looked at them, she was happy. She couldn't look at them enough!

As time went on, the cloth bag bulged with more and more things, and the time for Zhima to go home drew closer and closer. The pale yellow of the cloth wrapper reminded her of the brilliant golden wheat fields, and she could smell the wheat's full-blown scent. It was the fragrance that came from the sun shining on the straw, the fragrance from the wheat paste pressed from kernels of wheat. When she closed her eyes, she saw Gang and Yan jumping on the bales of straw. Zhima closed the cloth wrapper, and looked at the wall calendar. Harvest time was drawing closer by the day and she still had to buy a few clothes for her parents and in-laws . . .

Feng's voice jumped from Zhima's brain: five hundred *yuan*. How many things could she buy for her family with five hundred *yuan*? At a minimum, she could buy two tires for the tractor and pay a year's tuition for Gang and Yan. To earn five hundred *yuan,* one ordinarily had to raise two big fat pigs and thirty large roosters. It was a month's wages for Zhima in the city . . .

Why did she feel as if she'd lost something?

That evening, she had just finished watching the news when the telephone rang. Since Auntie Li was home, Zhima didn't answer it. Most of the phone calls were for Danni. Auntie Li answered the phone, listened a moment, and then shouted toward the kitchen: "Young Guo, it's for you."

Zhima stuck her head out of the kitchen, and gestured. Auntie Li didn't catch on and shouted again. Zhima slipped quietly over to Auntie Li and whispered, "Is it a man or a woman?" Auntie Li answered loudly, "A man. As soon as I heard the Henan accent, I knew it must be Xishu." With that, she handed the receiver to Zhima.

Xishu? Zhima trembled. Was Xishu phoning her? She grabbed the receiver, and a man's hoarse voice immediately roared into her eardrum: *"Zhima, how dare you? Why is it so hard for you to do a favor for someone else?!"* Zhima's lips quivered. Before she had time to say hello to Father-in-law, he said, "Apricot is in difficulty. We have to help her out. Even if her family wasn't going to give you money, we'd have to help. Isn't it just a matter of taking one bus ride? We aren't asking you to walk to the pregnancy-testing place!"

While he was wheezing, Zhima interjected, "Father-in-law, it isn't that I don't want to help. It's just that what Apricot wants me to do is against the law."

Father-in-law interrupted her: "Tut-tut. Lots of things in this world are against the law. When you had Yan, you said it was against the law. Now she's already growing up, isn't she? In the villages, relationships are the law. You must understand that our laws and Beijing's laws aren't the same."

Zhima's heart was pounding. She thought her voice was so soft that it must be almost inaudible. She said, "Apricot should get an abortion. Otherwise, if she has the child, she'll be fined so much money that it won't be worth it. They should save this money so their other children can go to school. That would be much better . . ."

Father-in-law grew even angrier. "*Don't you worry about them!* Just tell me: will you do it or not? If you do it, our whole family will feel a lot better. If you don't, how will your mother-in-law and I still have the face to see people?"

Zhima didn't say anything for a long time. He kept shouting *Hello!* Finally, Zhima said, "Let me talk with Xishu." Father-in-law responded, "He's gone to work. There's no point in your talking with him, anyway. If you don't do as I say, I'll tell your parents! If you don't do this, you . . . I don't see how you'll have the face to come home . . ."

In a flash, Zhima's tears gushed out. Listening to the tut-tutting coming from the receiver, Zhima felt her eyes blur. For a minute, she couldn't even see where the phone was. Danni walked over quickly, took the receiver, and sighed. "*Aiya.* Your Henan people are just too much. They take turns with their bombshells. They're really bullheaded. It seems that if you don't impersonate Apricot, you'll be taken off the village rolls . . ." Auntie Li nodded her head. "Yes indeed. Don't we see the Henan people being criticized all the time in the press? Now I see why." Uncle Liu put his newspaper down and corrected Auntie Li, "Don't always say 'Henan people, Henan people.' This phenomenon is rife in China . . ."

Zhima didn't hear one word of what the family was saying. She went back to the kitchen, sat down on a small stool, and covered her face with her hands. She wanted to cry, but couldn't. There was no place for the anger inside her to go. If she were a pressure cooker, she would explode.

What was wrong with Henan people? Zhima thought resentfully. Suddenly, she recalled what Uncle Liu had told her once: Henan has nearly one hundred million people. How many a hundred million were, Zhima couldn't imagine. It must be similar to when the locusts invaded: the whole sky was like a sandstorm, and when the insects fell to the ground, they covered the wheat seedlings in a dense mass. You couldn't see one bit of green. At Spring Festival, when Zhima went home, the train was like a hemp bag—jam-packed with people. People sat on the luggage racks and under the seats: it was more crowded than a chicken coop. Once, Zhima couldn't get a ticket, and had to stand up all the way from Zhumadian to Beijing. Her legs were swollen from standing, and Zhima thought it was because she hadn't been able to get to the toilet. You didn't dare drink any water on the train, because there was no way to use the toilet. Before the train even started moving, four or five people had squeezed in there. Every time Zhima took the train home, she stuck her money into her socks. Although it hurt to walk, still with every step you took, you knew the money was there; you felt safe. It was more secure than sewing it into your clothing. Someone from another village had sewn his money into the front of his trousers. At midnight, when he dozed off, someone pulled it out. How skilled thieves were these days!

Zhima had no idea how there could be so many people in the world. She just knew that most of them were so poor they fought over a pot of rice. Not everyone could get some. For those with nothing to eat, stealing was the only alternative. People always say that rabbits won't eat the weeds near their own nest. That wasn't so. If rabbits were starving, they'd eat food wherever they could find it. It didn't matter if you were a fellow villager or a relative. In Zhima's village, someone had made off with the high voltage wire that ran all the way from the village to the town. And so, just when Zhima's family had finished building their new home, electricity in the village was cut off, and it was most of a year before the villagers could get hooked up again. Everything was dark until the county government approved the budget. Then the electricity was reconnected. Everyone knew that the thief was hiding right under their eyes, but if you didn't catch him in the act, you could do nothing but stare at him. You could curse him as much as you liked, but he pretended not to hear.

Another year, Zhima's family was raising a pig. When it weighed more than a hundred pounds and was almost ready to be butchered, an opera troupe came to the village. People in the family took turns watching the pig while other family members went to the opera. The last night of the opera, Zhima just had to see it. When she came home, she was so sleepy that she fell right into bed and went to sleep. When she got up the next morning, she couldn't open the door. She shouted to someone to help, and he discovered that the door had been wired shut: when the thief stole the pig, he had locked Zhima inside so that she couldn't chase after him.

And then there was the case of the simpleton called Jughead, who lived on the west side of the village. He was raising an ox to plow the land, and he slept in the same room with the animal to keep anyone from stealing it. But Jughead slept like the dead—never heard anything. Someone suggested that before going to bed he tie two ropes to the ox's horns and then fasten the ends to the pillars on each side of the room. As if this wasn't enough, he should also tie a rope to the ox's leg and fasten the other end to the leg of his bed. Sometimes Jughead wasn't so stupid. He followed this routine faithfully every night. One night, sure enough, a thief came. The thief didn't go in through the front gate, but hollowed out a hole in the wall in the back. He came in and took his time untying the ropes on the ox's horns. Then he dragged the ox toward the hole in the wall. Even with so much commotion, Jughead just went on snoring and dreaming. Luckily, the thief didn't notice the rope running from the ox's leg to the bed. As he tried to pull the ox through the hole, the bed got stuck. In the struggle, the ox swung its tail against Jughead's head, and Jughead woke up with a start. He saw the big hole in the back wall and hurried through it, but the thief had already run off. This sort of story was common enough at home. As Zhima saw it, when bad guys like this were caught, they should all be executed.

Zhima raised her head and massaged her eyes. She felt as if something were leaping in her heart: her chest felt hot and cold by turns. And yet her head felt as if she had just awakened from a good sleep. It was absolutely clear. No matter what, Zhima didn't want the people from the countryside to lose face. She didn't want to make Uncle Liu's family look down on Henan people. She knew she had to test her will against the Zhao villagers' will. And she'd been in Beijing for five years—she knew what she had to do.

The next morning, after the family finished breakfast, Zhima washed the dishes and deftly tidied up all the rooms. Then, carrying a bulging mesh bag from her room, she walked into the living room. She lowered her head and called out to Auntie Li.

Startled, Auntie Li looked up at Zhima and then at the mesh bag on the floor. "Young Guo, what are you doing?"

"I'm leaving," Zhima answered, still looking at the floor. She had polished the floor until it was brighter than the pot rack at home. Her lips were quivering, but she didn't say anything. She wanted to thank Auntie Li and the others for their concern for her in the past three years and for helping her learn so much about proper conduct. She wanted to say that she didn't want to leave, either, but if she didn't, Feng and the people at home would keep pressuring her so much she'd have to take the pregnancy test for Apricot. She was leaving only because she had no alternative. If she hid in a place where Feng couldn't find her, Feng wouldn't phone anymore . . . She had so much to say, but she didn't know where to start.

With difficulty, Uncle Liu shifted his walker and said in a quavering voice, "You're leaving? Why?"

"After I go, Feng can't find me," Zhima said.

Everyone was stupefied. Danni, who had stayed home that day, walked in and heard what Zhima said. She began chuckling. But Danni's laughter was interrupted by the urgent ringing of the phone, which sounded like a rooster announcing the dawn and urging Zhima out the door. She said, "Listen. It's Feng again—I can't argue with her. I don't want to talk with her."

When Danni picked up the phone, Zhima had already turned to leave. Danni shouted at her, "Wait. It's Xishu! If you want to go, at least wait until you've talked with him." Zhima stood stock-still. "Is it really Xishu? Are you sure? I'm afraid this time it's my own father calling." Danni was a little annoyed. "It's really Xishu. I know his voice, don't I?"

Flustered, Zhima put her things down and took the receiver. So many complaints were suddenly gushing up in her heart; something mixed with acid and bitterness was stuck in her chest. She wanted to curse Xishu: *You skunk, you swagger foolishly all day long as you drive the tractor. You go to hell! Not until now did you think about calling me. If you'd waited any longer, you couldn't have found me.* But what she said was, "Xishu."

She heard his familiar voice, like a big bell ringing next to her ear. Xishu said, "Zhima, I want to ask you something: Are you Apricot?" Zhima answered, "No, I'm not Apricot. I'm Zhima." Xishu's voice shook Zhima's ear until it hurt: "I don't want you to change into Apricot. You aren't Apricot. You're Zhima. See?" Zhima said, "Uh." Something seemed stuck in her throat. Xishu said, "Just stay out of it. I'm here and I'll take care of it." Then he added, "If we could turn the clock back seven or eight years, we shouldn't have had Yan, either. Actually, Apricot doesn't want to have the baby, either. She won't blame you." After a pause, he said, "Zhima, are you there? Say something."

A heavy stone was falling from Zhima's heart. It hit the ground with a thud. The cotton she was walking on became as solid as the snow-covered ground. Suddenly, Zhima shouted, "Xishu, why didn't you tell me you'd bought a tractor?" Xishu cleared his throat. "How did you find out?" Zhima said, "Never mind how I found out. Anyhow, I did." Xishu said cheerfully,

"I had my reasons for not telling you. First, I was afraid you'd worry that we didn't have enough money and wouldn't let me buy it, and then I wouldn't have it in time for the farming season." Xishu went on, "All these years, we've had a plow and rakes, but we haven't had a four-wheeled tractor. For turning over the land and harrowing it, we've had to borrow a vehicle from others. Now that we have our own tractor, we can haul fertilizer and seed and transport foodstuffs. After the harvest, we can turn over the land whenever we want to. We don't have to beg from others anymore. This is much better than buying anything else."

Zhima didn't say anything. She thought Xishu was right. The last several years, they were always worried during the busy season. You could borrow a tractor from others, but they needed to use it, too. You had to wait until they were finished with it. You waited and waited. On top of that, you were in debt for the favor. Zhima had been wanting for a long time to buy a tractor for Xishu, but there wasn't any money. She couldn't make the dream come true.

"Okay. And the second reason for not telling me?" Zhima didn't intend to let Xishu off the hook lightly.

"The second . . . ," Xishu swallowed hard. "The second is that I wanted . . . I wanted to wait until you came home for the harvest. I would drive the tractor to Zhumadian to meet you. It would be a surprise for you. You'd be so happy. Just like on TV shows—I'd have a pleasant surprise for you."

"Forget the TV show. You're just buttering me up." With her mouth, Zhima was blaming him, but in her heart she felt a rush of peppery heat. All at once, she remembered one time when she went home and had decided to visit her mother. At the edge of the village, she ran into Little Bud, who asked where she was going. Zhima said she was going to see her mother. Little Bud said, "Do you have a mother?" Zhima said, "Who doesn't?" Little Bud said, "If you do, why doesn't she pick and wash your quilts? The quilts in your home are so filthy, and yet she doesn't come to help you out." Zhima said, "My mother is sick, and she lives across the river. How would she find the time?" With that, Zhima went to the ferry crossing. Later, she thought about what Little Bud had said. The more she thought about it, the more she thought something wasn't quite right. She felt uneasy. When she got home, she ripped into Xishu: "Tell me, does Little Bud come over here a lot? How does she know our quilts are filthy? Tell me the truth!" Xishu was dumbfounded. "As soon as I open my eyes, I'm up and working. The two kids are anxious to get to school. I count myself lucky if I can eat breakfast. The quilts are never folded and put away during the year—just thrown on the bed. Whoever comes over sees them. How was I supposed to know that Little Bud would notice?" Zhima wasn't ready to let him off. She said, "How come it's just Little Bud who knows our quilts are filthy? Who knows what she's been up to under our quilts?" Angered, Xishu said, "Don't go looking for trouble. It's been so many years since you've lived at home that if I'd been fooling around, it wouldn't have been just with Little Bud, but also with Flower and Leaf." In his fury, Xishu was lighting one cigarette after another. Gang and Yan both started yelling, "Little Bud hasn't been here, and neither has any other woman!"

Mulling it over now, with Xishu on the phone, Zhima realized that Xishu didn't have an easy life, either. All these years, he'd been bringing up two children, acting as both father and mother to them. And night after night, the quilt was cold, without anyone to even warm his feet. Yet, Xishu had never once complained to Zhima. All of a sudden, Zhima was determined to buy some cloth and have a seamstress make it up into two quilt covers. When she got home, she would slip the quilts into the covers—just like city people—and it wouldn't be necessary to pick and wash and mend the quilts. This was an expedient way to keep them clean. It would also enhance Xishu's "quality of life" a little. If someone like Xishu—a man who neither drank nor gambled—was bent on buying a tractor, was that too much for him to ask?

But Zhima didn't say this. She shouted, "*Who did you borrow from to buy the tractor?!* Couldn't you have waited until our debts were paid off? Why did you have to be in such a hurry?" Xishu wasn't at all ruffled. He just said calmly, "The pigs have brought good prices in the last few days. I got more than two thousand *yuan* for them. I also borrowed three thousand from my brother. Altogether, that was enough. Just think about it: now that I've bought a tractor, my work is much easier. Isn't it a lot better than waiting? Isn't it worth it? I talked with the people we owe money to. They said it would be okay for now to just pay the interest."

Zhima still wasn't ready to let him off the hook. "And what about the trailer to go with the tractor? You need at least that, and probably it'll cost another two or three thousand." Xishu began to stammer a little. "Oh, that's a cinch. Later this year, the old mother pig will have more piglets. After I raise them and sell them, I'll have the money for the trailer. For now, I've hammered a wooden frame together and added two old tires, and the tractor pulls it just fine." Zhima couldn't help but laugh. "If I don't do what Apricot's family wants, how will I have the face to come home for the harvest?" For a second, Xishu was flummoxed. Then he said, "Well, then, don't come home. I'll hire a combine to harvest the wheat. That's okay." Zhima said, "What about the autumn harvest?" Xishu said, "Don't come back then, either. Now that I have the tractor, I can swap labor with others." Zhima said, "Then what about Spring Festival? If I don't go home then, either, I'll be stuck in Beijing all my life and never go back to Zhao Village. You'll have to find someone else to wash and mend the quilts for you."

Xishu didn't say anything. It seemed he hadn't thought this far ahead. After a long time, she heard his voice coming from far away. "It's okay if you don't come home. After I've saved some money, I'll go to Beijing to see you!"

Zhima put the phone down, and sat down in a trance on the mesh bag in the doorway. She thought it was Xishu who understood her after all. After talking with him, she was no longer afraid. But should she leave or not? If she didn't, Feng would call her again. All of a sudden, Zhima regretted that she hadn't had her tubes tied after having Yan. She shouldn't have believed her mother-in-law, who had said that women who had their tubes tied were useless. Auntie Li had told her that was really ignorant. If Zhima had had her tubes tied, she wouldn't have to have a pregnancy test every three months, and she could have saved quite a lot of money. And if she'd had her tubes tied, Feng wouldn't be making so much trouble for her. Why was it that it took so long to understand some things?

Auntie Li walked over and patted her on the shoulder. "Okay. Take it easy. Take your bag back to your room. You have to get lunch ready." Zhima hesitated. Looking up, she asked, "If I don't go, then what will we do when Feng calls again?" Suddenly, the whole family roared with laughter. Zhima was confused.

Auntie Li said with a straight face, "Just look at you. You see why I call you a little idiot. How come you don't know even a little strategy? Do you really think that leaving here is the only way to duck the issue with Apricot? Let me tell you what we'll do. Beginning now, don't answer the phone for a few days. Listen up, everyone. When you answer the phone, if someone wants Young Guo, say she's left and isn't working here any longer. If the person asks where she's gone, say you don't know. Have I made myself clear?" They all said they understood. Smiling, Danni put in a word, "This time, it's our turn to cooperate in being devious."

Embarrassed, Zhima began smiling. She thought that she actually was quite idiotic. This way, they'd defeat Feng and Apricot and even Father-in-law. In the end, it was the city people who were "thief-smart."

Zhima went to the kitchen. While she was washing the rice and picking out the vegetables, she felt a small piece of grit rubbing against her heart: if they did things Auntie Li's way, wouldn't Zhima be lying? The only ones fooled would be Feng and Apricot. Wouldn't someone as quick as Feng realize that Zhima had "disappeared" on purpose to avoid her? Feng certainly wouldn't have anything good to say to Apricot about Zhima. And who knows how angry Father-in-law would be? It wouldn't take even three days before all the villagers would know that Zhima had no heart. Even if you had a hundred mouths, you wouldn't have any way to explain yourself.

It had been more than a year since she'd last gone home. She had been looking forward to going home for the wheat harvest. But now she couldn't go back.

A life could be extinguished before it was even born. That was really sad. Zhima sighed lightly. *But in the end, what's the point of a life coming into this world?* She thought, *If life means only suffering, probably it's better not to be born in the first place.* Thinking of it like this, she hardened her heart.

A little worried, Zhima looked out the window. The city's buildings were piled on top of one another. Cars were chasing cars. People were jostling people. Looking south, she saw a gray sky filled with clouds. She felt that all at once Zhao Village had become more distant—so far away that she felt estranged. Over that great distance she could no longer locate her home.

Atop Beijing's Mountain of Gold

Walking sideways through the alley, Li Da felt like a crab.

An electric rice cooker—suspended by a plastic rope—was hanging from his neck onto his chest. Tucked under his left arm was a flattened carton that had once held a TV set; it was as big as a window. All he could do was drag it forward a step at a time. Tucked under his right arm was a bundle of old newspapers tied loosely together, so every few steps he had to stop and reassemble them. He was holding a thermos bottle in his left hand and a plastic stool in his right. On his back, he was carrying a mesh bag with a hole in it. It was like carrying a hill, and it was bulging and swaying. If he didn't have to walk with his feet, he might have carried something on his insteps as well.

Li Da wished he could grow a hundred hands and feet so that he could lug everything away. Whatever he couldn't take tonight wouldn't be here tomorrow. He was carrying too many things, all seemingly glued to his body. He breathed heavily with each step. Li Da had once seen a crab walking sideways in a glass tank at a roadside restaurant. He'd also seen crab shells in a garbage bag—a heap of big feet, little feet, hairy feet, and feet with pincers: they grew only feet—no flesh. He moved his body sideways, shifting himself step by step. This way, it was easier for him to move all the big and small objects, but his view of anything behind him was obstructed. When he heard any movement nearby, he stuck close to the wall to make room for the shadows to pass by. Li Da preferred the dark. When the street lamps were on, this city took on a different appearance: it became somehow friendlier. The trash cans reflected in the light at the corner of the wall were like hidden gold gleaming in the dark.

When he got home, it was already midnight. Afraid that his appearance would frighten the soundly sleeping girl, he stood outside the door and unloaded everything and then very quietly dragged the things into the house. If he left them in the courtyard, tomorrow you wouldn't be able to see even one fiber. In this place—not part of the city but not quite like a village, either—people stole even from their neighbors. However someone got something into his bowl—whatever it was, it was his food. With a *hua-la* sound, things spilled out from the bottom of the mesh bag. The light went on inside. Shuanzi

143

rubbed his eyes, and in a blur saw the things scattered on the floor. He said, "Hey, Dad, you've struck it rich!"

Li Da poured a dipper of cool water down his throat, and said, "I caught up with some people who were moving. These city people—they throw everything out."

Shuanzi called him to dinner. After searching briefly through the things on the floor, he kicked them and said, "How come you didn't bring a TV set back?"

Li Da's mouth was busy slurping the congee, but finally a few words slid out: "TV? I wanted to get a cell phone, too, to make it easier to call home."

The girl woke up, jumped down, and ran toward a stuffed bear. All its hair had fallen out, so it was like a mangy dog. The girl hugged it tight, and said, "Grandpa, you're great. You're like Santa Claus. You give me presents every day."

It hadn't been a year since the girl had come to the city to go to school. Although she hadn't learned anything else, she'd learned to say Santa Claus. "You're full of nonsense," Li Da scolded the girl. "If I'm Santa Claus, then what's left for your dad and mom to do? Go to sleep!" Instead of going back to sleep, the girl squatted on the floor, single-mindedly picking through the heap of things. She wanted to find a little something more. Li Da put his bowl and chopsticks down. He was quite satisfied with his haul from today's efforts:

A pair of almost new leather shoes, just missing some stitches at the toes; a pair of walking shoes that were in good shape except for a hole burned into one upper; a sweater with a zipper—so what if the zipper was broken; a blanket—just a little dirty in one corner—would be like new after it was washed; the rice cooker's electrical switch was probably kaput; the thermos bottle surely wouldn't keep water hot, but it could hold cool water; the plastic stool wasn't missing any of its legs, and when Li Da sat down on it, it didn't collapse . . . These things were all good things—things that everyone used every day. He couldn't understand why anyone would toss them out.

Li Da was satisfied with today's take. He put his bowl down and lay down and went to sleep. Dazed, he heard Shuanzi ask, "Dad, it's almost time for the autumn harvest. When are you going to go back home? It'll take at least ten days to harvest the seven *mou* of corn. Fengmei takes care of an older couple and I'm delivering drinking water. Neither of us can get time off. If you're going to go, I have to get your ticket a few days ahead of time . . ."

Li Da didn't answer. He was snoring.

Actually, Li Da seldom went into the city's hutong—alleys. The people living in the old homes there were frugal: they collected old newspapers and bottles and sold them at the recycling center. You'd better not expect them to throw out even a nail.

Li Da had his own territory, a top-notch place overflowing with good things. He strolled there early every morning and again in the evening, and he never came home empty-handed.

Half a year ago, the first time Li Da touched the plastic garbage bags next to the wall, his fingers had shaken badly, and he'd sweated a lot before finally opening the bags. They were filled with vegetable leaves and cigarette butts— things like that. The choking, rotten smell forced him to turn his face away. He picked up a flattened tin can, and straightened up to go. Suddenly, spotting something shiny, he couldn't keep from looking into the plastic bag.

Under the vegetable leaves was a small box without a lid. A gleaming silver watch chain shone out from it. Li Da's heart thumped. He looked in all directions, and his hands trembled as he carefully weighed the box in his hand. He opened it and saw a watch face the size of an apricot and encircled in gold. It lay in Li Da's large palm. Nothing happened when he held it up to his ear. Could it be broken? But there were so many long and short hands moving with such vigor on the watch that he couldn't see the time. Dumbstruck, Li Da couldn't take a step. Should he put it down and go home? That'd be stupid, he couldn't give it up. Then take it and go. But could this be a trap? How could something so good happen to him? Li Da felt as if he were holding a time bomb in his hands; he didn't dare move.

I just picked it up. It belongs to whoever picked it up. It was just like picking up a radish at the side of the road, or a mushroom in a clump of grass: who would you give them back to? *Who deserves it more than I do? This was what people called a "lucky day!" The old saying "you shouldn't pick up things people left behind" meant you mustn't take things that others had lost, but if it was something someone had thrown away and you didn't pick it up, someone else would. If you picked it up, it was valuable. If you didn't pick it up but just left it in the garbage bag, before long it would go to the dump.* Convinced, Li Da squared his shoulders. He looked down happily and carefully at the watch and wiped the traces of sweat off it with his sleeve.

Suddenly, a window opened in a nearby light yellow house, and a woman with permed hair stuck her head out and shouted, "Hey, you. After you finish picking through the garbage, you have to tie the bag. Don't leave everything in a filthy mess!"

Li Da answered briefly, deftly slipped the watch into his pocket, and ran off.

He had picked up this watch; *he hadn't asked anyone for it*, thought Li Da as he ran off. If you stuck your hand out and asked someone for something, it was begging. Li Da's family had farmed for generations; they weren't beggars. Only when disaster struck did they beg. Some people would starve to death before they would beg. When Li Da had come to the city to take care of his granddaughter, he had looked for a little work. He hadn't come here to beg. The wheat at home would soon be ready to harvest. City people didn't have a chance to eat fresh wheat: why would he come to the city to beg? Li Da hadn't stuck his hand out and asked any city person for a watch: it was the watch that had come to Li Da. He couldn't have avoided this.

From then on, Li Da's skinny wrist sported a big, dazzling bright watch. Now and then, he lifted it up a little. Li Da liked to raise his arm up high and trace a large circle in the air, and then bring it level with his eyelid and look down at his watch again. That way, he made sure that everyone he ran into would see his watch. His arm ached from holding it up, and yet he couldn't get enough of seeing it. Li Da gradually discovered that with a watch to take charge of the time, people all did things by the time of day. When it said it was a certain time, you had to eat; when it said it was a certain time, you had to go to sleep. This watch was even more intimidating than the village mayor. After a few days, the girl came home from school crying, saying that she was late every day, and the teacher scolded her. Only then did Li Da realize that this watch didn't keep the right time: it was half an hour slow. The girl was crying. Li Da smiled: sure enough, this watch was one that someone didn't want and had thrown away, it wasn't something that Li Da had stolen!

From then on, Li Da kept thinking about the plastic garbage bags at the side of the road. In the small district called "Xiushui Garden," every morning and evening—like clockwork—the people in two- and three-story Western-style houses would bring out black garbage bags and set them down in front of their doors. If you didn't see this, you wouldn't know it: several times, Li Da opened the bags and was stunned at what they held.

So Li Da had work. At the same time he picked up the watch, he picked up work.

This "work" was a lot better than Li Da's former "work." He strolled in the small district every day, going about his "work." People who didn't under- stand said this was picking up garbage. People who did understand knew that Li Da was picking up money.

The first two months that Li Da was in the city, he had changed "jobs" several times. The work that Shuanzi gave him was to escort the girl to and from school. Shuanzi and his wife had been working in the city for a few years, and now their daughter, whom they'd left at home, was school age. Fengmei insisted on bringing their daughter to the city; she said there was a primary school here for children of migrant workers. The tuition the school charged was reasonable. Shuanzi and Fengmei rented a place and arranged for Li Da to come and cook for the girl and do the laundry. There were lots of criminals in the city. If no one took her to and from school, she might be kidnapped and sold. Shuanzi's mother had died years ago, so Li Da was responsible for both the home and the land. At first, Li Da hadn't wanted to move to the city. Shuanzi's two brothers, Suozi and Lianzi, were both married and had sons. Li Da thought it was a ridiculous idea to leave the family home and the grandsons behind and come here to look after his granddaughter. Li Da wasn't one bit happy when Shuanzi applied a lot of pressure. Over the phone, Shuanzi said, "Come, come. The wheat is all planted. What else can you do there? There's work in the city. I guarantee that if you come here, you won't want to leave." Li Da finally changed his mind.

Li Da went to the city by car and train. Not until he got to the city did he learn that city cars weren't called cars, but buses. Li Da thought this was a very odd name for them. They came gasping along, halting slowly at each stop, taking much longer than they should have. Looking out the window, you saw tall buildings—one after another—stretching toward the sky. They were so tall that you were afraid they'd collapse and the gawkers' necks would soon break. The streets were crowded with cars, crouched briefly like locusts and then leaping to life again, one following the other. The roads all over the city were covered with these "locusts." Looking at them made people dizzy. Shuanzi, who had come to meet him, kept talking, telling him the names and histories of this and that. Here and there were the office buildings of all kinds of scary authorities. Li Da was thinking giddily, *sure enough, this city is a great place. In the corners of the streets and the cracks of the walls, there are countless opportunities for work.*

Later, Shuanzi said, "Here we are. We're here." Disembarking from the bus, Li Da stood there like an idiot.

Opposite the bus stop stood a sheet-iron sign that said "Six-*li* Hamlet." Under the sign was an uneven concrete street. The power poles next to the street, the low red-tiled houses and yellow earth walls, the pigpens and chicken coops in the courtyards, the emaciated dogs and the garbage in front of the doors—everything was like his home village. Li Da felt he'd returned to the Li family village.

"This is called the suburbs. It was all we could afford," Shuanzi said. "Apartments in the city rent for at least a thousand *yuan* a month. Between what Fengmei and I earn every month, if we paid that much for rent, we'd have nothing for food. This place is better than places in the city. Look over to the east: that's where Fengmei works—" Looking in the direction that Shuanzi was pointing, Li Da was once more dumbstruck.

On the east side of the village, separated by a small river, was a long white fence, on which there were a lot of green leaves and clumps of pink flower buds. Through cracks in the fence, one could see a large, low-lying vegetable plot and a lot of small two- and three-story houses built in the center of the green field. One roof was violet blue, one bright red, and one jade green; the roofs weren't made of separate pieces of tile, but were a whole expanse of color. All the houses had black iron doors, and jets of water spurted out like mist from the ponds. They were like the foreign houses in movies.

"Fengmei works in that home, the one with the blue roof." Shuanzi's tone was happy, but then he lowered his voice right away. "She earns quite a lot, but she isn't allowed to come home. It's good that you've come, Dad. I feel better . . ."

Li Da interrupted unhappily, "You feel better, but I don't! I've left the wheat behind, and what for? Just to come to the city and waste time? In the time I'm going to be here I would have raised several pigs which would have been butchered. And then there are your two brothers' sons. They all say I'm playing favorites . . ."

Shuanzi gave him an ingratiating smile, lifted the baggage up to his shoulder, and said, "They're jealous that you've come to the city. They think you've come here just to enjoy yourself."

Li Da's face fell. After walking a short distance, they stopped in front of a tilted wooden gate. The courtyard wall was on the verge of collapsing. The sound of the girl's sharp laughter came rushing toward them. Li Da couldn't keep from turning around again to look at the white fence next to the river, the small houses' rooftops floating in the treetops like colorful clouds: they didn't seem like houses inhabited by people, but like places being offered to the gods . . .

"What's it called?" Li Da raised his chin, pointing at the houses on the riverbank, and asked coldly.

"That's . . . 'Xiushui Gardens,'" Shuanzi answered. "Only rich people live there. The houses are called villas."

Li Da snorted and said, "Another odd word!"

At the time, he didn't realize that just the garbage thrown out of these houses would feed him well.

A couple of weeks after Li Da went to the city, he secretly looked for a second job. In those days, while the girl was in school, he strolled all over for miles around. His search was frustrating. Restaurants were looking for young dishwashers and bus boys, beauty parlors wanted young girls to wash hair, and then there were also electricians, plumbers, and bricklayers—all skilled work, all requiring licenses. Construction companies were looking for ditch diggers and earth movers. When foremen saw him, they looked amused, and said, "Grandpa, what are you coming around for? This isn't an old folks' home." He stood for a while in front of a vegetable stand in the farmers' market. The vendor asked, "Do you want to buy something? If you don't, then stop blocking the way." He heard that all the vendors had come from villages and moved to government housing. It had been a long time since they'd farmed. They were like him, looking for work all day long. In the eyes of long-time residents, a new arrival was no different from a looting bandit. If you can get work, what will other people eat? In this world, someone was always starving while someone else was eating his fill. Li Da had been aware of this principle from the time he was young.

Work, work. There were a lot of buildings and a lot of cars in this city, but there were also a lot of doors. The kind of work that you could make money doing was all hidden behind closed doors. Li Da was strolling around listlessly, when without knowing why, he circled around a little creek and walked up to the main entrance of the villas.

The main entrance to "Xiushui Gardens" was imposing: its high, decorated archway was engraved with bronze characters. In front of the cast iron gate, which was painted black, was a horizontal red wooden pole, which kept cars out so that the drivers could be questioned first. Standing next to the entrance was a middle-aged man in paint-covered clothes; he seemed to be waiting for someone. He and Li Da took stock of each other, and then the man walked over and asked, "Can you sift sand?" Astonished, Li Da was speechless for a moment. When the man asked him again, Li Da hastened to say, "Yes, yes, I can." After saying something to the guard, the man told Li Da to follow him.

The first time Li Da strode into the complex of villas called "Xiushui Gardens," he was so dazzled by the clusters of forsythia along the roadside that he couldn't keep his eyes open. In the thickets, the small houses—with their pale yellow walls, their stainless steel window frames and balcony railings, their bay windows as large as walls—were like golden caskets in the sunshine. While he was walking, Li Da avoided looking around. He thought the whole of Xiushui Gardens was brilliant. He didn't know what kind of stones formed the surface of the path—they were bright enough to reflect a person's shadow, and so clean there wasn't even an ant to be seen. If you spat on them, they would probably turn slippery. Li Da was walking slowly with his heels stretched tight, as if he were walking on a table and if he took a misstep he would smash the bowls. Villas, ah, villas. Villas were really wonderful: the work he'd been looking for had been hidden in these villas all along.

In the courtyard in front of an empty house, coarse sand was piled up—spread out on the east side to be placed on the west side after being sifted. The interior of the house was being finished, and it was a lot of work to tear down walls and create open spaces. The foreman told Li Da what to do, and Li Da buried his head in the work. Never mind that Li Da was more than sixty years old. He could hoist a bag of wheat to his shoulders with no more effort than throwing a towel. In a short time, Li Da had sifted out a small pile of fine sand and had put the coarse sand to one side and then shoveled it outside the courtyard. He put everything in order. Sitting on the steps of the courtyard for a cigarette break, he narrowed his eyes to look at the three-foot-high pile of sand that he had sifted: it was sticking up like a small hill. In the sunshine, a mountain rose from the land, delicate and golden yellow, like fresh, just-ground cornmeal. From a little farther away, it was like wheat drying in the sun in the backyard, each grain fully ripe. For a moment, Li Da couldn't tell whether it was sand or wheat. He had to grab a handful of sand and smell it. Then he let go, and the sand slipped through his fingers and turned as colorless as water. *How could sand be compared with wheat?* he kidded himself. Both cornmeal and wheat were fragrant. Their scent was the scent of green grass, wheat straw, chicken shit, brushwood, and the sun-baked earth all mixed together with human odors from the whole village. It was the scent that could bring people back to life from the verge of starvation. But sand had no smell at all, and all sand—even fine sand—was abrasive . . .

He sifted sand for two days—always on tenterhooks because at noon and late in the afternoon, he had to slip away like a thief and meet the girl when she got out of school. He cooked lunch for her, but didn't take time to eat anything himself. He just rushed back to work. The third day, before work had even begun, the foreman walked over and handed him a fifty-*yuan* note.

He said, "We have enough sand now. You don't have to come back." Taking the money, Li Da smiled at the foreman and said, "If you have any more odd jobs, just let me know." The foreman turned and walked away. Li Da looked back at the pile of sand he had sifted—earthen yellow, like a lonely tomb that no one visited.

Li Da stood up resentfully and slowly walked away. Since he was inside the garden, he didn't have to rush to leave. After leaving, it would be hard to get back in. His hands behind his back, Li Da walked deliberately, feeling a little like the village mayor. *You don't want me to work here anymore, but I guess it's okay to patrol and look around for a while.*

While he was thus "patrolling" the area, Li Da figured out what he could do: he had found work for himself that no one could take away from him.

With the girl's soft hand in his, Li Da shuffled toward the primary school outside the village. When they drew near the school door, the girl wriggled away from him and, as enraptured as a little bird, flew into the school. Li Da bent down and picked up a scrap of paper; it made a *huala* sound as he shook the dust from it. *Don't look down on a scrap of paper. After all, the grains of rice that went into a burlap bag were also collected one by one.* Now Li Da's eyes were as sharp as a snipe's: nothing escaped his eyes. But a lot of people took this path and a lot of people picked things up here: it was just like harvesting the crops in the fall—not many corncobs were left behind. The place where Li Da "went to work" was Xiushui Gardens. He could work only before daylight or at night. A few guards went back and forth like dogs in this little place, especially to catch people like Li Da who came out at night to pan for treasures. As soon as they saw that it was Li Da, the guards lifted their electrified truncheons to drive him out. Li Da said, "My cat's lost. I'm looking for my cat!" The guards would say, "Cat? What do I look like? Do I look like a cat? I'm here especially to catch rats like you!" Li Da was frightened whenever he saw a uniformed guard.

But Li Da knew a lot of cat and mouse games. After a few days, Li Da found a small opening in the white fence where there was a broken iron rod: a skinny person could get through. After he went through, Li Da replaced the iron rod. Later on, after he finished his work, he picked up some things, removed the broken iron rod, squeezed himself and the things he had taken through the opening, and got out. Below the fence was a small path along the riverbank. Rounding the curve of the river, he reached the area where he lived. This was a first-class secret path for moving things without anyone noticing. Even if the cat had sharper eyes, it wouldn't be able to catch an experienced rat like Li Da. One time, he picked up an old radio, went home and tinkered with it, exchanged its batteries for several that he'd picked up, and suddenly the radio started playing. It was so loud it almost shook the ground with its vibrations. After that, when Li Da had nothing to do in the daytime, he listened to the radio. Once he caught a new word from it—"trade secret." He thought to himself, *why is it that some people are able to pick up things and others aren't: in this there is also a trade secret.*

Within a fortnight, Li Da, having developed a knack for dealing with Xiushui Gardens' garbage, became passionate about his new business. Trash was like crops: you had to take pains with it. For example, some people liked to throw their garbage outside at night. If it was gone the next morning, then the third day they threw garbage out again. The recycling station here was quite far away, and carts for collecting discarded goods weren't allowed in. Some people piled up their used plastic oil bottles and pop bottles, cardboard boxes and newspapers at the entrances to their homes, waiting for the morning trash collectors to take them away. Li Da had to act before these trash collectors showed up. What a pity it was to see good stuff turn into real garbage if you made your move a minute too late. One time, chancing upon a sofa that had been thrown out in front of one home, Li Da went up and sat on it. Half his body sank comfortably into the softness. After fiddling with it, he found that it was doubled up and folded into itself: when he opened it, it became a bed. Li Da went home and stayed up until midnight, and then went back with two lengths of rope to get the sofa. In one breath, he hoisted the sofa up on his shoulders and lifted it up onto the fence. He tied the sofa shut and then went through the fence, and carefully pulled on the ropes. It took all his strength to get the sofa over the fence and down the other side. Then, carrying it on his back, he transported the sofa back to Six-*li* Hamlet.

Now, Li Da often sat on the sofa, leaning back with his eyes narrowed as he listened to the radio and drank cool water from the thermos bottle. Li Da felt that the city was really a good spot. If you needed anything, you just had to move quickly and pick it up. It might not be easy to find cash on the roadside, but there were plenty of other things. If you didn't mind their being old or broken and if you didn't care about self-respect, you could set up a whole household by helping yourself to them. Your home would be furnished more completely than the village mayor's.

The sound from the radio was too soft: you had to press it hard against your ear to hear anything. If it didn't work, you could try hitting or shaking it a little, and then it might suddenly let out a sound as loud as the loudspeaker in your home village.

No wonder everyone wanted to move to the city.

This time, Li Da went back to the village with scrap paper and empty plastic bottles. He was swaggering, flaunting the things he was holding as if he had just come back from shopping at the supermarket. Every time Li Da entered the village, he walked like this on purpose. He didn't think picking up trash was a disgrace. He didn't feel he was losing face by doing this. Face was always where it usually was. From under a tree, the guy with a gimpy leg called out to him, "You've picked up trash again!" Feeling a little unhappy, Li Da answered, "I've told you time and again. This isn't trash. It's all useful!"

The gimpy-legged guy mocked him, "Oh, oh, who do you think you are—the environmental protection official?"

Li Da pushed open the gate to his courtyard and went in the house. Forgetting to stoop over, he bumped his head against a stiff plastic bag. His head hurt. He had more than ten of these plastic bags hanging from bamboo poles that he had set up especially for this purpose. With his eyes shut, Li Da could tell what was in each bag just by feeling them. This one had all kinds of toys—more than ten little cars that were missing wheels and couldn't move; seven or eight dolls that were missing arms or whose heads were askew. There were also plastic slates that could be written on, a stuffed rabbit with long ears and a fuzzy tail, plastic puzzle pieces, colored pencils, and a pilot wearing a helmet (the gimpy-legged guy said this was called "Aoteman"—a Japanese cartoon character.) After Li Da took them home, cleaned them up in the river, and dried them in the sun, they looked just like new to him. With these things spread out all over the floor, his room was like a toy store. If he took them back home, every one of them would be a treasure; his two grandsons would fight over them. One plastic bag held all kinds of ropes— long ones, short ones, coiled and straight, round and flat, and rubber bands. All were useful in daily life. There was also a bunch of colorful ribbons, which he'd seen someone remove from a large bouquet of fresh flowers and throw into the garbage. The ribbons must be made of silk, for they were fresh and smooth. He intended to take them back home. At New Year's, when he gave presents to relatives, he would tie a couple of these ribbons onto the gifts. How much more valuable the gifts would be! There were also clothes for all the seasons. He even had several dozen hats—leather hats, cloth hats, wool hats, straw hats—enough to cover half the heads in the village. Padded jackets were big items: each one would fill one plastic bag. They hung all over the house.

The little empty space in the small house would soon be so filled that it would be hard to turn around. Aside from the places where they ate and slept, every spot was crammed with things. It wasn't like a residence but like a storehouse. Li Da was worried: he didn't know how he would get all these things home. Cardboard boxes, newspapers, plastic bottles, wine bottles, scrap copper and iron: whatever could be sold, he'd sold long ago at the recycling station. What was left was what couldn't be sold. Li Da found that actually the things that couldn't be sold were the most useful. For example, shoes: cotton shoes, sandals, rubber boots, leather shoes, slippers, travel shoes, men's shoes, women's shoes, children's shoes . . . Every two or three days, Li Da could pick up a pair of old shoes from the villas' garbage, brush them clean, stitch the broken parts back together—and they could be worn. After collecting for more than six months, he had shoes of all sizes. Some had to fit one or the other of his two sons at home. And if not, their wives could try them on. He even saved some shoes for when his grandkids were old enough to go to school. Now, under the beds in Shuanzi's rented house, three mesh bags were filled with all kinds of shoes. One time, Li Da's nephew who worked in the city came to see him. He bought fruit for the girl. She ate it happily and then said, "My grandpa has lots of shoes under his bed. I'll ask him to choose a pair with platform heels for you!" Li Da paled, distressed at the thought of giving away any shoes that he planned to take home. Li Da couldn't sell the shoes to the recycling station, but he prized them greatly. On peasants' feet, shoes wore out easily. Who could bear to wear new shoes to work in the fields? But without spending a penny, Li Da had shoes for all seasons for the whole family. Not to mention that each pair was a hundred times better than the shoes back home. From now on, no one in his family would have to worry about shoes. Li Da slept on a bed under which shoes were stored, and he rested very well every night.

But it was hard on the seven-year-old girl. Li Da sighed. Since he had found himself this job, like a donkey working at a mill, he went all around Xiushui Gardens all day long, so as not to miss out on any good items. He didn't have time to cook a hot meal that included soup and vegetables for the little girl.

All of a sudden, he heard the gimpy-legged guy shout at him from outside the window, "Li Da, when are you going home for the autumn harvest? Are you going to abandon your grandsons for the garbage?"

Li Da didn't enjoy talking with the gimpy-legged guy. Gimpy didn't do anything all day long, and yet he was always eating at restaurants and smoking good tobacco. He didn't act like a decent man. The last few days, he'd made a habit of going to Li Da's home. This really irritated Li Da.

Gimpy pushed the door open a crack, stuck his head in, and said, "In the southeast corner of the residential area, a family is putting in new security windows. A pile of rusty iron bars is piled up about three feet high outside the door . . ."

Looking at the top of the fence, Li Da rolled his eyes and snorted.

Gimpy continued, "The sanitary workers think the iron bars are too heavy to move in a small cart, and passed me a message about this."

Li Da sat up in bed. "You? They wanted you to move them? Isn't the real-estate management responsible for this kind of thing?"

Gimpy said happily, "Sure, they'll take care of transporting them, so by tomorrow morning, you'll have lost your chance."

Li Da pondered this. If he went, it would take at least two hours. The girl would be home alone: how would he handle that? After thinking a while, he said to Gimpy, "Do it yourself if you want. Shuanzi is working overtime tonight and will be home late. I have to stay home and take care of the girl."

Without saying anything, Gimpy tossed him a cigarette and left.

On the bed, Li Da stared blankly for a while and then made up his mind: he had to give up a few days of work and go back home for the autumn harvest. While he was at it, he could take all the things he'd collected with him and make room for continuing to collect things when he came back.

It grew dark. The girl came back from school, and after eating dinner, she bent over the table and did her homework by the light of a reading lamp. This lamp was another thing he had picked up: it was a porcelain bottle with a voile lampshade, quite pretty. It's just that the light bulb flickered on and off— bright for a while and then dim for a while. It made Li Da feel unsettled. He couldn't help looking out the window, as if seeing those rusty iron bars—piled up like a hill—brightening the darkness in the distance.

Li Da looked at his watch, and taking into account that it was half an hour slow, he realized it would soon be nine o'clock. Gimpy had a lot of tricks up his sleeve, and knew several of the guards, too. If Li Da waited much longer, Gimpy would have taken the iron bars away.

Li Da couldn't sit still. He told the girl to wash up and go to sleep. Then he locked the door and walked to the riverside. When he went outside, he sensed a shadow dodging at the base of the wall. He rubbed his eyes: it was only a telephone pole.

When he got to the fence, Li Da moved the iron bar and made his way through the opening. He went to the spot Gimpy had told him about, and found the right place, but there was nothing in front of the house—not even a nail. He walked around the house a few times and stood on tiptoe to look through the windows. In the light, the stainless steel security windows didn't seem to be newly installed. He looked carefully at the neighbors' homes on either side. There was no sign of any construction taking place. It was then that Li Da realized that Gimpy had tricked him. Gimpy had made a fool of him. Tomorrow, he'd get Shuanzi to deal with him. Li Da spat on the ground, bent forward, and took a few steps. Not resigned to going back empty-handed, he turned around, avoiding the path that the guards regularly took, and headed toward a different corner. All he paid attention to were the garbage bags in front of the small Western-style houses. He had walked only a few steps before he nearly bumped into a little tree. He stopped at once. Actually, it was a couple in such a tight embrace that they were like a single shadow. Flustered, Li Da steered clear of them, and then saw that there was also a tree next to him. This tree was a real one, and under it was a garbage can. He thrust his hand into it, and felt a soft package. Exerting all his strength, he pulled it out and looked at it under the streetlight. It was a mosquito net. Feeling pleased, Li Da took the mosquito net with him. Most of his anger vanished.

How could it be that the people in this city didn't know that you could repair ruined household goods and go on using them? Li Da whispered to himself. City people just knew how to dump things. He'd heard that the cart hauling garbage away from Xiushui Gardens every day had to pay the garbage dump seventy or eighty *yuan*. Where on this earth did you have to pay to throw things away? Someone would buy a new dress today and throw it away tomorrow. Or someone would buy something packed in a big box, and after tearing off layers and layers of wrapping materials, would finally pull out a tiny item, leaving a large pile of plastic bubble wrap which didn't even have recycling value. People worked day and night to earn money: was it just to turn money into garbage? Look at cars: in a few years, they'd be turned into scrap iron. Old buildings were demolished and turned into rubble. In restaurants, platter after platter of delicious chicken, duck, and fish were left over and emptied into slop buckets. This noisy, confusing city was like a factory specializing in producing garbage. Li Da thought indignantly, a few years ago in his hometown, no one even knew what garbage was. Everything grown on the land could be returned to the land. Wheat and corn straw became brushwood, their husks fed pigs, vegetable leaves and leftover rice fed the chickens, and bones fed the dogs. Pig and chicken manure was good fertilizer. Worn-out clothes could be used for making shoes and diapers. Even fertilizer bags could be used to make trousers. Bits and pieces swept up from the floor served as cooking fuel . . .

As he mulled it over some more, he decided his ideas just now hadn't been completely right. If the city didn't have garbage, what kind of work would he have had in the city? And if the city didn't have garbage, wouldn't it just become a village? Life in the city was really better than life in the village simply because city people could throw out good things that then turned into garbage. If a household could throw out garbage, it must be quite well off. Only if there was affluence was there garbage, and if there was garbage, there was affluence—the more affluence, the more garbage, and the more garbage, the more affluence. If it were possible to move all of this city's garbage back to his hometown, all the people of the county would benefit from it for generations. People spoke of golden mountains and silver mountains. Li Da hadn't seen them: Li Da just knew that the city's garbage was his golden mountain. Not once when he dug into it with his spade was he ever disappointed. He would never ever give up doing this.

As Li Da was woolgathering, he suddenly kicked something, which slipped to one side. He squatted down and felt it all over. He finally felt something cool and hard, about half the size of a cigarette case. Excited, Li Da ran over to the streetlight, lifted the object he was holding and took a look. *Mother of God, you did get what you wanted: sure enough, it's a cell phone!*

Was it real? It couldn't be just a toy, could it? For a second, Li Da wasn't sure. He weighed it in his hand; it was light. It was a diaphanous silver case. He held it in his palm and shook it a little; nothing happened. He waved it, and nothing happened then, either. It looked like the real thing, but was it broken? If it was still working, why had it been tossed away on the road? If it was broken and he took it, would he still have to spend money to have it repaired? Now he had a cell phone, but who could he call? And the phone bill would be another problem.

He sat down on the cement shoulder of the road and turned the cell phone over and over in his hand, as though picking up a hot sweet potato.

Unexpectedly, the sweet potato started quivering lightly in his palm, and then it began ringing, scaring Li Da so much that he nearly threw it away. The ringing grew louder and louder; it was like a loudspeaker spreading noise in all directions. At night, the Xiushui Gardens area was so quiet that you could hear mosquitoes far and near. Now this ringing was stabbing his ears. Li Da held the tiny object tightly, wishing he could pinch the sound to death, but he couldn't: it was earth-shattering, like a singing grasshopper. Now Li Da could finally hear it clearly: it really was singing. It kept singing a line like this:

Brilliant splendor, on the golden mountain of Beijing . . . Brilliant splendor, on the golden mountain of Beijing . . .

Li Da was flustered out of his wits. He had no idea how to turn off the sound. His palm was soaked with sweat, and he couldn't find the right button to press.

After singing a few times, the sound finally stopped. Li Da sighed with relief. He had no sooner hidden the cell phone in his pants pocket than he heard running steps thudding toward him. A square-faced guard was running as he shone a flashlight on him. "Hey, you. Hand over the cell phone!"

Li Da was annoyed. "What the fuck are you talking about? A cell phone? Where?"

Displeased, the guard said, "I heard a cell phone ring. Don't lie to me!"

Li Da said perversely, "You heard it? Why didn't I? Make it ring so I can hear it!"

Just as he was saying this, something stirred in Li Da's pocket, as if a tape recorder on his body had been turned on:

"Brilliant splendor, on the golden mountain of Beijing . . . "

Li Da quickly covered it with his hand. The guard moved fast and took the cell phone from Li Da's pocket. Square-face turned on the phone and shouted: "I've got it. Hurry over to the southeast corner of No. 18."

It was a while before Li Da figured out that it was the ringing of the phone that had tipped the guard off. Before long came the sound of footsteps, and a boy and girl ran up out of breath. The guard handed them the cell phone and asked if it was theirs. The boy took it in his hand and kept saying, "Absolutely, absolutely." The girl added, "I picked this particular old song for the cell phone's ring. Nobody else has this ring." After saying this, they still didn't leave, but asked the guard how he had found it. The guard pointed at Li Da and said, "If the cell phone hadn't rung, he still wouldn't have admitted having it." The girl screamed at Li Da, "You! Don't you know that people get really worried when they lose something?" The boy shouted gruffly, "Who knows if he picked it up or if he stole it? Just now, I saw this old guy wandering around. He brushed past us . . ." With that, he raised his arm to punch Li Da in the chest. When Li Da dodged, the blow landed on his shoulder. Li Da felt all his blood boiling up to gush out his throat. Clenching his fist, he charged the young guy, but the guard pulled him away . . .

Li Da was shivering all over, and stammering when he talked. "It's not fair. I picked up this cell phone on the side of the road. Every day, I pick up things in this area . . ." As proof, he nervously took out the mosquito net that was tucked under his arm. He saw the three of them stare at the net, then disdainfully at him. Li Da had been in the city for six months, and he was used to being looked at like this. He hastily changed his tune: "Stealing is one thing. Picking things up is another. I picked it up. It isn't stealing. Stealing is against the law. Even if I were dying of poverty, I'd never steal . . ."

The boy broke in, "Only broken things can be picked up as garbage. This cell phone is in good working order. You have to give it back. If you don't, it's against the law. Hunh. Just look at you. I was flattering you by saying you stole it. You'd better learn from the beggars in the subway—kneeling down to beg for mercy. That's certainly not against the law. Old man, if you kneel down in front of me, I'll give you this cell phone!"

Li Da didn't know what to say: he was fiery hot all over. Just then, all he wanted was to slap the lad's face.

The cell phone started singing again: "Brilliant splendor, on the golden mountain of Beijing . . ." The girl walked to one side to answer the phone. She paid no more attention to Li Da. She hadn't finished talking when the boy hurried over and put his arm around her waist. Then they walked away. The square-faced guard, who spoke in the same country accent as Li Da, pulled a long face and asked, "How do you get in every day? Tell the truth."

"No way." The fire in Li Da's throat turned into phlegm and he coughed hard and spat it out on the carpet-like grass. He twisted around and left. Hurrying to catch up, the guard followed him at a leisurely pace. With nowhere else to vent his anger, Li Da deliberately played a trick on this young fellow from his hometown who seemed to have put on airs after getting a job in the city. He took several turns around the buildings until the guard grew tired and irritated and quietly gave up. Only then did Li Da remember his granddaughter who was sound asleep. He hurried toward the fence. As he was walking, something hard hit him in the ankle. He swore, "Fuck" and stopped to look at it closely under the streetlight. What he had stepped on was iron grating used to cover a drain—a corner was sticking up and had scratched his foot. Li Da knew at once what had happened. Someone had prized up the four sides of the iron grating and was waiting until midnight to move it away. Pressing down on the iron grate, Li Da bent his head and stood there for a short time. Then he carefully looked around in all directions. But darkness had risen, and the streetlights were all dozing. He couldn't see anything even a few paces away. Gritting his teeth, Li Da bent down and pulled up the iron grate and slowly dragged it off, finally stuffing it through the gap in the fence. Then he wrapped it in the mosquito netting, hoisted it onto his back, and ran toward the rented house in the village. He was planning to find a distant recycling center the next day and sell it; it could bring quite a few bucks. As he walked, he muttered: *you little bastard, I'll make you understand what stealing is and what picking things up is! You blamed me for stealing: now you want to know what stealing is? Someday, when the mood strikes me, I'm going to rob a couple of banks so you can see what stealing really is!*

Sweating all over, Li Da took the iron grate back to the village. Since the house was dark, he knew his son hadn't come home yet. He took out his key to open the door, but before he had inserted it into the lock, the lock gave way. Puzzled, he pushed the door lightly and entered the room. Even before groping for the light switch, he sensed an emptiness, as if something were missing. When he turned on the light, there was a buzzing in Li Da's head, and he felt confused—

He didn't see even one of the more than a dozen full plastic bags that had been hanging from the pole. It was as if a flock of crows on a telephone pole had suddenly all flown away. Not even one remained. He was dumbfounded. Confused, he bent down and looked under the wooden bed: nothing. Not one of the three tightly wrapped mesh bags could be seen. On the floor there were only a few traces of dirt left behind when several things had been dragged away. Li Da bent over again and looked. There really was nothing under the bed: it was so empty that several grown pigs could be hidden there.

All of a sudden, the room was a lot more spacious, just the way it had been when Shuanzi brought him here from the depot. All the good things that Li Da had laboriously collected for more than six months had been lost in one evening. They were all useful things that he had wanted to take back home, things that he had planned to give to everyone in his family. How could they all be gone? All taken away? This wasn't taking, it was stealing. No, it was robbery! Whoever had robbed Li Da of the things he had picked up had no conscience!

A gimpy shadow flashed before Li Da's eyes. He shook his head again: how could a gimpy-legged guy move so many things?

The girl was still sound asleep on the wooden bed. Even when Li Da shook her hard, she didn't wake up. It looked as if even thunder couldn't wake her up. Angry, he lifted the sheet and pillow, and the girl fell to the floor. Finally she opened her eyes. He asked her if she'd seen someone here. The girl rubbed her eyes, thought for a while, and said that she had dreamed that a lot of Santa Clauses had come, all talking in the hometown dialect . . .

Li Da went out the door. It was dark outside, so dark that he couldn't see even the shadow of a ghost.

Holding his head, Li Da squatted down. Everything in both the room and his head was dark and indistinct. Everywhere in the vicinity of this village were people from his hometown. They said they'd come here to work, but who knew what kind of work they were doing? Those people were all the sort who were capable of stealing an ox without a sound. He could do nothing but blame himself for not being wary earlier. He had always told people that what he picked up wasn't trash but good useful stuff. See, those people had believed him. It seemed that the little trash from the villas wasn't enough to divide among the people from his hometown, and some of them were really more destitute than he was. Had anyone been robbed of trash before? Now he had been. Someone had robbed him: didn't this mean that he was already better off than others from his hometown? Li Da didn't beg, nor did he steal. Since coming to the city, he just kept picking things out of garbage. Finally, he had picked up a bunch of thieves. He didn't know whether to be angry or happy . . .

The girl climbed into bed and went back to sleep. Those villagers who'd stolen the trash apparently hadn't harmed the little girl at all; it looked as if they still had something of a conscience. And luckily, he had long ago given Shuanzi the money he made from selling waste to save for him. Recalling this made it a little easier for Li Da to accept what had happened.

He went out the door and—hands behind his back—strolled through the village. The moon emerged from the clouds, and the villa across the river looked as if it were covered in a large piece of plastic film. It reminded Li Da of the circumstances of his leaving the Li Family Village six months earlier. At night, he had arisen soundlessly and gone to his wheat field. The full moon had arrived there before he had: it was suspended high in the heavens like a lantern. In the bright moonlight, it was as if the wheat fields were also covered by a very large piece of plastic film. When the evening breeze rose, the dense wheat seedlings stirred, *hualala*. He could see only silver-bright, slippery white waves, no longer the jade-green color of the daytime. Li Da squatted on the ground, stretched out a hand, and tried to lift the plastic. His hand came up empty. He tried again. His palm was filled with a wheat seedling. The sharp, fine leaf blades threaded themselves between the cracks in the old man's fingers and pricked his hand like daggers. The moonlight wasn't the way it used to be, for it had made the wheat field look like a large plastic tent, a preposterous camouflage. Li Da was whispering. When he stood up, he felt quite happy. What he was weighing in his hand wasn't a rough, green wheat seedling, but was evidently a heavy spike of wheat. The low, sturdy, fat seedlings in the wheat field were actually lying under his feet. If you put your ear close to the seedlings' roots, you'd hear the wheat stalks leaping up impatiently. Narrowing his eyes, he saw the golden yellow wheat kernels trickling everywhere like rising rivulets, and the scene was even more beautiful than the full moon. When the wheat was ripe, it would be harvested. After the wheat was harvested, corn would be planted. Six months would flash by, and the corn would be ready to harvest . . .

Now, Li Da sat down on a hillock and gazed at the moon. Suddenly his eye sockets ached: he was going to go back for the autumn harvest, but he was empty-handed. He hadn't saved anything. All that remained was the watch on his wrist. How could he divide it between his two sons? What could he do? Should he return to the city after the autumn harvest and figure out a way to pick up another watch?

And so do I have to come back after the harvest? he asked himself. But if he didn't return to the city, where else could he go? In any case, the villas had trash every day; why not come back? As long as he stayed in the city, the gold and silver mountains would always be gloriously radiant. Li Da snorted, musing that the song on the cell phone was so familiar that it seemed he'd heard it somewhere years ago. He thought hard for a while, but he couldn't remember where.

✻✿❧

About the Author

Zhang Kangkang was born in 1950 in Hangzhou, Zhejiang. After graduating from high school in 1969, she was one of the urban educated youth "sent down to the countryside and up to the mountains" to learn from the farmers. As part of that Cultural Revolution program, she worked for eight years on a government farm in Heilongjiang. In 1977, she was sent to the Heilongjiang Arts School to study playwriting for a year. In 1979, she became a member of the Heilongjiang Writers' Association, and began to devote herself to writing fiction. She had already published her first short story in 1972 and her first novel in 1975. Since then, she has published numerous short stories and novellas, as well as novels. Her works have been translated into English, French, German, and Japanese.

In conversation with Karen Gernant in October 2003, she said that her writing focuses mainly on the Cultural Revolution years, and on the experiences of women in urban China. She has recently begun mining the stories her Henan housekeeper tells of rural life, and indeed that housekeeper appears to be the prototype for Zhima. Zhang Kangkang believes that, over time, as more and more people from the countryside move to the cities to work, they may take city values and practices back to their homes and thus serve as conduits of change in the countryside.

Ms. Zhang moved to Beijing in 1983 and now lives in the suburbs with her husband.

She is vice-chair of the Chinese Writer's Association and also serves as a counselor to China's State Council.

About the Translators

Chen Zeping Professor of Chinese Linguistics at Fujian Teachers' University, holds a master's degree from Beijing University. He has published numerous books and articles in his field of Chinese dialects. Professor Chen also taught Chinese language and history at Southern Oregon University in 1988–1989, 1991–1992 and 1995, and taught Chinese language at Ehime University in Matsuyama, Japan, from 2000 to 2002. He directs the Ph.D. program in Chinese linguistics at Fujian Teachers' University.

Karen Gernant Professor Emerita of Chinese History at Southern Oregon University, earned her Ph.D. at the University of Oregon, and studied Chinese at the Stanford Center in Taipei. Her book, *Imagining Women: Fujian Folk Tales,* was published by Interlink in 1995. In 1999, she received the Fujian Provice Friendship Medal. She now divides her time between homes in Fuzhou, China, and Talent, Oregon.

Together, Professors Chen and Gernant have translated more than thirty stories for the literary magazines *Chinese Literature, Manoa, Conjunctions, turn-row, Black Warrior Review, Ninth Letter,* and *Words without Borders.* Their translations of stories by Can Xue were published as *Blue Light in the Sky* (New Directions, 2006) and their translation of Can Xue's novel *Five Spice Street* was published by Yale University in 2009.

༷

CORNELL EAST ASIA SERIES

CORNELL
East Asia Series

Order online at www.einaudi.cornell.edu/eastasia/publications